ALEX MILLER is one of Australia's best loved writers. *Prochownik's Dream* is his seventh novel. His work includes *Watching the Climbers on the Mountain* (1988), *The Tivington Nott* (1989), which won the Braille Book of the Year Award, *The Ancestor Game* (1992), which won the Miles Franklin Literary Award, Australia's premier literary prize, the Commonwealth Writers Prize, and the Barbara Ramsden Award for best published book, *The Sitters* (1995), which was shortlisted for the Miles Franklin Literary Award, *Conditions of Faith* (2000), which won the NSW Premier's Literary Award, the Christina Stead Prize for Fiction, and was shortlisted for the Miles Franklin Literary Award, *Journey to the Stone Country* (2002), which won the Miles Franklin Literary Award.

Prochownik's DREAM

Alex Miller

ALLEN&UNWIN

This edition published in 2006
First published in 2005

This project has been assisted by the Commonwealth
Government through the Australia Council, its arts
funding and advisory board.

Allen & Unwin
83 Alexander Street
Crows Nest NSW 2065
Australia
Phone: (61 2) 8425 0100
Fax: (61 2) 9906 2218
Email: info@allenandunwin.com
Web: www.allenandunwin.com

National Library of Australia
Cataloguing-in-Publication entry:

Miller, Alex, 1936– .
    Prochownik's dream.

    ISBN 978 1 74175 013 3.
    ISBN 1 74175 013 X.

    1. Artists—Fiction. I. Title.

A823.3

Set in 12/18 pt Requiem HTF by Bookhouse, Sydney
Printed in Australia by McPherson's Printing Group

10 9 8 7 6 5 4 3 2 1

For Stephanie

&

To the memory of Max Blatt

We cannot arbitrarily invent projects for ourselves: they have to be written in our past as requirements.

Simone de Beauvoir

I

The Mistress of Trees

one

I should like to understand myself properly before it is too late. The phrase arrested his attention and he stopped reading and looked up from the book. He was standing in the doorway of his studio, posing for his daughter, who was sitting at her little table within the shadows of the studio's interior. She was drawing a picture of him with her coloured pencils, her black and white Snoopy Dog propped in front of her. When he looked up from the book the little girl also lifted her head and studied him, raising her hand and shading her eyes from the light, her expression serious and concerned. 'Are you all right, Daddy?' she asked.

'Yes, darling, I'm fine,' he reassured her. He was touched by the earnestness of her inquiry.

But perhaps she was not reassured after all, for she continued to examine him for a long moment before returning to her work, her head bent close to the paper, her free arm around her drawing, shielding it within the circle of her embrace. 'You can move now, if you like,' she said.

He looked at the book in his hand, wondering if he might go on reading it. He had picked it up at random from the table by the door, to occupy himself while he posed for her, and had not registered either its title or the name of its author. It was one of many that had belonged to his father. On the cover there was a reproduction of a familiar painting by Salvador Dali, *The Triangular Hour*. The unearthly glow of the yellows and greens of Dali's imaginary landscape. He read: *A novel of the alienation of personality and the mystery of being.* Inside the front cover at the top of the page, above the brief biography of the author, his father had pencilled his name, *Moniek Prochownik*. He could see his father now, seated on the couch in the evening, exhausted after his shift on the moulding line at the Dunlop factory, staring vacantly before him, the book face down in his lap, lost in the thoughts inspired by the words in the book, at that time of the evening needing only one good phrase in order to surrender himself to the uncertain universe of the book. His father's apologetic smile on such occasions at finding himself caught gazing absently into space.

He stepped out of the sunlight into the studio and stood looking down with distaste at the pile of old clothes and timber racks that filled his workspace. There were overcoats shagged with use, frayed skirts and blouses, dresses stained and un-hemmed, the dark trousers and jackets of men's suits; and,

4

here and there among the grown-up things, the small garment of a child. The summer heat was drawing from the old clothes the dispiriting smell of napthalene. It was a smell that reminded him of the closets of old people and of their preoccupation with the preservation of their things against the inevitability of decay, as if by preserving their most intimate belongings they might thereby contrive the preservation of themselves. His wife had urged him weeks ago, a touch of impatience in her voice, *Why don't you begin a new project? Take all this stuff back to the op shops and forget about it, or it will depress you.* Although he knew that it was good advice, he had been unable to summon the resolve to act on it. He was still troubled by a resistant element of these dismantled installations, something unremembered that tugged at him and awaited resolution. He had been unable either to continue with them, or to conceive a convincing new project to take their place. The smelly pile of old clothes had begun to sicken him. He realised it was beginning to stand in his mind for his failure as an artist. Teresa was right, he must get rid of it.

He looked away. Out in the courtyard the water was spilling from Teresa's stone fountain and splashing into the sunlit basin: the courtyard and the house in the sunlight, the tall windows of the kitchen and the French doors reflecting the studio. How carefully, how lovingly, Teresa had planned it, speaking of it as their home and as his place of work while it was still little more than an idea in her mind. She did not reproach him, but he knew that he had not fulfilled his portion of her dream. He had begun to wonder lately if it might be the very perfection of the conditions she had organised for him that had silenced his imagination. He had felt a traitor for even thinking it. He hated and feared the silence in his mind, but he could not pretend to work when there was really nothing there. He could not do that. Not even for Teresa's dream.

His daughter called to him and he turned from the doorway. She was standing behind her chair holding her drawing by its top corners for him to see. He beckoned to her with the book.

The little girl crossed the studio and handed him the drawing, then she stood in front of him, watching him examine it. Her manner was expectant, reserved and attentive. She had drawn the figure of a man, the man's outline rendered by a single firm blue line. There had been no attempt at a likeness of himself, no reference to his pose in the doorway. The figure had no hands and its pointy feet were poised, like a ballet dancer's feet, on a green sward of spiky grass. It leaned to one side from the waist up, as if it were being bent by a powerful wind, or was about to execute a difficult leap that would test its agility to the limit. Spears of red hair issued from its head like flames—its hair anticipating the violent energies of its intended leap, or perhaps the panic in its mind. Above the portrait, in black pencil, she had written the word *Dad*. The confidence of her line astonished him, and he envied her the unconsidered liberty of her pencil. There were no crossings out, no correcting, no second thoughts. The image must have stood whole and complete in her imagination before she made her first mark on the paper.

'It's wonderful, darling,' he said with feeling.

'It's you,' she said, the certainty of her work in the assurance of her gaze.

The telephone rang and he reached past his daughter and lifted the handset from the wall by the door. 'Hello,' he said.

'Is that you, Toni? It's Marina Golding.' There was a slight pause, 'We're back.'

He was very surprised to hear from her. 'Yes, it's me. You mean you're back in Melbourne?'

'We're back in our house in Richmond.'

'You're living here again?' He held his daughter's portrait of him at arm's length and smiled. It was so absolutely right. Her Dad was a perplexed and desolate pixie with his head on fire and no hands to beat out the flames.

'For the moment, yes,' Marina Golding said. 'I'm sorry, Toni, we should have been in touch sooner.' Her apology for their neglect was sincere. 'We thought you might have heard by now. We've been back a few weeks.'

He wondered why it was Marina and not Robert who had called. It was a year, more, since he had heard anything from them. 'How's Robert?'

'Robert's fine. He's incredibly busy. He says to give you his love.' She allowed a pause. 'I'm interrupting your work?'

'I'm in the middle of getting a big new project under way.' It was a lie, of course, or rather it was a joke, but a joke addressed to himself. A private irony he was unable to resist.

She made an exclamation of satisfaction. 'Robert was sure you'd be working on something big.'

Marina had taken him seriously, but he let it go. Within a month of Robert and Marina going to Sydney four years earlier, his daughter had been born, his father had died, and he had given up painting and turned to installations. His world had changed forever. Now, suddenly, Marina's voice on the other end of the telephone, reminding him of those years of hope and excitement that they had shared.

'We've got some news,' she said. 'Can you come for lunch? Say next Wednesday?'

'I'd love to. Wednesday would be good.'

'Come about one.'

His daughter tugged at the pocket of his jeans. 'Can we go to the swing park now, Daddy?'

He cupped the phone and leaned down to her. 'Yes, darling. In a minute.' He straightened. 'I have to go now. I'm taking Nada to the swing park.'

'She must be four already. Is she at school yet?'

'She's at kinder. We have this bit of time together before Teresa gets home.'

'And how is Teresa?'

'She's fine. Busy.' He resented the forced, unnatural, stilted manner of the conversation with Marina and wanted to say something that would provoke a bit of reality between them. He could think of nothing that would not sound crass and pushy, however, so he said nothing.

Marina said, 'I saw your installation at Andy's.'

He waited. He would not ask her what she had thought of his work.

Nada dragged at his pocket with both hands, her head thrown back, presenting the pale curve of her throat, pulling away from him with her full weight.

'It was powerful,' Marina said. 'I found it very disturbing.'

Powerful and disturbing! He let the book drop to the floor and transferred the child's portrait of him to his telephone hand, then he leaned down and took hold of her wrist. Bending to her level, he begged her, 'Wait for Daddy a minute! *Please*, darling! I'm coming!' The puerility of his eagerness to hear what Marina had to say about his work shamed him.

'There was no one else there. It was a weird feeling being alone in that vast space of Andy's with your crowd of faceless people. I could smell them. They seemed to be standing there sweating and waiting for me to do something. I felt I was being accused. Of inaction, I suppose, was it? Something like that? A failure to acknowledge their plight? Is that what we were supposed to feel? Were they supposed to make us feel guilty? Well *I* felt guilty anyway. But perhaps that was just me. Though we've all got this guilt nowadays, haven't we? About everything. I don't know whether that's what you meant.

I should have called you before this and said something. There was a kind of eerie silence about it.'

Nada released her grip, suddenly, and his hand slipped from her wrist. She walked over to her little table and began putting away her coloured pencils, her manner poised and self-sufficient, her head down, concentrating on her task, ignoring him.

'Robert didn't get to see it?' He was dismayed to hear the self-pitying resentment of his tone.

'It's not been easy, Toni. The move back, I mean. It hasn't been straightforward. There's nothing wrong between us, it's not that. It's just that Robert hasn't had a minute. He *meant* to go. You can't imagine. He just didn't get a chance. Then you'd dismantled it and taken it away.'

'You needn't explain. It's okay.'

'It's not okay.' She allowed a pause. 'I'm sorry, Toni. We seem to be like strangers.' There was another pause. 'Robert's father has come to stay with us. So that's complicated things as well.'

'I thought Robert's father lived in Germany?'

'He did. He's ill. He's dying.'

He watched Nada put her pencil case in the drawer of her desk and close it. She picked up her Snoopy Dog and, holding the toy to her chest, set off towards the door.

'Sorry, Marina, I'd love to talk but I've absolutely got to go. See you Wednesday.'

'See you Wednesday, Toni,' Marina said. She sounded disappointed. 'It's good to at least be in touch again.'

He hung up the telephone, stepped across the studio and swept the little girl into his arms. 'Gotcha!'

She cried out with delight, 'Daddeee!' She clung to him and bit his shoulder hard.

He set her drawing of him on her table, then carried her across the courtyard into the house. On the way to the front door along the passage he paused beside a small framed gouache that hung on the wall. It was a modest tonal image of a straight-backed chair and the corner of a kitchen table with a jug and a bowl.

Nada pointed at the picture. 'Granddad!'

'Yes, Granddad, darling. He would have loved you like crazy.' At the door he set Nada on her feet. 'Let's have a really big swing.'

They went out through the gate and walked hand-in-hand along the footpath. At the main road he scooped Nada up and waited for a gap in the traffic, then he ran across with her held against him. On the other side he set her down on the grass. 'There's no one on them!' he shouted. 'They're *ours*! I'll get there first! I'll get there first!'

She screamed in terror and excitement and ran from him across the dry summer grass towards the safe ground of the empty swings. He followed her closely, watching anxiously as she clambered onto the swing. Marina's phone call was a distracting resonance in his mind behind his anxiety for his daughter. What was Robert and Marina's news? Did they want to share it with him? Did they want to pick up the old friendship where they'd left it four years ago? He could see them both: Robert's faint smile, knowing something. Marina standing by his side admiring him. They were focussed people. A successful team. He had never known them to be without ideas and projects. The telephone call puzzled him. What did they want? He caught Nada on the back swing and pushed her away gently.

'Higher, Daddy! Higher!' she demanded.

He caught her and pushed her higher, the tails of her red jacket flying out behind, the wind of her flight lifting her brown hair, her friend Snoopy Dog clutched against the chain of the swing. His heart contracted in his chest with love for her.

two

A little after midday on the following Wednesday he bought a bunch of expensive out-of-season Iceland poppies at the florist and drove across town to Richmond. It was hot again and his car was not airconditioned. He worried that the delicate flowers would wilt before he reached Robert and Marina's and thought that he had made a mistake buying them instead of robust proteas or natives; except that there was for him something emblematic in the vivid fragility of the poppies, and their name, Iceland. In the relentless heat it seemed like a message of hope.

Before he reached the river he turned out of the traffic into a side street. Three blocks later he turned right again and pulled up at a small square of park tucked between a row of houses. He sat looking through the windscreen, gathering his thoughts and remembering the park. Theirs was the last house in a terrace of painted brick and timber cottages, dwellings that had once been the homes of factory workers but which had been expensively restored and redesigned to accommodate young professionals. The scene before him was unchanged from his memory of it. The withered oleanders in the park and the small patch of bleached grass shimmering in the heat, the solitary palm tree, and beneath the palm tree the bench, still broken . . .

That summer night four years ago, Robert and Marina's friends had spilled from the lighted house into the park. Robert Schwartz and Marina Golding, the brilliant collaborative team, were relinquishing their position of influence in Melbourne's art scene for the vertigo of the great metropolis. That, at any rate, had been the understanding, a sense that it was Robert's largeness of vision that compelled them to go. A feeling that it wasn't so much that they had *decided* to go as that they were being drawn along the golden path of those who had found success in Sydney before them. There had been, among some of their friends that evening, a feeling of being left behind. Of being abandoned even. And, for a few, no doubt the departure of Robert and Marina for Sydney must have seemed a confirmation of their own failure. For the older ones especially. For it was what they had all aspired to. So there was a certain envy among the less-generous spirits. Despite their worldliness, despite their fervent scepticism, they had all privately clutched at a shamefaced hope of that sign of a divine care that placed upon a body of work a recognition that was not disputable.

When the last guests were leaving, Robert entreated him to stay with them in the park under the stars. It was he whom Robert had chosen to be the very last to sit with them on the grass, drinking wine and talking far into the night—Had it been that he and Marina could not bear to arrive at that moment when they would be alone with their happiness and without a witness to its splendours? Now they had returned.

Today the park was deserted.

He reached across to the passenger seat and picked up the bunch of flowers. As he lifted the blooms a scatter of petals was left on the grey nap of the seat. He was nervous now at the thought of seeing Robert again. He stepped out of the car, locked it and walked the few paces to their verandah. He pressed the bell and stood waiting.

Marina opened the door. 'Toni! How lovely to see you!' She stepped forward eagerly and embraced him lightly, touching her hand to his arm, touching her lips to his cheek. She moved away and examined him. 'It's cruel the way the critics ignored your show.'

'It's okay. It's their loss.'

'Exactly. And you've got your new project. Good for you.'

He handed the flowers to her.

A gust of wind tore off a scatter of bright petals. Marina exclaimed and sheltered the flowers protectively in her arms.

'You remembered! I love being given flowers. And Iceland poppies are my favourites.' She was moved. 'Thank you.'

So the Iceland poppies had been for Marina after all. He had not remembered, but had imagined himself to be choosing the flowers at random.

'What is it?' Marina asked. 'Have I changed so much?' She was older than he, by as much as ten years, slim and dark, her short hair freshly styled.

'No,' he said. 'You haven't changed at all.'

She smiled, enjoying the exacting quality of his attention.

The passage was narrow and she walked ahead of him. The disconcerting sensation of stepping back into their world, the familiar, elusive, clarified smell of their lives, a smell of cleanliness and good order. Today she was being welcoming and encouraging. Previously she would have stood aside, her manner silent and interior, observing him with Robert. Marina had seemed to him in those days to be in Robert's shadow. A faithful collaborator, content to be the apprentice of Robert Schwartz's studio. Perhaps, after all, she had stood within the shadow of some private inhibition of her own, an uncertainty too intimate to be disclosed. And of course she was older now.

She said over her shoulder, 'Robert's running late. He apologises. He rang to say he'll be in a meeting. We'll have a minute or two to catch up before he gets here.'

He followed her through the archway at the end of the passage into a lofty rectangular room. It was cool in here, the light filtered through pale blinds. The faint background hum of an airconditioner. An old man was sitting by a wall of books on a set of folded library steps. His loose cotton robe had slipped from his shoulders. He was barefoot, craned forward unsteadily over the book that he was holding open on his knees.

Marina stood beside a circular table in the centre of the room, the vivid poppies held against the white of her blouse, the tips of the fingers of her free hand touching the table beside her, steadying herself. She watched him, interested, her feet neatly together in smart Italian sandals.

'You *have* changed,' he said.

'Yes. I'm older.'

'That's not what I meant.'

The table was set for lunch, a chair at each of the four places. On the table were breads, Greek dips, a green-glazed bowl of olives. There was the faint aroma of dill.

'What *did* you mean?'

'I suppose we're bound to have changed,' he said. 'In some ways. All of us, I should think.'

'You're being evasive.' She laughed. 'Come and meet Robert's father.'

The old man did not get up but stretched an arm around Marina's waist and drew her to his side. It seemed to Toni to be a gesture of possession rather than of fondness. He was trembling, his head jerking and nodding. The lower lid of his left eye drooped, disclosing the livid weeping membrane. 'I've come home to die,' he said and laughed, his breath catching in his throat, his glance quick and amused. 'I shan't be around to bother you for much longer.'

'This is Theo Schwartz,' Marina said. 'Robert's father. Toni is an old friend, Theo. He was one of Robert's most gifted students.'

He took the old man's hand, catching a whiff of body or bowel rising from the gown where it fell open. As he stepped away his eyes were drawn involuntarily to the gape of the material, his eyes encountering a glimpse of what he should not see, a mound of coiled and yellowed flesh, the inadmissible disaster of old age and disease.

Theo Schwartz smiled and released Marina. 'Gifted and in his prime,' he said in a tone of mild irony. 'Did you know that Nero murdered his wife and mother, Toni? People do such things.' He patted Marina's arm. 'My son's wife.' He might have wished a connection to be registered by them between the present situation and Nero's murderous violence towards the women of his household, the idea that murder, giftedness and youth were commonplaces of existence.

Toni read the title of the book. It was a German edition of the diaries of the artist Paul Klee, Klee's *Tagebücher*, the spidery inked lines of an illustration between blocks of text, Klee's occult signs and portents. Toni considered making a comment, but Theo turned his shoulders away and re-entered his reading, lifting one hand to them in gentle dismissal, preferring the company of Klee's immortal journal.

Marina said, 'Let's put these in water before they wilt. They're beautiful.'

He paused to inspect a bronze figure of a running man that stood on a small table. He grasped the heavy figure around the waist and picked it up, turning it and examining it. 'This is new. Whose is it? I have a feeling I should know it.'

Marina said, 'You should. It's Geoff Haine's. His show followed your installation at Andy's. We were at his opening. We thought we might see you there.'

He remembered the preoccupied, offhand greeting of the famous Sydney artist when Andy had introduced them. He set the heavy figure down on the table. 'I met him.'

Marina reached over to adjust the figure's line of flight, as if she knew its secret destination. 'Robert wrote a piece on his sculpture for *Art & Text*. Geoff gave him this by way of thanks.'

'Haunted,' Toni said unhappily. 'Isn't that the word they always use for Haine's work?' He stood looking at the bronze running man. He recognised it now as the figure that appeared and reappeared in the artist's monumental post-industrial landscapes, a solitary fugitive human presence in vast wastelands of rusting machinery and empty office towers aglow with the unearthly light of the end-of-days, visionary scenes calculated, perhaps, to impress the viewer with the towering moral authority of the artist himself. They had been hanging Haine's pictures at Andy's when he was carrying the last of his own dismantled installation out of the gallery, his arms filled with the wooden racks and old clothes, a rag-and-bone man. He had been feeling dismantled himself that day. Helpless. Gutted. Angered by the deathly silence with which his work had been received. He turned away from the sculpture, the enormous weight of Geoff Haine's reputation too much for him to deal with generously.

'So Sydney didn't work out for you two, then?' he said. 'We all had the impression you were doing brilliantly. I'm sorry!' He apologised quickly. 'I didn't mean that the way it sounded.'

'No, it's all right. I know you must be wondering.'

'I was thinking earlier of that great send-off we had for you two on your last night in Melbourne.'

'Wasn't it terrific! It was like being students again.' She spoke with enthusiasm of the memory. 'You stayed and we talked in the park until dawn.'

'Teresa was ready to kill me when I got home.'

'Of course. Teresa wasn't with you. I'd forgotten.'

'She was home with Nada. Nada was only a few weeks old.' His guilty reluctance that night to leave Robert Schwartz's magic circle. Staying until dawn, knowing Teresa was alone with their new baby waiting for him. Teresa had made plain to him her satisfaction that they had seen the last of Robert and Marina. *They're not our kind of people.* He had defended himself with the claim that they were his friends.

'It's funny, but I always picture you on your own,' Marina said. She smiled to soften her remark. 'I mean, we don't seem able to separate what we actually remember from what we invent about other people's lives, do we?'

She might have observed that it was not possible to ever know one's friends except through one's own imagination. A comment on the slight awkwardness between them, the lapse of time and the failure of the friendship suddenly being reversed.

Theo cleared his throat and turned a page.

'This house is still very much you and Robert,' Toni said. Their lives childless and mess-free, the assurance of their fastidious idiom persisting.

'I'm glad you feel that,' she said.

The room was bare of ornament except for Haine's running man and a solitary canvas leaning against the wall on the mantelpiece above the fireplace.

She turned to him. 'We *did* do well in Sydney. And of course we had that wonderful six months of Robert's residency at the university of Minnesota. He finished his book. Lots of good things happened.' She considered him. 'I missed Melbourne. How frivolous does that sound? I only realised once we'd left how deeply I belonged here. I still remember our first night in the apartment in Glebe, looking out the window at the lights of Sydney and knowing, suddenly, I was never going to be at home there.'

He looked at her.

'I couldn't possibly justify such a feeling, so I didn't try to. I didn't say anything about it. Sydney was very beautiful and everyone made us welcome. And I was supposed to rejoice at being there. After all, wasn't Sydney where everyone wanted to be? I went along with the idea that I'd eventually get used to it, but I knew I was never going to. I should have had the courage to say so that first night. I should have said, *I can't do this, we have to go home.*' She was silent a moment. 'Robert loved it. It had taken him an enormous amount of energy to plan the move. I could see that Sydney was everything he'd hoped it would be. He had his job and his connections. For Robert, Sydney is the heart of the world. It's where the main game is. It always will be. But I knew that in Sydney I was not in my right place and that I would be cast as an onlooker for the rest of my days. Anyway I don't know that I belong at the centre of things. Not everyone does. *The main game!* What a pompous idea that is, really. As if anything can be the main game for everyone. Last Christmas I told him I needed to move back to Melbourne for a period. For a few months of each year. I need to feel at home somewhere at least for some of the time. I didn't insist he come with me.' She turned and looked at him. 'After a very long silence he said, *If that's the way it is for you then we must go back together or this will become a trial separation for us.* Neither of us wanted that. So here we are. Trying things out in Melbourne again. It's not fair to be unloading all this on you.' She turned away. 'I've needed to tell someone. I must sound terribly selfish. Robert's Sydney friends are convinced I'm being manipulative. But I'm not.' With a sudden impatient fling of her hand she indicated the painting above the fireplace. 'Well, what do you think of it?'

He said, 'I would have thought being cast as an onlooker is something you *allow* to happen to you, isn't it?'

'Don't! Please! Look at the painting! Tell me what you think.'

He turned to the large two-metre square unframed canvas. It was an image of a naked man falling upward into a sombre sky of deep lustrous black. The figure sharply defined against the sky, suspended in a place without atmosphere. The luminous blue curve of the earth infinitely distant below. The man's body foreshortened, viewed from underneath, a perspective from the Sistine ceiling, his genitals and grey skin chilled by the life-neutralising forces of outer space, the wrinkled soles of his feet presented to the viewer. He was not dead, it seemed, but was a man adrift. An ironic *ascent of man*. A suggestion of crucifixion, but without the cross. Below the wrinkled soles of the naked man's feet a *trompe l'oeil* of an open book, the deckled edges of the pages casting a delicate filigree of reflected light onto the black sky, so that it appeared as if an actual book had been artfully attached to the canvas. Toni recognised the complicated ideas of Robert, the exemplary theoretician and assiduous practitioner of the contemporary, the *post*-postmodernist absenting himself from his works. His pictorial images a comment on the outmoded act of putting paint on canvas. The painting was a beautiful, sardonic self-apology for the abstracted hand of the artist, the absent master of his own designs. Robert's generous, calm and reliable good sense behind the carefully articulated idea of the painting. He could see Robert now, considering Marina's nervous announcement that she wanted to return to Melbourne, soberly reflecting on the realities of their situation and concluding that his choice was either to lose his beloved Sydney or to lose his beloved wife.

'You two have always been serious about wanting people to enjoy looking at your pictures,' he said and moved in close to the painting to examine its surface. He turned to her. 'But is it still both of you?'

'You guessed!' She was pleased. 'No. It's just me. Robert doesn't paint any more. I do all the painting now. The subjects are still Robert's. The ideas are still his, but the brushwork's all mine these days.' She laughed. 'That was very good, Toni.'

'Your technique's fantastic,' he said.

'I love painting.'

'You were always good, but you're way ahead of where you were four years ago. It doesn't look like a painting by someone who is unhappy.'

'Oh, I'm not unhappy! For goodness sake, don't think that. Please!' She turned to him, reproaching him gently. 'You don't like it, do you?'

'It's brilliant.'

'You don't like it, Toni. Why don't you say so? Or can't we tell each other the truth anymore?' She watched him. After a moment she asked, 'Why did you never come to Sydney to see us in the early days? You promised solemnly that last night that you would come and visit us. It was almost a sacred vow. Do you remember?'

'Of course I remember.'

'You and Robert swore to remain friends forever.'

'We'd all been drinking pretty solidly that night.'

'That wasn't all it was.'

Did she believe, he wondered, that the neglect of his old friendship with Robert had been deliberate? He was silent for some time, meditating on the injustice of such a view. 'Once you've got a child,' he said, 'you can't just drop everything and go whenever you feel like it.'

'No, I suppose not. I'm sorry, I didn't think of that. We're such incredibly selfish creatures, aren't we? We only see the complications in our own lives.'

'I often thought of coming up. Teresa wouldn't have minded. It wasn't that.' But in fact Teresa would have minded greatly if he'd ever suggested going to Sydney to stay with Robert and Marina.

Marina held up the poppies and said, 'I'd better go and put these in water.' She turned abruptly and walked out of the room, as if she were leaving him to consider what had been said.

He did not feel invited to follow her. Robert's father gave his cough; the dry metallic comment of a sceptic. Toni turned and looked at him. There was something in the old man's style that attracted him; his age and his nearness to his end, no doubt. There was an uncanny likeness of father to son in the shrunken frame of Theo Schwartz. It might almost have been Robert himself present in the room in the transfigured form of his dying father, Robert's features locked in behind the mysterious mask of old age and sickness.

Marina called from the kitchen, 'Come and see!'

As he went out the door he was unable to resist a backward glance at Theo. The old man was watching him.

There was a short passage. On the left side of the passage a closed door, on the right an open door. He might easily have walked past the open door and gone straight through to the kitchen and on to the studio, where Marina would be waiting for him. He paused and stood looking into the room. Framed in the mirror of the dressing-table was the reflection of the single bed in its old position, pushed against the wall behind the door. *Toni's room* they had called it in the years before Nada, before Teresa, before the installations, when he was still living at the flat with his mother and father in Port Melbourne and tutoring part-time under Robert at the art school. He had been a painter of pictures in those days, before his father's sudden death. Now, as he stood looking in at the room, he might have been a traveller from the future *then*, his presence unsuspected by the young man asleep on the bed; a young man without self-irony, trusting implicitly to the necessity of success and to the potency of his gift. Toni could almost taste on his palate the pungent memory of that young man who had been himself then, crashed on the bed in the grey dawn light after talking and drinking all night with Robert and his friends, his head reeling with the effects of alcohol and the delirium of ideas. Something of him was still here in this house, something of his own life persisting in their lives, a sense of something unfinished between them.

He turned and walked along the passage. Marina had never taken part in those nights of drinking, but had gone to bed early and let them get on with it. He had thought her then too self-effacing, too lacking in enthusiasm, too comfortably in the shadow of Robert's vivid intelligence to be interesting. But perhaps she had merely been bored with the frantic adolescence of their ambitions and had preferred the company of a book in her own bed to the company of her husband's admiring ensemble of young friends.

The passage opened into the kitchen.

The Iceland poppies stood in a yellow and blue Picasso vase on the benchtop. Beside the flowers was a dish of antipasto covered with a membrane of cling-wrap.

Beyond the kitchen he emerged into a long room. The smell was intense; a mixture of Belgian linen, damar varnish, turps, paint extender and the faint essence of cedar. It was Duchamp's olfactory art. His own craft that had fallen silent in him on the day of his father's death. There were no windows. The panes of a lantern roof dispersed an even illumination from above: the controlled light of illusion with which to seduce the eye of the beholder. A timber easel and side table stood at an angle against the end wall. An oil painting in-progress was mounted on the easel, a coloured photograph from a newspaper pinned at eye-level to the right-hand upright of the easel. On the side table the paraphernalia of the craft. A hard-backed chair by the left-hand wall, and two prepared canvases. Behind the chair a white-painted cupboard. The chair faced the easel, as if it had been placed there for someone to observe the artist at work.

Marina was standing beside her painting.

She might have been testing her own presence in the composition, or posed with her work for a publicity photograph—*see the artist, see her work*. She did not step forward and stand beside him to view the painting with him but remained where she was.

A menacing young man confronted Toni from the centre foreground of the large canvas. Above his tight blue jeans the young man's naked torso was soft and feminine. He gripped a stone in each clenched fist, a black bandanna masking the lower half of his face, the likeness of another man, but of calm expression, printed in white on the bandanna. The crazy eyes of the half-naked young man blazed above the calm face of the man on the bandanna. Behind him, flames lit up a disordered streetscape in which the indistinct forms of fighting men struggled in front of burning buildings. Red, yellow and green points of light struck suggestively through the smoke above the struggling figures. The painting lacked the detail and finish of the painting in the other room.

Marina watched for his reaction, as if it were she herself who was on display.

The image, he saw, was a greatly enlarged copy of the newspaper photograph. CHAOS RULES was written like a title or a headline across the top of the canvas in pale letters, a simulacrum of the graffiti in the photograph.

There was a movement of air and the distant sound of the front door slamming.

'Robert's home,' Marina said. She walked across to stand beside Toni.

A moment later Robert came in. He was holding his father by the hand, his manner solicitous, respectful and deeply attentive towards the old man, who was having difficulty walking without his son's assistance. Robert looked across at them, acknowledging them with a lift of his chin and a quick smile. When Robert's father was seated on the chair facing the easel, Robert came over to them. He held out his hand. 'Toni,' he said. 'It's really good to see you. I'm so glad you could come.'

'Welcome back,' Toni said. 'It's going to be great having you two in town again.'

'You've met Dad?' Robert half-turned towards his father and said with mild astonishment, 'He came home.'

They stood looking at Robert's father, as if he were with them by some freakish twist of fate, an object of their peculiar and intense curiosity. Theo looked at the painting on the easel before him and might have been unaware of them.

'My dad,' Robert said, a tenderness and something of regret in his voice. He might almost have said, *My son*.

Robert was a lightly built man of fifty. He was youthful and alert. His thick greying hair was cropped close to the dome of his skull and he was wearing an expensive grey business suit with a black silk shirt and green silk tie. An ample handkerchief of the same material as the tie flopped from the breast pocket of his jacket.

'I'm sorry I'm late,' he said. 'I'm sure Marina's been looking after you.' His tone and his manner were friendly and encouraging, but behind the lenses of his spectacles his pale eyes were hooded, tired and distracted. 'Marina told me you're working on a big new project. I knew you would be. That's wonderful, Toni.' Without waiting for a response to this he kissed Marina on the lips, then turned and faced Toni, his arm through Marina's arm, holding her to his side much as his father had. 'Has Marina told you?'

'I haven't said anything,' she said.

'You remember Oriel Liesker?'

'Sure. Of course.'

'Oriel's partly our reason for coming back to Melbourne just now.'

Marina said quickly, 'Not the whole reason.'

'No, not the whole reason.' Robert frowned. 'But I don't think we'd have actually come back, would we, darling, if Oriel hadn't been so persuasive?' He turned back to Toni. 'Oriel's been working on us for a while. We've finally been seduced. She's curating the new Bream Island sculpture park and art space.' He allowed a moment for effect. 'She's offered us the inaugural show.' He paused again. 'It's going to create a lot of interest. Sydney's jealous.' He looked at Marina, as if he asked for her confirmation of this improbable claim.

'No wonder you came back then,' Toni said. 'Congratulations!' He shook hands with them both. 'I've heard a lot about the space. It should be brilliant.' Robert insisting on a purely professional reason for their return, their move back to be viewed as a considered opportunity in the advancement of their careers, rather than merely satisfying Marina's vague need to feel at home.

'So you've been out to the island?'

'No, I've just read about it.'

Robert waited for the space of two heartbeats. 'Marina and I would like you to join us. We'd like it to be a group show. The three of us. Our paintings and your installation.' They watched him, like parents who have given a favourite child a present. The collaborative team of Schwartz and Golding, seduced back from the main game to lead this minor advance in the artistic life of their mother city. They might almost have not been away, Robert's manner implied, their absence from Melbourne an unsettling dislocation, this the steadying reality. It seemed that Robert would rejoin the fractured ends of the disjointed narrative of their friendship, as if nothing, after all, was to be irrecoverable.

'That's incredibly generous of you,' Toni said. He was perplexed by the offer. He had not expected anything like it. He should tell them now that he was in fact without ideas and his work at a standstill. He did not want to relinquish the attraction of the situation, however—at least not just yet. 'But is Oriel okay with it? She doesn't know my work.'

Robert said firmly, 'Oriel's fine with it.' He stepped away from Marina. 'Let's go in and have a drink. The opening's in two months. You can have something of your new installation ready by then, can't you? A section? An aspect? We're putting in three paintings. These two you've seen and another one.' There was something just a little bullying in Robert's brisk tone now, something of the dean of the faculty demanding his own way, insisting his plan be adopted by his subordinates without modification.

Toni wondered if he had been Robert's first choice of a partner for the show. 'I'm flattered, Robert. Really. Thanks. It's wonderful of you.'

Robert smiled slowly. 'Good!' He was the concerned teacher once again, their old leader at art school pursuing the project of his vision, ever proposing to his students and his staff the sense behind what happens. A man of high certainty and composure, the person whom they were glad to have in charge in a crisis. Against all the prejudices and fashions of the day, it had been Robert who had opened out a moment in their lives when it had been possible for them to believe in something they might have called authority, something, in an earlier age, which they might have been content to refer to as his *school*. But that was in the past now and would not be recovered, Toni was suddenly sure of it, though it seemed

Robert had not noticed, or *would not* notice. And yet, almost against his will, Toni wanted to believe in the idea. *The Bream Island Inaugural Show—Schwartz, Golding & Powlett.* It *was* seductive.

Robert said, 'It's a great opportunity for all of us.' He held both hands out palms up, considering two weighty objects. 'The space needs a three-dimensional installation, or a sculpture, to bring it up. Our paintings would be lost there on their own.'

Over Robert's shoulder Toni could see the old man, his hands gripping his knees, his head craned forward, his jaw slack, his body jumping and jiggling, his attention anchored to the floor.

'I'm sorry I didn't make it to your show. Truly sorry,' Robert said. 'It was just impossible for me to get there.'

'I wasn't expecting either of you to get to it.'

'Marina told me I missed something important. I believe no one reviewed it? If things hadn't been so chaotic, I might have written a piece for *Art & Text*. Have you got photos or studies? Perhaps I could still do something.'

'No. I just put it together. I knew what I wanted. I didn't do any studies.' Toni found that he did not want to talk about his last installation with Robert.

Marina said, 'I couldn't decide whether you meant them to be a crowd of victims in need of help or a sinister mob.'

There was a silence.

Robert said, 'You'll have to see the island space before you can finally decide whether you'll do the show. Marina can take you one day next week, if that suits. What do you think, darling? There's that business of getting the keys from the park ranger. Can you organise it?'

Toni realised that his viewing of the island was to be purely a formality for Robert.

They turned at the clatter of Theo Schwartz's spectacles hitting the floor.

They watched Robert hurry across the studio and lean to pick them up, one hand on the old man's shoulder.

Marina said, 'Why don't we go in? He won't be a minute.'

In the room where the table was set for lunch she moved from place to place, adjusting the position of a knife, a glass, brushing at the cloth with her fingers. A sleek silver-haired cat emerged from the passage and pressed itself against her legs. She bent and picked it up, cradling it in her arms like a baby. 'You've abandoned me, haven't you, darling?' She set the cat on the floor again. 'Misty's fallen in love with Theo.'

They watched the cat patrol the room.

He considered asking her if their plan was to return to Sydney after the island show, but she no longer seemed accessible. She spoke softly to the cat, coaxing, lightly teasing, accusing it of betraying her, as if she and the cat were alone in the room. The cat responded to her voice with a low sound in its throat, as if it reassured her of its continuing fidelity, as if indeed fidelity were a delicate game they played.

Robert came in from the kitchen. He had taken off his jacket and tie and carried a bottle of white wine and a corkscrew. 'Dad's having a lie down. He's too unwell to join us.' He drew the cork from the bottle. 'Wine, Toni?'

'Thanks. You finished a new book while you were in Sydney?'

Marina set her glass on the table and went out to the kitchen.

'I can't stay long,' Toni said. 'I have to pick Nada up at two-thirty. Kinder finishes early on Wednesday.'

Robert looked at him. 'I'd very much like to meet her.' He was silent a moment. 'I've often wondered what it would be like to be a father.' He gestured at the chairs. 'Why don't we sit down? So it's still portraits with you then? These costumed racks that Marina is so enthusiastic about?'

Toni shrugged. 'It's always been people with me.'

'You've dispensed with likeness, is that it?' Robert reached for an olive and chewed it, moisture glistening on his lips, his desire to understand, to be informed. 'Can we have a true portrait without likeness? Without personality? Without the individual?'

'What's a true portrait?' Toni asked.

They laughed at the unanswerable question, a spark there suddenly of the old attraction, the competing visions of master and pupil.

'It's always been the interesting question for me, how we depict ourselves,' Toni said. He had no theories about his work. He supposed that the faceless presences of his installations had represented for him something like his own unofficial history, a kinship history of displacement. A story of losers, not winners, of those who had drifted into the dark without a trace, his fascination not with personality but with the *im*personal. It had been something like that. He was not clear. He did not want to be clear. Clarity about such things offended his sense of their authenticity. His abandonment of paint and canvas and the switch to installations on the death of his father had been as much a surprise to him as it had been to everyone who knew him. He had not planned it. Indeed he had attempted to keep on painting after his father's death, but had not been able to. He lost his confidence and the paintings he did were empty. Painting didn't work for him anymore. So, reluctantly, for he loved it, he gave it up. He had never been able to share his deepest feelings about his work with anyone but his father. He looked at Robert. 'I'm not actually working on anything. I haven't been able to work for weeks. I've done nothing since the last installation.'

Robert examined the olives. 'You're saying you don't have anything on the go at the moment?'

'That's right. Sorry. You'll have to get someone else to do this show with you.'

Robert was thoughtful. 'We have these black spaces,' he said after a moment. 'That's all it is. They feel like the end, but they're usually a prelude. You know, to something important.' He smiled. 'We won't be asking anyone else. You'll come up with an idea when you've seen the space. I know you will. And so you told Marina you were working on a grand new project.'

'She took me seriously and I let it go.'

Robert laughed softly.

His assurance that black spaces were not ends in themselves had been given with his old conviction and Toni found himself wanting to believe him. It was the way things had once been between them; something reliable and perceptive in Robert that he had offered generously to those he cared for and believed in. Robert had not changed. Toni said, 'Thanks.' It occurred to him that Robert had always had a mixture of ambition and authority alongside a deep private modesty in his personality.

Marina came in and set the dish of antipasto on the table. 'Here we are. All my own work.' She sat down. 'Not really. But I did choose the ingredients.' She eased the dish towards Toni. 'Please.'

three

He waited for her at the chainmesh fence, watching the slow brown river with its cargo of floating garbage, the tall trees of the sunlit island fifty metres out bending in the wind. *You're doing their bidding*, Teresa had accused him scornfully that morning, working herself into a state. *You're just letting them interrupt your life. In a couple of months they'll go back to Sydney and forget about you again.* It was harsh but she had never liked them. An aluminium dinghy with an outboard rode at a timber jetty the other side of the wire, dipping and bobbing to the little waves. On her way out she had turned at the front door and shouted back into the house, *You're a bad judge of character!* Teresa believed he needed protecting from what she confidently referred to as the real world; that place, in other words, where she spent her own working days. He said maybe she'd prefer it if he never left his studio. But the truth was he had no legitimate room for complaint, so he shut up and let her do the talking...

Behind him, his old green VK station wagon was parked alongside a concrete pylon under the roadbed of the freeway. Beyond the VK, deep within the darkness under the columns, a slope of rubble. When he'd stepped out of the car he had noticed a dark-stained mattress humped with old clothes, or maybe a recumbent figure slumped in the monochrome of shadows. The scene put him in mind of Geoff Haine's apocalyptic landscapes. The underbelly. A netherworld of empty Coke cans, discarded packaging and plastic bags. A theatre for drunks and the homeless. Fugitive figures. A family resemblance between the featureless people of his own installations and Haine's anonymous running man, another human portrait-without-likeness. Robert was surely right to suggest that it was time to be doing something else. But what? His father had said, *To work is what matters to the artist.* And it was true. He would have given anything to be working right this minute, instead of hanging around here waiting for Marina to turn up.

Two kilometres to the north, the glass towers of the CBD shone in the midday sun. He could almost see Andy's converted biscuit factory from where he stood. If it weren't for Andy's support, he would have had nowhere to show his work these days. Andy had never offered an opinion on his installations one way or the other and, when Toni pressed him after a few beers one evening, Andy said, *You show your stuff here, whenever you're ready with it. You do what you do.* Feisty little Andy Levine, making a nice fortune supporting some of the least commercial and some of the most commercial artists in Australia. Supporting people he liked. He and Andy Levine had been staunch friends since first grade at Nott Street Primary. Andy's father a backyard car dealer in those days, dreaming of a franchise with the big boys out along Burwood Highway, and no one at all surprised when his son converted the old Port Melbourne biscuit factory into one of the most successful contemporary art galleries in Australia. *It's your space, mate. Whenever you need it.* That was Andy's attitude, and Toni was grateful for it.

He turned from the fence at the sound of a car coming off the blacktop onto the gravel slope behind him, the tyres losing grip and popping the stones. The sun was against her windscreen, then she rolled down into the shadows and he saw her sitting behind the wheel, a big sunhat on her head.

He stepped away from the fence and walked across to meet her.

She parked beside his wagon and swung her door open.

'Good morning,' he said. 'Is it still morning?'

She took off her sunglasses and squinted up at him. 'I'm not late, am I? What a beautiful day we've got for it!' She stepped out of the car and grabbed at her hat. Her dress was sleeveless, grey cotton, light and summery. On her feet flat-heeled sandals. She turned and leaned into the car, one knee on the driver's seat, putting the strap of a denim satchel over her shoulder. She reached across to the passenger side, saying something he did not catch, and lifted out a basket covered with a blue and white tea towel. She turned, resting the basket against her stomach, the wind lifting the edge of the towel. 'I brought us some lunch.' She handed him the basket and took from the satchel an orange float with a bunch of keys attached to it. She flourished the keys. 'One of these fits the padlock on that gate over there.'

At the end of the jetty she took the basket from him and he got down into the dinghy. She handed the basket to him and stepped into the boat. While she was starting the motor he unfastened the mooring rope and slid it through the ringbolts on the dock. She opened the throttle and the boat cut through the water, slipping out of the shadow of the freeway into the sunlight.

'It's wonderful to get out of the studio for a day,' she said.

The island presented a dense margin of trees, willow branches trailing in the river and snagging the garbage. As they rounded the southern tip of the island a landing stage came into view, a canopied barge moored next to it. The barge was decorated like a fairground boat that might ply the make-believe waterways of Luna Park or Disneyland, *The Tunnel of Love* or *The Pirates Cave*. BREAM ISLAND PUNT in blue lettering along the side of its canopy.

He took hold of the rope and tied up alongside the barge. Marina cut the motor.

He secured the boat and climbed out onto the landing stage, taking the picnic basket from her and standing to read the sign. *Bream Island Environmental Sculpture Park and Art Space. All native plants and animals are protected.*

'It's like playing truant.' she said beside him.

The smell of the dry incandescent bush in his nostrils.

Her features were uplit by the reflected sunlight within the shadows of her hat's brim. In this modelling of her features, something of the burnished softground of an etching needle. *In art, beauty is everything*, his father had told him. *The artist's enterprise is to refuse the world's ugliness.*

'I bet you never played truant,' he said.

She laughed. 'Come on, let's go and see the space.'

She walked ahead of him, climbing the levee that was set with redgum sleepers for steps, rising diagonally across the face of the bank.

He followed her, admiring the free swing of the grey dress against her legs—the dress she had chosen to wear for her truant day. Taking it from her wardrobe this morning and holding it against herself, considering how she would look. Robert sitting on the edge of their bed admiring her. She telling him, *They said on the radio it's going to be hot.*

She waited for him on the crown of the levee. 'Look! It's amazing. An island of native bush preserved in the middle of the city.'

Below them a sweep of dry grass and tall eucalypts. A *plein-air* vision trembling in the golden summer heat.

'We never went to the bush when I was a kid,' he said. 'I don't think Mum and Dad knew the way.'

They walked along the top of the levee.

'What time do you have to pick Nada up?' she asked.

'Three-thirty.'

'Good, we'll have time for our picnic.'

They followed the track down into the hollow of the island. Electric barbeques with tables and bench sets, and here and there among the trees the environmental sculptures. Constructions of local stone and timber suggesting the work of shamans, something to do with the sanctity of wilderness.

She reached out with her straw hat, pointing. Ahead, through the trees, a pale building reclined along the verge of the timberline.

A few minutes later they came up to the building and she unlocked the door with one of the keys on the orange float. She waited and he went in and set the picnic basket on the floor.

It was a large empty space with narrow vertical windows looking out on to the surrounding bush. There was the smell of fresh paint.

She stood beside him. After a minute she asked, 'So what do you think? Can you see your work here?'

'It's a good space,' he said. He was not enthusiastic.

She walked away from him, impatient. 'So you haven't really got a project?'

He watched her standing on her own in the middle of the expanse of vacant floor, the hard light from the windows behind her, isolating her. The human figure, isolated and vulnerable. He said playfully, '*You* could be my installation.'

She swung around, making a sweeping gesture at the space with her extended arm, the broad brim of the hat, her skirt swinging around with her. 'Come on, Toni! What do you really think? Be serious!' She stood, considering him. 'It's the silence of the critics, isn't it? God knows it's hard enough when they *do* notice us.'

'It's not the silence of the critics,' he said. 'Nada's got more idea of what she's doing at the moment than I have.'

'You can't let this opportunity go by, Toni. I can't believe you won't think of something.' She walked back and stood beside him. 'Robert and I don't want someone else doing this show with us.'

They looked out the narrow window together. Two magpies walking about stabbing at the leaf litter.

'I hated Melbourne our first day back,' she said. 'I thought I'd made a terrible mistake. I panicked. I went to your show that day to reassure myself that you were still here doing the things you do.' She looked at him quickly. 'I needed to know there was some sort of continuity. In my life, I suppose. I was being selfish. But when I stepped through the door at Andy's and saw what you'd done I almost turned around and went straight out again. That awful napthalene smell of those old clothes. The way you'd set up those racks, like a crowd of forlorn refugees standing there waiting for something impossible to turn their fortunes around and make them whole and happy again. But you could see that theirs was a lost cause. They were like someone's memory of people. People from a dream. It was almost too personal to be on display. I thought, no wonder no one's here. I wanted to leave at once.'

He liked the way she talked about his work, vehement, angry. As if it had meant something to her. 'So why didn't you?'

'I forced myself to stay half an hour, then I fled. I didn't tell you, but I went back again the next day. But you'd already dismantled it and they were hanging Geoff Haine's pictures. Geoff's pictures were a relief. I was glad your empty people were gone. I had to make an effort to believe I'd actually seen them. And then, of course, they began to haunt me and I couldn't get them out of my head. That was when I began to realise you'd done something impressive.' She stood looking out at the encompassing bush. 'I know just how you're feeling. I know what it's like. When you can't work, life stops.'

The warbling of the two magpies. The birds peering curiously through the glass, or perhaps looking at their own reflections.

'Let's go and have our picnic,' she said with decision. 'I don't have the right energy for this.'

He picked up the basket and they went out of the building into the sunlight.

She slipped her arm through his and they walked together through the crackling bush, as if they were strolling down

Brunswick Street among the crowds. 'You were always observing us,' she said. 'Drawing and watching, that's what you used to do. You never stopped drawing and looking. You were so certain of your gift. So sure of what you were doing. You had no curiosity about the world. We couldn't believe it when you wrote and told us you'd given up drawing and painting. You turned everything into drawings in those days. Everything can be drawn, you used to say.'

'I was quoting my dad. I only drew people. Nothing else.'

They walked on in silence.

'Dad always said drawing is superior to painting. He never drew people. He never drew us, his sons or his wife. I think we were too precious for him to risk our likenesses.'

The magpies stood looking after them, heads on one side then on the other, considering, making a judgement.

He was sitting with his back against the trunk of a gum tree. She was drawing the group of pale gums in front of them, seated cross-legged in the shade of a wattle, her drawing block on her lap. She checked her subject, then touched her pencil to the paper. Beside her a half-empty glass of wine. The remains of the salad and chicken and the last of the bread were spread on the blue and white tea towel between them, the empty wine bottle on its side on the grass. She eased her back and set the pad and the pencil aside on the grass and reached for her wine.

'Can I see?' he asked.

She passed the pad across to him. 'When did you first know you were going to be an artist? I don't think I've ever heard you speak about how you came to it.'

'This is good,' he said. 'I can't do trees.' He handed the pad back to her. 'Kirchner turned to landscape near the end. I might have a go at it one of these days.'

She looked at her drawing then set the pad aside. 'Tell me. I want to know. You don't mind?'

'It was my dad,' he said. 'He used to have nightmares and couldn't sleep. He'd get up in the middle of the night and sit in the kitchen drawing and painting. It was his night world, his escape. Watercolours and gouaches. He taught himself. He'd paint these modest studies of the domestic items around us. Our stuff. Cups and saucepans. The kitchen chairs. Tea towels Mum had left drying over the stove. The bag of flour or box of cereal. You know? The tins on the shelf. He had dreamed of being an artist when he was a boy, but the war ended all that for him. With his art he was reclaiming something of his boyhood dreams out of that landscape of ruins, something of his innocence. I'd see the light under the door and I'd get up and come out to the kitchen and watch him. To me it was magic. I'd hold my breath. He wouldn't say anything, but he'd slip his arm around me and press me to his side and keep working, and I knew he was glad to have me there with him in the night. Just the two of us. It was a picture in his mind, the perfect picture, father and son safe together. For him it was the greatest blessing that I was interested in his art. Emotion was always close to the surface with my dad. He would weep and smile at me and wipe his eyes and I'd give him a cuddle. But he never talked a lot about himself. About what had happened. It was too much for him. I soon started doing drawings of my own. His stuff. Copying him. He never tried to teach me. *You don't teach drawing*, he used to say. *Drawing is something you learn by doing it. There's no other way.* We'd be there in the night together doing our drawing and painting and he'd tell me about the great artists he admired. Max Beckmann and Kirchner. It haunted him that Kirchner killed himself at the age of fifty-eight because he realised he was never going to be in the first rank of the artists of his day. The art and the struggles of these men to make sense of their lives fascinated him. And Giorgio Morandi, of course. He loved Morandi's solemn still-life etchings.

Those artists helped Dad sustain his belief in himself. With them he was never alone with his art. He loved them. He loved their passionate vulnerability and the tenderness of their work. He recognised himself in them. *The dream is to have made sense of one's life at the end*, he used to say. *That is all.* He would whisper it: *To have made sense of it.* To me it was as if he had discovered the secret of existence. He would get their books out of the library and study them. Those self-portrait pencil drawings of Kirchner's that Kirchner did during the last weeks of his life. Those simple poignant line sketches of the man's features held him. He would stare at them for hours, lost in them, as if he were touching Kirchner's despair and sharing it with him. Dad made me see the point of art, showing me how Kirchner was groping his way towards a meaning in the reflection of his own features. It was beautiful. I loved it when he talked like that. He would pass his fingers over the reproductions of Kirchner's features in that book, and sometimes he would weep for the man. Dad believed art was something noble. Something with the power to lift humanity out of the factory and the prison. Which is where he worked, in a factory that was his prison.'

'Toni. I've never heard you talk about any of this before. You change completely when you talk about your father. It's astonishing.'

He had never spoken in this way about his father. Not to anyone. He was surprised to have heard himself say these things, as if he had achieved a sudden clarity.

'Did he ever show his work?'

'No,' he said slowly. He was a little reluctant to continue. Perhaps he had already said enough.

'Why not?' she persisted gently.

'Art was a private thing with Dad. It wasn't the way it is for us. It wasn't something for outsiders to admire or for strangers to buy. Dad was building a temple with his art. A temple of our lives together. The intimate things of our daily use. To be a family was something deeply precious to him. The domestic realities. He never took any of it for granted. He never complained. The Dunlop factory was like his second prison. He was more familiar with prisons than he was with temples. Mum told me that when he was fourteen he was separated from the rest of his family and was transported to a labour camp in Poland. Then, after the war, he was in a refugee camp in England, which was where she met him. They both worked in England for ten years, then they had the chance to emigrate in the fifties and they came out here. That's when they had Roy. And then me, of course, but much later. Mum still says I was her surprise package. After a while I took it for granted I was going to be an artist when I grew up. Dad did too. It became our joint project. My future. We worked on it together. Drawing. Always drawing.' He fell silent, thinking back.

Marina watched him.

He looked at her and smiled. 'I used to think I was going to build the temple of my father's dreams with my art. But it's not that easy, is it?'

'No, it's not. It's not easy at all. You had that intensity about you when we first met you. I thought you were aloof.'

'Keep drawing,' he said. 'I like to watch you working.'

Marina resumed drawing the trees. After a while she paused and looked across at him. 'Go on. Don't stop now. Tell me the rest. What happened to your father's pictures?'

'In the mornings, when he'd left for his shift, Mum would gather up the previous night's batch of pictures and carefully put them between sheets of newspaper, then she stacked them flat in his old suitcase. That suitcase had travelled everywhere with him. She told us it was the one thing he had with him when he arrived in England. I guess someone had given it to him. They kept it under their bed—which is where his pictures still are. Mum let me have one of them. *They belong together*, she said. *He wouldn't want them scattered around the place.* I had it framed. It's hanging on the wall in the passage at home. It wasn't there when you and Robert came over for dinner that time. You can see it next time you come over.'

'I'd love to see it.'

'Dad painted the same things over and over. *It doesn't matter how skilled you become*, he used to say, *you can never paint the same thing twice. Look at the work of Morandi!* He'd tell me, *A thing will always surprise you when you look at it again. There will always be something new each time. And the more you look, the deeper the mystery, the deeper the silence of the object of your contemplation.* Those were Dad's words to me. *Nothing in art is ever finished*, he'd say. *Everything is always a work-in-progress. Even if you never go back to it. The artist is not interested in completion, only in the work.* That was my dad. *The artist is not a priest*, he warned me once, when he saw how seriously I was taking it. *Remember that! But the artist must have something of the priest's irrational persistence. A faith that doesn't ask why but just is.* Art was my dad's answer to the cruelty and the ugliness of the world.'

She was silent a while, drawing, then she said, 'You must miss him very much.'

'I've never talked about him like this before.'

She looked at him. 'I feel very privileged. Thank you.'

'I don't know why, but it all seemed to be suddenly there for me to say.' She was a picture herself. The sketching block on her knees, her pale legs bare in the sunlight where her dress was rucked up. 'Trees,' he said. 'I remember you drawing those big old trees at your parents' place that time.'

'The elms at Plovers. Yes. I've always loved to draw trees. They don't get fidgety sitting for you.' She looked around at the bush. 'Isn't it beautiful? We're so lucky. What you just said was beautiful, too.'

He stood up.

She was startled. 'You're not going?'

He grinned. 'I need to take a walk.'

'Oh.'

He walked off some way into the timber and took a leak. The wind had died and, on an impulse, he kept walking, drawn into the warm aromatic stillness of the bush, picturing Marina back in the glade under the wattles alone, doing her drawing; the scene of their own private *déjeuner sur l'herbe*. Sharing with her his memories of his father had made her seem more real to him. In the telling he had recaptured something of the intensity of those early years, his passionate hopes for his art and for his father's dream. Teresa would be fiercely jealous if she knew he had shared something like this with Marina. He had not meant to, but had just found himself suddenly able to talk to her. He stopped and looked around. He and Andy would have loved this place when they were boys. Marina was right, it was a truant's island. A place for escapees. Full of little hillocks and hollows and hidden glades where the hunter could hide or approach the enemy's camp unseen.

A pulsing of bullets through the leaves and the felled bodies lay twitching on the grass. Step in and finish them off. The *coup de grâce* . . . He realised he had no idea which was the way back. He was amused at the notion of being bushed in this island remnant of wild Australia in the middle of the city. It was an uncanny feeling of being suddenly alone. A loss of direction. An absence of familiar reference. A white-eyed crow observed him from a nearby tree, the malevolence of the opportunist in the bird's eye.

He walked on, feeling stimulated and excited by the talk. He was restless now to be doing something. A few minutes later he topped a low rise and she was there below him, lying in the broken shadows of the wattle tree on the bleached grass. He stood on the rise among the trees looking down on her. She was a stranger, really. They had never been close, not as he and Robert had. She was lying on her side in the silver wattle's overhang, her straw hat under her head. Her left leg drawn up under her, her right leg thrust out, the sandal fallen from her foot. Her sketching block and denim bag abandoned on the grass beside her. The blue and white tea towel with the two plates, chicken bones and scraps of lettuce. The empty wine bottle and two glasses on their sides on the grass catching the sunlight. The bright orange plastic float with the keys to the island.

He made his way down into the hollow.

The heat of the afternoon and the wine had felled her. He stood admiring her and wondering about her, his eye drawn to the back of her knee in the cast shadows of the wattle's foliage, a dimple in her bare flesh where ligament and muscle were linked in tension to the bone beneath the skin. With care he stepped to her side. It was the cautious action of someone who did not wish to be discovered. He stood above her, the body of the woman lying on the grass. Robert's wife sleeping in the sun at his feet. After a moment he leaned to pick up her sketching pad and pencil case. He carried them back to the gum tree and sat with his back against its trunk. He recognised the pencil case. It was the one she had carried during his holiday with Robert at her parents' house at Mount Macedon all those years ago. He had been in his first year at art school then, and a little awed by the grand manner of Marina's parents, the ample style of their lives, the imposing gabled front of their enormous old house with its tall chimneys rising from twelve acres of winter garden, hundred-year-old laurels and a ground mist of bluebells. The red-brick bulk of the house and its gardens set against a rising woodland of leafless elms and oaks. He remembered making a drawing of Marina one afternoon while she was sleeping off a migraine on an old-fashioned cane chaise longue in the conservatory.

For some reason, he and Marina had been alone in the house that afternoon. Perhaps Robert had been taken by Marina's mother to visit an 'interesting' neighbour. Migraine seemed to him then to have been Marina's excuse for avoiding doing things she did not want to do; her excuse for staying quietly out of the main game, just as her return to Melbourne now was a retreat from similar demands. But perhaps the migraines had been real, too, for she had emerged from them grey-faced and washed out, purple half-moons under her eyes, her gaze glassy and absent. As he had passed the conservatory that day he had seen that the shutters were half-closed across the tall windows. The figure of a woman lying on the cane chaise longue asleep, her form a tonal arrangement among deep shadows. He had paused at the door—then, as now, the unobserved voyeur—and had decided to take her likeness.

He sat with his back to the gum tree and examined her pencil case. The seams were hand-stitched and it was held closed by a row of four large wooden buttons that might have come from a woman's expensive overcoat. One of Marina's mother's old coats. A camelhair coat that women of her style used to wear. A coat his own mother would admire but would never put on her own back, even if it were a gift. Not a coat he would have included among his featureless mob. The pencil case was a thing that a woman who had learned to sew as a girl might make if she were thinking back to her schooldays. It was an article intimate to Marina's hand, suggesting to him the image of a domestic moment in that grand house, Marina sitting in a deep armchair by the fireside sewing and dreaming, the black rain of Mount Macedon streaking the windows, the dog asleep on the hearth rug at her feet.

He laid the case open across his outstretched legs and tested the feel of an ink pen between his fingers. But the pen was not right and he put it back. He touched the pencils, the broken pieces of pastel, her sooty stubs of charcoal. Everything in Marina's pencil case was toned to a smoky hue by powdered charcoal. He picked out a thick stub of soft pencil and fitted it to the grip of his left thumb and two fingers, the pads of his fingers in contact with the lead, something at once familiar and potent in the feel of it. He set the open pencil case aside on the grass and took up her drawing block. He flipped it open, his thumb smudging the page of her abandoned study of trees.

He turned to a clean sheet and sat holding the stub poised over the pad for a long moment, his knees raised, his eyes narrowed, examining the rising curve of Marina's thigh beneath the folds of her summer dress, the swelling line of her hip and midriff, the turned obliqueness of her shoulder, his eyes lingering on the dimple behind her knee. He braced his shoulders against the tree and, without looking at the pad, his eye following the line of Marina's form, he inscribed a series of lines on the page with the soft pencil stub, the nail of his forefinger touching the paper lightly, his guide, steadying the line, keeping his hand obedient to his eye ... After a few minutes he looked at what he had done, holding it up and squinting at it, then he bent close and began working on the suggestion of form, giving it volume.

As the summer afternoon slipped by, Toni scrubbed out his drawing repeatedly and reinscribed it, his eye returning again and again to Marina's sleeping form in the drifting shadows of the wattle. The knuckles of his fingers scuffing the paper, working his line into a softground *chiaroscuro*, establishing the volume of her form that would permit the expression of the alluring dimple, the substance and structure that would coax the tension of ligament, muscle and bone behind her knee to emerge. He was not a draughtsman of light but of shadow. He scrubbed out with the side of his hand, his familiarity with the drawing increasing with each erasure, the line of Marina's bare toes, the curve of her instep . . . It was elusive, exhausting and exhilarating, and he was lost in his task. *The more you look the deeper the mystery*. His father . . .

The two magpies delicately removed the remains of the picnic item by item.

Marina woke, suddenly. She rolled over and sat up, turning and looking at him.

The magpies ran away, looking back over their shoulders in alarm.

On Marina's cheek a red mark, like a birthmark, where she had been lying on her hat. A spike of sweaty hair sticking out sideways from behind her ear. Her broken dream in her eyes.

He flipped her sketching block closed.

She frowned. 'Did you say something?' Her gaze went to the block in his hands. 'You've been drawing me! What time is it?'

He looked at his watch. 'Shit!'

'You forgot Nada!'

'Christ! It's after four!'

'I've got my mobile.' She searched in her bag, took out her phone, and handed it to him.

It was picked up on the first ring. 'Welcome to Greco Travel. Tanya Bacovic speaking. How can I help you?'

'Hi Tanya, It's Toni.'

'She's not here, Toni. The kinder called. She's gone to pick Nada up.'

'How was she?'

'Yeah. You know? Not so good, eh? They called her out of a client conference.'

'Shit!'

'Yeah.' The young woman laughed nervously.

'Thanks, Tanya. See you.'

'No worries, Toni.'

He handed the phone back to Marina. 'Teresa's picking her up.'

'That's okay, isn't it?'

'How could I have forgotten her?'

She was watching him. 'Can I see your drawing?'

He was shocked at himself. 'I've never forgotten her before.'

'It's all right, isn't it? Teresa's picking her up. Let me see what you've done.'

He handed the sketching block to her. The act of drawing her had excited and disturbed him. He knew already that what he had achieved on the page was an offer, an authentic mark. He waited now for Marina to confirm it. The drawing was a beginning. It was an offer of work.

She said admiringly, 'No one draws like this anymore.'

He leaned down and reached for the wine bottle. He held the empty bottle up to the sun, squinting through the green sunburst in the glass. 'Teresa's going to kill me.' He set the empty bottle on the grass and straightened.

Marina held the drawing at arm's length. 'I can't believe you haven't done any drawing for four years. It makes me so happy to see this, Toni. Suddenly there's something definite to be happy about. For the first time since Sydney I feel as if coming back is really going to work out. Don't look so grim. Teresa will forgive you. She'll be glad you're drawing again. That's the main thing, isn't it?'

He saw how she was seeing herself as the sleeping woman in the transformed shadows of his mind's eye. Confusing the erotic illusion on the page with her own reality. His wishful seeing beguiling her. 'You were dreaming,' he said. 'You kept jumping. You don't mind, then?'

'Mind?' she said emphatically. 'Of course I don't mind. God, it's wonderful.' She was silent, looking at his drawing. 'Today is the first time I've relaxed properly for months. For years. it feels like! You can't remember what I was dreaming, I suppose? Can you? I can never remember my dreams.' She looked at the drawing again. 'I'd love to keep this. Can I?'

He hesitated, his eyes going possessively to the sketching block in her hands. 'Sure.' He waved his hand. 'It's yours.'

'No,' she said and held it out to him. 'No. You don't want to let it go. I can see that. You did it for yourself, not for me. I'm sorry. I shouldn't have asked.'

He took the sketching block from her. It was his reference. He needed it. He examined it. He was thinking of his father. Those first crushing days of his bereavement. His blind grief. The uncharted life without his father that had stretched ahead of him. The emptiness when he had attempted to return to work, the enervating sense of futility draining him. He looked up from the drawing. With the drawing in his hands he was beginning to feel whole again.

She said seriously, 'What made you do it?'

'I was just filling in time.'

'I don't believe that.'

He considered her. 'Let's say I'm glad to have you around. Let's say Melbourne's a more interesting place with you and Robert in it. Is that better?'

She looked at him levelly. 'Yes. That's much better. I like that. Just filling in time has never been you, Toni.'

He was still reading her, his eye awakened, tracking her, following the line of her shoulder as if his eye had a will of its own, noting the slightly double-jointed backward angle of her elbow where she was resting her weight on her hand, the invitation to exaggerate, to rearrange her likeness, to imagine her . . .

She laughed, self-conscious with his scrutiny. She reached down and straightened her dress. 'I must look a fright.'

He watched her bend and put on her sandal. The curve of her back a unique trajectory describing who she was, her history coded in the way she moved, the way she had grown, the woman she had become. Bits of grass and small twigs were sticking to the back of her grey dress, as if she had been rolling in the summer grass with her lover. She had felt herself welcomed home by his drawing.

She kneeled on the grass, her hands resting on her thighs, and said regretfully, 'I suppose we really do have to go. What a shame today has to end.' She put the orange key float and her sunglasses in her hat and set about gathering the remains of their picnic, packing the things away neatly into the basket one by one.

He did not offer to help her.

She put her shoulder bag on top of the plates and the cups and bottle and she smoothed the tea towel over the packed basket. When she had done this she got up off her knees and stood picking the leaves and grass from her dress. 'When you're young you think you can do this sort of thing whenever you like,' she said. 'Then when you're older you realise days like this are never to be repeated. You realise *this* is what beauty is. Something that catches you off-guard and is gone almost before you've had time to see it.' She stepped across and stood beside him. 'It has been our special day,' she said. 'Hasn't it?'

They waited for something to settle between them.

'We'll come out here again,' he said.

'No. It will never be the same. How could it be? Today you did your first real drawing since the death of your father.'

It was true. He saw the shadowed uncertainty that was in her eyes now and which had not been there before. Something of sadness or reflection, or perhaps discontent. A ghostly offset from those old purple half-moons of her youthful afternoon migraines. The indelible mark of her concealed history.

He reached to take the basket from her and they walked together through the trees. She did not take his arm this time; sensing, maybe, that the gesture might no longer have the simple neutrality it had possessed for them earlier.

four

Teresa's Honda was not out the front of the house in its usual place. As he was crossing the courtyard the sun went in and he looked up. The storm front of an approaching southerly change divided the sky from horizon to horizon. When he opened the door of the studio the humid stench of the old clothes hit him. He went in and put on the light. Setting Marina's sketching pad on Nada's table beside her drawing, he bent and took hold of one of the timber racks by the base and dragged it out of the tangled pile of clothes, as if he were dragging a body out of a bomb site. He dumped the rack in the doorway and went back for another. He worked steadily, sweat soon running down his cheeks, his T-shirt sticking to his back, the light dimming and brightening, thunder rippling across the city.

He made a pile of the clothes and racks in the doorway, as if he were building a barricade. He was working his way back through time, down through four years of dismantled installations, clearing his way towards the plan press against the wall at the back of the studio.

The storm broke over the city, a gust of cold wind from the Southern Ocean whipping through the studio and clearing out the smell, snatching Nada's drawing from the table. He retrieved the drawing and weighted it with Marina's sketchbook. The barricade of old clothes in the doorway was soaked in moments by the downpour. The rain thundering on the tin roof. He tossed the clothes and racks behind him now without caring where they fell.

He was down to the last of the old garments when he stopped. He realised, suddenly, that he was looking at his father's old Sunday suit. He read the display sign that was still attached to the rack: *Moniek Prochownik's Outsize Sunday Suit.* He lifted the rack tenderly and stood it upright in front of him. He might have been helping a fallen man back to his feet, brushing at the jacket as if he'd had a hand in the man's fall. This was it then, the resistant, unremembered element of the installations that had been holding him back. With care, he removed the jacket from the rack and pressed the dark serge to his face. His dad was still there; faint, elusive, but there, the deep familiarity of his father's smell lingering in the tight weave of the material: the telephone call that afternoon four years ago telling him bluntly that his father had died on the moulding line at the Dunlop plant. In his blind grief he had got hold of his dad's old Sunday suit and hung it on a rack out in the middle of that great empty space of Andy's gallery. What had he intended by the gesture? To deny the loss of his father? He was not sure. But that was it, and his dead father became his first installation; the old suit standing out there on its own like Everyman. A man's defeat exposed mercilessly in death for the world to see. A power in that old suit, something more real than reality. His dad's workmates from the plant had come to stand and look at it, silent, awkward and abashed. His older brother, Roy, the only one who did not flinch to see it there. When he took his mother along she told him, *Your father would not have wanted this, Antoni.*

He held the suit jacket out in front of him, moved by the memory of his father, then he slipped his arms through the sleeves and put it on over his T-shirt. The jacket fitted him. It had been a size too big for his dad. The other kids' dads wearing T-shirts and jeans at weekends, and his dad dressed in a three-piece suit that was too big for him. The terrible sense of his dad's vulnerability in that suit. His oddity and isolation. His own agony, longing for his dad to be like the other fathers and at the same time loving him for not being like them. He looked down at himself and tugged at the lapels, just the way his dad used to tug at them, the little smile his dad would give him, a secret between them with this sign, the gods of fire and vengeance placated once again. His father's morbid fear that his nightmares might once again invade the day.

Toni was seeing his father in his mind's eye so clearly he could have drawn his likeness from the memory. He possessed no likenesses of his father, no drawings, no paintings, no photographs. All he possessed of his father was in his memory, but at this moment it was sufficient, a vivid recollection of the expression in his father's eyes. He turned around and faced the door.

Teresa was standing in the rain on the other side of the barricade watching him. She was clasping Nada to her and holding a coat over them both. The rain blowing against them, her dark hair drifted across her face. Nada was clutching Snoopy Dog, her expression shuttered and unhappy.

'Why didn't you pick her up?' Teresa yelled, shouting over the noise of the rain.

'I forgot. I'm sorry!' He spread his arms in a gesture of helpless contrition.

She stared at him, flinching from the driving rain. 'We thought you must have had an accident! What are you doing?' She was angry and offended, demanding a convincing explanation for his behaviour.

'It's okay. I'm just looking for my old Macedon sketchbook,' he yelled back.

The thunder of the rain on the tin roof.

'What Macedon sketchbook?' she shouted.

'Don't worry about it. It was before your time.'

She stood clutching Nada, cringing away from the vicious slap of the rain, the slap of his words.

He yelled, 'Sorry, darling!'

Teresa was a big woman. She was physically strong and sure of herself. He knew her to be a willing, generous, forgiving, loving and emotional woman. And she was loyal. That above everything. Loyalty was the big thing with Teresa. She was hard-working and loyal. And she was beautiful.

The rain drove into the doorway with redoubled force, lashing them. Nada started crying.

Teresa yelled, 'You *forgot* her!'

'We got caught up.'

'What do you mean, you *got caught up?*'

'I'm sorry.'

'You're a shit, Toni Powlett!'

'Sorry.'

'I was in conference with these people! They want to do bulk travel. Don't you care? You and I had an agreement! What happened to our agreement? How am I supposed to keep this thing going for us?'

'Sorry.'

She shouted fiercely, 'You don't give a shit!' Nada was struggling in her arms, the rain sweeping in, gusting against them, Teresa ducking away from it. She yelled, 'All I do is work!' She flung the word *work* at him like a stone through his window and turned and ran for the house.

He stood looking out across the barricade through the grey downpour. He should follow her and apologise. He was thinking, suddenly, of the night they met. She was still teaching then. It was at one of Andy's famous parties in the biscuit factory. Teresa arrived with an older man, a friend of Andy's, a Chinese painter who was the art teacher at the school where she was working. There was a band and people were yelling and drinking and dancing, and there was a lot of dope and other stuff going around. He did not remember what he and Teresa said to each other, but in the early hours she was walking him home through the empty streets and they were holding hands. They did not make love that night—she told him, *We have the rest of our lives*—but lay naked beside each other on her bed. She was very calm and sure of what had happened between them. The next day she took him to meet her family. *Me and Toni are getting married*, she told them. Her father asked him, *What do you do, Toni?* When he said he was an artist, Teresa's father said, *I meant for a living, son*.

He turned away from the door and picked up Marina's sketching pad from Nada's table. He flicked the pages until he came to his drawing. There was an immediate recognition in him, the attraction of something unfinished, something begun, the mysterious offer of a work-in-progress. It excited him to see it.

The rain ceased as abruptly as it had begun. A moment of silence followed, then a drift of air through the open door, chill and clean, the smell of the country in it. Nada was wailing over at the house, Teresa's voice raised, still putting her case to the ear of universal justice. He should go over and offer them comfort. Take Nada in his arms and weep with her. Take them both in his arms. Weep together, then laugh together. Show them how much he loved them and how sorry he was to have caused them this distress.

He carried Marina's sketchbook to the back of the studio. His bookshelves and his old work table and, the centrepiece of this arrangement, the timber plan press Teresa had bought for him with the settlement of her first big account at the agency. It had been an extravagant gift, her rebuttal of her father's scepticism, a sign to her family of her faith in Toni Powlett's art. Her four brothers carrying the heavy piece solemnly across the courtyard, one at each corner like pallbearers, the plan press wrapped in silver foil and tied with a white silk ribbon, as if it were an Italian funeral casket. He wiped at the dust with the flat of his hand. He had not stood on this spot since the death of his father. The back door to the lane was misted with cobwebs, his easel leaning in the shadows covered with a sheet. The white frame of a painting showing in the gap between the bookshelves and the press. He put Marina's pad on the press and reached in and pulled out the painting. He set the painting up in front of him and stood back. It was oil on a 40 × 30 cm piece of cheap masonite from the hardware store in Bay Street. The portrait of his mother that had won him the Kingsgate Prize at art school.

There she was! The woman he had known back then when he was an ardent young student. Mrs Lola Prochownik leaning on the parapet of their balcony at the rat flats, taking a break, a cigarette between her fingers. Her dark eyes looking out of the frame at her son painting her, an expression of knowing disbelief, and of abiding love, and just that touch of pride. His mother. Still a believer despite everything. Her skinny arms brown and wrinkled, reminding him of her brown wrinkled stockings. The black dress under her wraparound apron. The model for the treatment had been Max Beckmann's stern-faced Duchessa di Malvedi from the exhibition at the National Gallery of Victoria in eighty-nine. There was a postcard of that painting in a drawer of the plan press somewhere. He had studied Beckmann's painting until he knew every brush stroke by heart, going back to the gallery day after day and examining it until his eye fused with its texture. Feminine beauty without softness, that was his portrait of his mother, a woman's beauty rendered as the determination to survive against all odds. The kind of beauty that spoke of an undisclosed and private self that had withstood the erosion of great suffering. How had he done it? Rendering the kind of quiet beauty his father disclosed in his modest studies of their domestic items, works achieved in that place where his father was alone with the silence, at the moral centre of his beliefs. It was not a quality that could be freely exposed to the casual observer. He had asked his father, *What should I paint?* And his father had said, *Paint what you love.*

When Robert had told him his painting had won the prize he had felt a surge of delight, a little triumph—then was humbled by the mysterious power of his gift. He felt a fugitive echo of that emotion now, the confirmation that had emboldened him to say for the first time, *I am an artist!* Robert had been one of the prize's judges. With success, it seemed there was always the element of luck, chance working with you or against you, what his father had called *Fate*, as if with that word he solemnly pronounced the name of God.

Behind his mother on the balcony were her bits and pieces. The tools of her trade. Her mop leaning in the corner where it would catch the sun later in the day. A slack arc of clothes line strung from one side of the balcony to the other, small items of underwear pegged to it. *Smalls*. Her long-disused word returning to him now.

He had never painted a portrait of his father. He had not believed himself ready for that task. Then came the day they told him his father had died on the line, and it was too late for a portrait. His beloved father was gone. The unpainted portrait of his father was still in him, however, still lodged in the eye of his mind as if he *had* painted it, an image of his father at the kitchen table at night, looking over the top of his spectacles, a paintbrush in his hand, in his eyes the consolation of his dream.

Toni opened the sketching pad again and stood looking at his drawing of Marina lying on the grass in the sunlit bush that afternoon, the invitation to his eye of the dimple behind her knee among the soft shadows of the wattle's overhang. He knew what it was now, this drawing. He understood what he had done. He set her sketchbook aside and opened the top drawer of the plan press. The drawer was filled with sketchbooks, sheets of drawings, photos, postcards, cuttings from newspapers and magazines, pages of pencilled notes, gouaches, watercolours, pastels. He saw his old Macedon sketchbook at once, his bold block lettering on the cadmium cover: MOUNT MACEDON, WINTER 89. He took the sketchbook out and flipped through the sheets until he came to the drawing of Marina asleep in the conservatory on the cane chaise. He placed the two drawings side by side on the press. Underneath the Macedon image, in his neat cursive script of those days, he had written: *Marina Golding in the conservatory at Plovers, June 19, 1989.*

It was a dark, confident drawing, vigorously made, with areas of heavy overworking and rubbing. The sleeping woman was half-turned away from the viewer, her right arm trailing on the floor, the backs of her fingers touching the white marble tiles. Her hair was long then, and lay loosely around her shoulders on the cushions. The sleeping woman in the silence, the weight of that big house under the shadow of the mountain holding her suspended in its stillness, as if some delicate unspoken thought waited to be expressed.

The trace of himself off the edge of the drawing, the cast shadow of the voyeur crouched by the sleeping woman taking her likeness. Something of guilt and secrecy in it that day. Art!

As if it were a vice against the sound governance of an orderly life. He stood considering the drawing a while, then he walked to the telephone by the door and dialled her number. When she picked up, he said, 'Remember Macedon?'

'I hoped you'd call. Of course. What do you mean, do I remember Macedon? Today was wonderful, Toni. I loved it. Thank you! Did you show Teresa your drawing?'

'The time I came out to your mum and dad's place during the winter break with Robert? It was the first time we'd met.'

'What made you think of that now? I was sorry Robert brought you. I couldn't believe it when he asked me if he could bring one of his first-year students with him. I'd been looking forward to some time alone with him. I scarcely saw him during term time in those days.'

'You and I were alone in the house one afternoon. Your mum and dad had taken Robert to meet some neighbours. I came past the conservatory and saw you asleep on that cane bed.' He waited. 'I did a drawing of you.'

'You were always drawing us.'

'This one was different.'

There was a small silence.

He said, 'You had a migraine.'

'I probably did.'

He could see her now, as he had not seen her before today, the woman on the telephone, his familiar subject of the afternoon, the visual knowledge of her he had gathered on the island.

73

'I don't get migraines any more.'

It was quiet over at the house now. In the courtyard a blackbird stood on the lip of the fountain celebrating the passing of the storm.

'You haven't lost your touch,' Marina said. 'I envy you. If I stopped painting, my technique would soon slip away.'

'Painting's something else,' he said. 'I don't imagine I haven't gone stale in that department.'

'You'd soon get it together again.'

'I'm looking at my Macedon drawing of you right here. I unearthed my old sketchbook. Things have come full circle.'

'What do you mean?'

'Me drawing you asleep again.'

'You never showed us those drawings. Not me, anyway.'

'Do you still have your sketchbook from that holiday?'

'It's sure to be here somewhere.'

'You were secretive about your drawings in those days.'

'So were you.'

It was true. His drawings had represented for him the private journal of his obsession, his experimentation and the record of his endeavour, his failures and his successes, the small, precious increments of the craft. With drawing he had been feeling his way towards the projects that had stirred his imagination and his ambition, inscribing the influences of other artists in the bare-faced copies of their work and the incorporation of material stolen from them. His drawings had been the record of his confusion and uncertainty as much as a record of his confidence. He had not, in the end, shared them freely even with his father, and to Robert and to his friends he had shown only a careful selection. It had been his painting that had been the public expression of his art. His private obsessions had not been masked in his drawings as they had in his paintings. Drawing had always been for him something of a solitary and even secretive act, a primary pleasure of the senses that had had little to do with his understanding, but which had fed on his dreams and those appearances and associations that possessed for him a private poetic or sensual reality; love, beauty, fear and the erotic had always been at the core of his drawing. When his drawings were transposed to paintings the subjects had invariably lost something of their intimacy. It had been a problem he had never learned to overcome. Until his father's death his art had been a magnificent mystery to him. 'I'm going to need more information,' he said. 'More visual information.'

'For what?'

'I'm going to do a painting of you from my old Macedon drawing.' *Was* he a bad judge of character? How was he to know the answer to this question without risking something of himself?

'It's for the show, isn't it?' she said.

'It could be. If it works. You don't sound too surprised.'

'You're a painter, Toni. What else is there for you except painting?' There was something of impatience in her voice. 'What else can you do? You've finished with the installations.

75

You as good as said so yourself. We come back to the things that have rewarded us in the past. We can't suddenly decide to be someone else.'

He laughed. 'I'm wondering if I can still paint.'

'Of course you can still paint! I'd love to see your Macedon drawings. Why don't you bring them over to Richmond one day next week? The three of us can have coffee and go over them together.'

'Do we have to wait till next week?'

'Is this what you really want?' she said. 'A painting of me from that old drawing? That young woman at Macedon isn't me anymore, you know.'

'No,' he said doubtfully. 'I suppose not.'

'So why don't you do something completely new?'

'Sit for me,' he said. 'And I'll do a painting of you awake.'

'I meant,' she said carefully, 'does it have to be me?' It was clear she had not quite meant this, or at least had not meant only this.

'Artists paint each other's portraits,' he said. 'We've always done it. It's a tradition with us.'

There was a considerable silence.

The blackbird had moved on.

'How about I come over to Richmond in the morning and do some studies of you working on that picture, *Chaos Rules*? If that's what you're calling it.' He waited. He was fearful of losing this possibility. 'I need to be working, Marina.' It was a confession of vulnerability. 'I need to be painting again.'

The sun had come out, steam rising from the barricade of sodden clothes, as if fires still smouldered within the pile of his discarded installations. He would miss them, he realised, his featureless people. In a way, of course, they had been the uncelebrated people of the flats, with whom he had grown up. The anonymous people who had left no trace. Something also to do with himself and his brother and his mother and father, and that terrible sudden end. The lost and voiceless people of his parents' pasts. All that. Loss and the past. But Marina was right, he had finished with it, or had finished with that particular form of it. Impossible to know when it is the last time for something, until we look back and, suddenly, we know it is finished, and then we experience this surprise and nostalgia for it.

'None of us ever imagined you'd turned your back on painting forever, Toni,' she said. 'But you don't need me to tell you these things. It might be less complicated, don't you think, if you asked someone else to sit for you? Why not Teresa? And what about Nada? Or your mother?'

He was impatient with these suggestions. 'What's so complicated about you sitting for me? You've sat for me twice already. I've done two drawings of you asleep. This project began when I drew you at Macedon all those years ago, not this afternoon on the island.'

'Project?' she said. 'It's hardly a project, is it?'

'Well whatever it is,' he said. 'It wouldn't feel right to be painting Teresa or Nada or Mum at the moment. I'll paint them one day, when I'm ready. Right now, I want to develop the suggestion that's in these two drawings of you. They're studies for something. I want to follow them up. I want to see where it takes me. There's an offer in it.' He waited, but still she said nothing. 'So,' he said at last. 'You don't want to do it?'

'I didn't say that. But perhaps it's something you ought to think about for a day or two.'

'I could try for a series of you. A suite. *The Marina Suite.*' The title appealed to him. A series of her from his old Macedon drawings set alongside a series from her life now. His imagination was running on with it. 'I might try for a series,' he said. 'Three, or maybe four, paintings. Three probably, to match the three you're doing. What do you suppose Robert would think?'

'Robert will support whatever you decide to do. You know that. But he's not expecting paintings from you. Paintings weren't what he was thinking about when he asked you. The idea was to have the contrast of your installation with our canvases.'

'Artists always do the unexpected. Robert knows that. He said so in his first book. *The artist always disconcerts our expectations.* He'll understand. Did you tell him about today?'

'He's not home yet.'

'Will you sit for me or not?'

'I'll have to think about it.'

'How about I come over in the morning and show the Macedon drawings and today's drawing to both of you? We can talk it over between the three of us. I can do some drawings of you working while I'm there. Your whole family is in this sketchbook, you know. There are several drawings of your mother and your father. And the interior of your house.'

She said, with a kind of heaviness, 'All right. But why don't the three of us meet at the Red Hat in Bridge Road in the morning instead of at our place? We can have breakfast. It's pleasant there. Do you know it?'

'It's that little place opposite the furniture auctions?'

'And Toni, I do think it's wonderful you're going to be painting again. Really. That's what's important.'

'But what?'

'I suppose it's just that I feel partly responsible. I know I'm not, of course. But I can't help feeling as if I am.'

'You've had a hand in it. Of course you have. I wouldn't be doing it if you hadn't come back. But that's good, isn't it? It's the way it is. You can't pretend you're not involved. These things always surprise us.'

He hung up the phone. The rack beside him was still wearing his father's buttoned waistcoat and trousers, reminding him of Sunday mornings in the kitchen before his parents went to the market, his dad in his shirtsleeves brewing a pot of coffee at the stove, classical music on the radio, last night's pictures already cleared from the table and stored in the suitcase. He picked up both sketchbooks, climbed over the steaming barricade and walked across the courtyard.

five

Teresa was at the kitchen bench slicing chicken breasts. She had changed out of her suit into jeans and a grey top, her blue apron tight around her waist, an open bottle and a glass of red wine by her hand. Nada was sitting on the rug in the living area watching the television. Teresa looked up as he came through the door from the courtyard, the blade of the knife paused in the yellow chicken flesh. 'You should see yourself,' she said.

'It's Dad's.'

'It's not just the jacket.'

He put the two sketchbooks on the bench, took off his father's jacket and hung it on the back of a chair.

Teresa set the knife on the bench and wiped her hands on her apron. She picked up his old sketchbook and examined the cover. 'So what were you two doing at Macedon?'

'We were staying at Marina's parents' place. Robert was with us.' He watched her going through the pages, pausing at each drawing.

'Who's this?'

'The housekeeper's husband.'

'And this?'

'Marina's mother.'

She stopped when she came to his drawing of Marina asleep on the cane chaise, his precise archival note underneath the image: *Marina Golding in the conservatory at Plovers, June 19, 1989.* Without taking her eyes off the drawing, Teresa felt for her wine glass and raised it to her lips. She took a sip and set the glass on the bench again, still looking at the drawing.

'I did it when I was a student,' he said.

'How come you never showed these to me?'

'This early stuff's been packed away.' He watched her. 'I did another drawing of her today. It's in the other book.'

Teresa put down his Macedon sketchbook and picked up Marina's. She turned the sheets, pausing once again to examine each drawing.

'I'm sorry I forgot to pick her up,' he said.

Teresa was looking at his drawing of Marina asleep in the shade of the wattle. She looked at the drawing for a long time. 'You did this today?'

'Yes.' He leaned over her shoulder.

She moved away from him. 'So this is what you were doing? On an island with her, doing this all day? You said, *we got caught up*. You got caught up on this island with her? Who else was there? Was *he* there? Was Robert what's-his-name there?'

'No, Robert wasn't there.'

'You were alone with her on the island? Is that it?'

He motioned at the sketchbook. 'When I said I got caught up I meant with doing the drawing. It's the first real drawing I've done since Dad died.'

'You said *we* got caught up. I know what I heard. Now you're changing it. You didn't say, *I got caught up doing my first real drawing since Dad died.* If you'd said that, it would have meant something else.'

'Marina was showing me the space. That's all. For the inaugural show. I've told you about it. It's going to be important. I'm thinking of doing some paintings for it.'

'Of her?'

'Maybe.'

'What's *maybe* supposed to mean? Are you planning on doing pictures of her or not?'

'That's the idea at this stage.'

'So that's a yes, is it? I can tell you, you're not making this look good.' She looked at the drawing again. 'I'd say she was showing you a bit more than the space.' She studied him. 'It's a good drawing. Anyone can see that.'

'Thanks.'

'So tell me, those two come back from Sydney and suddenly you forget to pick up your daughter? Then you throw your installations out the door into the rain? Now you come in here wearing your Dad's old jacket and looking half-deranged. So what's going on?'

He reached a glass down from the shelf and poured wine into it.

'I just want to know what's going on.'

He swallowed some of the wine. 'I'm going to Richmond tomorrow to talk over an idea for a project with them.'

'The project of doing pictures of her?'

'Yes.'

'So you're going to be a real artist again? Is that it?'

'I hope so.'

'You know what I was doing today while you were on that island getting caught up with her, being a real artist again? I was asking Dad for another ten thousand. Yes! That's it. Have you got any idea how that makes me feel after everything he's done for us with the agency, without ever being asked for anything? You know how it makes *him* feel? Do you have any idea what I'm doing to keep this thing going for us? Then I'm in conference with these people and I get a call from the kinder telling me Nada hasn't been picked up. *Come and get your daughter*, they tell me, *we're closing up. I'm sorry*, I say to them, and I tell my clients, *See you later, I've got to pick up my daughter from kinder*. And that's it. They look at me as if I'm crazy. Am I going to see *them* again? You've got to be joking! That's not the kind of service these corporate people are looking for. You've got no idea what I have to do to run this business. It's not just your dad's old jacket! You're like a stranger since those two got back from Sydney. I'm not in touch with you.' She put down the sketchbook and picked up the kitchen knife. She waved the knife in Nada's direction. 'If you want to do something useful, take your daughter for a walk. She watches too much of that. It's not good for her.'

He would have spoken but she overrode him. 'Just do it! Do *something*! Do something useful for once!'

'There's no need to get worked up.'

'You want to see me worked up?' She sliced at the chicken. 'I sometimes wonder if my father wasn't right about you.'

'Come on! Take it easy. You've had a massive day. Careful!' he said. 'Don't cut yourself. You work too hard. You should take a break.' He put his arm around her.

She twisted away and stood facing him, the knife in her hand, her shoulders tense, a rush of emotion in her eyes.

'I was going to fill you in with what's happening,' he said quietly. 'But when did we get the chance to talk until now?'

She gave a little gasp and turned back to the chicken. 'Take her for a walk!' She sliced through the chicken with a suppressed energy that made him wince.

He stood a moment, then turned and went over to the television and scooped up his daughter. Nada pushed at him and he put her down again. 'Don't you want to come to the swing park with Daddy, darling?'

She didn't look at him but stalked off down the passage.

Teresa was ignoring him, flouring the chicken fillets. He followed Nada.

Teresa yelled, 'Snoopy Dog!'

He came back and picked the toy dog off the rug. He straightened and met Teresa's eyes.

'This'll be ready in twenty minutes,' she said, and she stood looking across the room at him, her dark eyes glassy with tears. 'Go on. She's waiting for you.'

'I'm sorry, darling.'

She shrugged helplessly. 'Yeah, I know. It's me, too. I'm strung out with this money business.'

'I'll be back soon.'

She called out to Nada, 'Have a good swing with Daddy, darling.'

At the end of the passage he handed Snoopy Dog to Nada. She took the toy from him and tossed it aside. It hit the wall and fell in a heap.

'Poor old Snoopy Dog!' He leaned down and retrieved the toy. 'Looks like you're in the doghouse, old Snoop.'

'His name's not old Snoop,' Nada corrected him severely, unimpressed by his flippancy. 'He told me he doesn't want to come with us to the swing park.' She stood facing the door, waiting for him to open it.

He propped the toy with its back to the wall. 'There! You'll be okay till we get back. You don't think he might change his mind while we're out?' he asked her.

'He can't hear *you*,' she said.

'See you later, Snoopy.'

They went out and down the path. He tried to take her hand but she wouldn't let him. She walked ahead of him along the footpath, being independent; he stayed a couple of paces behind, reprimanded.

She stopped abruptly and looked back at her heel.

He squatted beside her.

The ribbon on her pink imitation ballet shoe had come loose. She did not say anything but stood twisted around, frowning at the trailing ribbon. He leaned her small body into him and retied the ribbon. She watched, making sure he was getting it right. 'How's that?'

She resumed her solitary progress, siding with her mother.

.

Toni and Teresa were standing together in the open door of Nada's bedroom looking in at their sleeping daughter. They had been curled up on the sofa all evening, drinking wine and watching a movie. There had been no big talk between them. They had been keeping to the privileged intimacies of the small stuff, staying within the safety zone.

Nada was lying sideways across her bunk on her back, the sheet thrown aside, an eerie glimmer of the whites of her eyes, her lips parted, her arms flung out as if she had been tossed, weightless, through the firmament by an elemental force and was no longer their little girl but a small stranger embarked on a journey that was not their journey.

Teresa whispered, 'Should we straighten her up, do you think?'

He stepped into the room, took hold of Nada and eased her around so that she lay lengthwise along the bed, retrieving her from the wildness of her dreams.

She frowned but did not wake.

'Don't wake her!' Teresa whispered at his shoulder.

They pulled the sheet and the summer doona up around the little girl's chin, placed her arms in under the covers and stepped back. She twitched but stayed straightened. Their little girl again. No longer flying away from them.

'That's better,' Teresa whispered.

They watched her, held by the fascination of their intense feelings for their child, a sense of their own frailty, the fragility of the link that was carrying them along together.

'We should give her a little sister or brother,' Teresa said. 'It's not fair to leave her on her own.'

'We're not leaving her on her own. She's got us.'

Teresa turned to him. 'Do you remember when you were her age?'

'No.' But he did remember.

'What happens to our first memories?' Teresa wondered.

He looked down at his daughter. His first memory was vivid; he had been Nada's age. He and his father were standing by helplessly watching his brother Roy fighting his father's tormentor in the entrance to the flats. The man going over backwards, his head hitting the kerbstone with a crack like a beam snapping. And they had stood, appalled, in the apocalyptic silence, knowing the man was dead and everything had changed for them . . . 'She doesn't need a brother or sister,' he said. 'She's okay the way she is.'

Teresa looked at him. 'An only child is not a real family,' she insisted quietly.

'I need a drink of water,' he said.

'Get me one too.' She touched his arm.

He turned and kissed her gently on the mouth.

She went down the passage and into their bedroom, and he walked back through the house to the kitchen. In the half-light of the living area his father's dark jacket hung on the back of the chair, as if his father were there working in the night hours, bending over his paints in his shirtsleeves and braces, lovingly disclosing the quiet beauty of the everyday in their lives, surprising them by making art of his wife's kitchen utensils. The wonder of how he did it. The whisper of his own childhood voice, *What are you painting, Dad?* The beautiful smell of his father in the night. His dad portraying his love for them through the objects familiar to their hands. He remembered a small rectangular watercolour of his mother's ironing board and iron, an image as poignantly the woman herself for those who knew her as his own carefully crafted portrait had been . . . He was not sure whether Marina knew the story of his brother's imprisonment. He could never remember who knew their family story and who did not know it. He went into the kitchen and filled two glasses with water from the tap and carried them back to the bedroom.

Teresa was under the sheet, her bedside light off, turned on her side, her face to the wall. He set the glass of water beside her.

She murmured sleepily, 'Thanks, darling.'

He undressed and climbed into the bed, and lay on his back beside her. Minutes passed and he was drifting into sleep when she turned to him, her voice coming out of the dark, husky and anxious, as if she had been building her resolve to put the question to him. 'Were you two lovers?'

He came out of the haze of his half-sleep. '*Who?*'

'You and her—Marina Golding? Back then, at her place at Mount Macedon? Before my time?'

'No,' he said firmly. He was alert now.

'How can I be sure?'

He thought about her question. How could she be sure? She had never sought such a reassurance from him before. They had never questioned each other's word. Now, suddenly, the certainty of each other was no longer there. He spoke carefully. 'I didn't like her back then,' he said. It was true. 'I was just doing a drawing.'

'And now you *do* like her?'

He measured his response. How to negotiate this sudden maze of uncertainties. How to reinstate the simplicity of their trust. He did like Marina now. She interested him. He had been surprised by how much he liked her, by how easily he had shared his memories of his father with her. It was important to him. 'Marina has changed,' he said. He was remembering her saying, *That young woman at Macedon is not me anymore, you know*. It was true. 'None of us is the same person we were back then.'

An empty gravel truck bounded over the railway crossing like a sudden beating of drums in the night.

When the echo of the truck had passed Teresa asked, 'So you *do* like her now, or you don't like her?'

He was slow to reply. 'I think she's probably more ambitious now—for herself, I mean, for her own work—than she used to be. That's bound to make someone more interesting. Even to themselves. I don't really know Marina all that well. She and I were never close. She was often there, but it was Robert and I who were friends in those days. Marina was content to go along with whatever Robert's plans were. Now she seems to be taking more of a lead. But I don't know. I'm only guessing. It seems to have been her decision that's brought them back to Melbourne.'

Teresa did not interrupt. When he fell silent, she said, 'That drawing you did of her on the island today. It's not *just* a drawing.'

'How do you mean?'

'It's suggestive.'

'What makes you say that?' What he had seen on the island this afternoon, Teresa was seeing now in her recollection of his drawing. In the mind's eye seeing is believing, the voyeur disclosing the hidden storyline whether he intends to or not. His own vivid recollection of the dimple in the back of Marina's knee, inviting his eye into the shade of the silver wattle where she lay on the grass.

'It's suggestive,' Teresa repeated.

He said nothing, the word spinning through his head.

'Do *you* think it's suggestive?' she persisted. 'Or not?'

'I drew what I saw,' he said. 'What seems suggestive to one person might not seem that way to someone else.'

The sounds of the night beyond the window, always somewhere a dog was barking.

Teresa said tightly, 'I couldn't bear it. You know that.'

He put his arm around her and kissed her on the mouth. 'You don't have to bear anything. Don't be silly! There's nothing to bear. I love you.'

She kissed him back. 'And I love you too. But I'm jealous of her. I can't help it. The thought of her makes my stomach crawl. It's not my fault. It's just how it is.'

'There's nothing to be jealous about.'

'You're sure?'

'Of course I'm sure. One hundred percent sure.'

'I wish you weren't planning on doing pictures of her for this show. I wish it was someone else.'

'Nothing's settled. The island show is a great opportunity for me. It'll attract a lot of attention. I could make some money at last.'

'I don't care about the money. You don't have to make money. I'm the one who's making the money while you establish yourself. That's what we agreed. I married an artist.

I know what I did. I believe in you. You didn't promise me money, you promised me you'd do your work. You have to do what you have the feeling for or there's nothing for either of us. Don't get sidetracked by money now. That's what Dad's waiting for. He's waiting for the day you dump your dream and go after the money like the rest of them, so he can say he told me so.'

'It's not your dad I'm thinking about. It's you. If you really don't want me to paint Marina, then I won't paint her.'

She propped herself up on her elbow and gazed down at him in the night glow from the window. 'It's no good talking like that. You're fired up with it. I can feel it. I told you weeks ago to take all that stuff from your installations back to the op shops and get on with something new and now that's what you're doing. And here I am complaining when I should be happy. What do you suppose you're going to do if you don't do this? If you drop this, you'll be at a loose end again.'

'I'd find something else.'

'No you wouldn't. Listen to you! I know you better than that. I'm happy that you know what you want. There are hazards, that's all, with knowing what we want. There always are. How many people know what they want? They don't look it in the eye the way you do. That's what I love about you. I see them every day. They wander in off the street and sit in front of me looking at brochures of Tanzania with dazed expressions, distracting themselves from what? They've made their money and now they're wondering what they can get from life with it. Like they finally earned enough frequent flyer points to buy anything they want, only they don't know what they want. So I tell them to buy a digital camera and go on safari and look at lions. Then they come back and they're still lost and they start to feel cheated. How come Tanzania wasn't the answer? It's a conundrum for them. So I say, *Maybe you should have gone to Paris instead of Africa*. I know all they're thinking about is escape, getting away to some place other than where they already are. And thank god, or we'd be broker than we already are. Staying home just makes them think of getting old and dying. Staying home they worry all the time.' She leaned and kissed him. 'I love you. You know why? You know what you want. It's not a conundrum for you. That's your gift. You'll have it till you die because it's you. That's your real gift, not drawing. You know what you have to do. You don't want to escape from it, you want to focus on it and do it. Sometimes it scares me. I felt good when you were doing your installations. I didn't understand them, but I felt good about you doing them. I always thought it was about your family, your love for your dad. That's what it was, wasn't it? I saw you putting those things together with love. And you never talked about making money or having a big opportunity or any of this stuff that you're talking about now. I'd look out the kitchen window and see you out there lost in your work for hours, and Nada sitting there in the courtyard with you doing her own thing. And when you two came in for your dinner you were both tired and happy.' She gave him a long kiss then pulled away. 'When I saw you at Andy's party that night I knew you at once. I knew who you were. Meeting you changed me. I was dancing with poor old Lang but I was only seeing you from the minute you walked in the door. Until then I was always going out with artists and wondering why I did it. When I saw you I realised I wanted you to live your dreams through me. I don't have that passion for my work that you have. But with you I'm part of it. We're a team. We're a family. When I saw you I knew I'd found the man I wanted to spend the rest of my life with and I could stop fooling around. I wanted to support you in your work.' She was silent a long while, then she said worriedly, 'This is not a trap for you, is it? The way I've set things up for you? Jesus, if I thought that . . .'

'Of course it's not a trap. Hey! Don't say that! How could it be a trap?'

'It's not me just keeping control over you is it? You never feel like that about us, do you? I couldn't bear it. There's always a price for these things. I know that. We don't get away without paying the price. It's not as simple as we think. That's what Dad always says. Sometimes I wonder how we can ever be sure of anything.'

'Don't talk like this,' he said gently. 'You're going to work yourself into a state again.'

She took his hand and placed it on her belly. 'I never liked those two. You know that. Of all the people you might have decided to paint, it would have to be Marina Golding! I think they're bloodless, the pair of them. I never worked out what you found interesting in them. I was glad when they left. Is it fate they came back? What is it decides these things? Why them? Why not someone I like? Why not your lovely brother, Roy? Roy's a man with a story in his face. That's what I always think. He is a man who has suffered and said nothing about it. If I were an artist, I'd paint a portrait of Roy and everyone would see his story in his eyes. In the old days in Calabria, when my dad was a boy, Roy would have been a hero.' She was silent a while. 'The idea scares me.'

'The idea?'

'You being out *there*! Being part of that scene out there with those people! With people like them. I don't know them. I never feel comfortable with them. I don't know what they're thinking. They're not my kind of people and they are never going to be my kind of people no matter how hard I try to like them or to understand them. They have agendas.' She was silent a moment. 'I don't trust them. It's really as simple as that. I wonder if, to be an artist, you have to spend your time with people like that or whether you can do it on your own. I would really like to know the answer to that one.'

They were both silent for a long while.

'You trust Andy?' he said.

'Andy's different. He's not like them. He loves you. He loves me and Nada.'

'He spends all his time with artists and dealers.'

95

'Andy doesn't have an agenda.' After a time she said, 'We need a holiday before you get into this new project. We need to *condition* ourselves for it.' She laughed. 'Just you and me. We haven't had a real holiday together since that trip to Tassie before Nada was born. There's a new resort promotion on Noumea. The people who are running it owe me. I can get the accommodation for free and half the airfares. I'll write a piece for them in *The Traveller*. There's child minding at the resort. You and me can lie on the beach all day. I'll get a new bikini. Remember when you said they invented the bikini for breasts like mine?'

'I remember.'

She rolled towards him and they kissed. 'When were you thinking of starting work on this show?'

'Tomorrow.'

They both laughed.

'*Tomorrow*, he says! I can't afford to take time off for Noumea anyway. So who do I think I'm kidding? Jesus! I don't know how I'd cope if you ever became successful.'

'And stopped being a failure, you mean?'

'You're not a failure. I don't see you as a failure. Failure's not the only alternative to success. People can go along leading a good life without being successful. We don't have to have success. It isn't everything. We make too much of success.'

'Success is good for you,' he said. 'I felt it when I won the Kingsgate prize. Otherwise I wouldn't know. I remember it doing me good.'

'Yeah, like drugs,' she said. 'It's a feeling for a moment. Like when I make a big sale. I know that feeling. I meant we get used to being who we are, that's all. *This* is who we are. This is us. If you were successful, *this* would change. It's changing already with the end of your installations and this new thing. I'm not saying what we've got is perfect, but I can handle being who we are now. Success out there in the world is the unknown for us. For the first time it seems to me you're aiming for the unknown and turning your back on what we know. To be honest, that scares me more than Marina Golding. I know in my heart you're never going to be unfaithful. I know that.'

'We both know that.' He kissed her. 'But I can't stand still and repeat myself, or do nothing.'

'We have to be honest about where we're going.' She moved his hand around on her belly. 'I want our other baby before it's too late. I've always felt it out there, waiting for us to decide to let it through. I've been hearing from it a lot lately. Nada's little brother or sister.'

They lay silently side by side, her hand holding his hand on her stomach. After a while she moved his hand to her breast. The night noises of the city out beyond the window.

six

He parked across the road from the Red Hat café. He was still preoccupied by the previous night's conversation with Teresa, the prospect of another child arousing in him a troubling contradiction of emotions. He was watching two men in grey dustcoats unloading furniture from the back of a truck parked in front of him. He realised suddenly, with a start of interest, that the men were lifting down an old-fashioned cane chaise longue similar to the one on which Marina had been lying that day, years ago, when he had made his first drawing of her asleep.

In the normal course of everyday life it might have been a weakness to have made something of this coincidence, he knew that, but he had no doubt that in the other world of art, with its kinship with dreams and illusions, the intervention of chance could signify that critical moment when a project might leap beyond the control of the artist; a moment, in other words, when the work ceased to be the banal projection merely of the artist's own fragile ego and took on a larger existence of its own. He grabbed the two sketchbooks from the passenger seat, stepped out of the car and followed the men into the auction rooms, where they were just at that moment in the act of setting the chaise on the floor. 'How much do you expect it to go for?' he asked. He reached and touched the back of it, as if he were already its possessor.

The older man considered the chaise with a professional glance. 'Maybe one-fifty?' he said and transferred the casual appraisal of his gaze to Toni. 'Two at the outside.'

'One-fifty to two?' Toni echoed him, considering the chaise as if he had a choice in the matter of whether or not to place a bid for it.

'You can leave a bid with me,' the man told him. 'The auction's Tuesday morning. I'll call you lunchtime Tuesday if I get it for you. It could go for less. Leave me your number.' The men watched him examining it.

Toni saw that it was not identical to the one at Macedon, but was nevertheless of the same style and period; an old-fashioned piece from that leisured era of shaded verandahs and conservatories. A regime of daily life that had permitted time for cool drinks in the afternoon; a bygone era, in other words, when well-to-do people such as Marina's parents had employed housekeepers so that they might be at liberty themselves to enjoy life. He could see that the chaise would sit nicely in a modern apartment or in his studio. It needed only one or two cushions and a colourful throw rug to give it back its life. He was imagining Marina asleep on it in the pose of his old drawing. Perhaps he would do another drawing of her in the same pose now? The idea occurred to him then of a naked portrait of her lying on the chaise. A woman alone in the privacy of her own room, lying on her couch, looking away from the viewer and thinking her private thoughts, oblivious to the gaze of the onlooker. He found it was not easy to visualise Marina without her clothes. He could only see her naked body in his peripheral vision, as it were, and at the very extreme of his imagination, an elusive impression of an anonymous woman. In the exquisite moment of such an image, he was sure she would be a woman open to the erotic intensities of her private desires; desires of the daydream world, to be sure, which she would share with no one and which she would have no wish to satisfy in the real world. Such a painting would lend intensity to the other pictures in the suite. A painting depicting the interior life of this woman, a life which the viewer might read in her expression rather than in the lines of her body. For surely there would also be a certain poignancy of human solitude, a vulnerability and sense of the failure of desire even, about such a woman, exposed to the viewer and no longer in the prime of her youth? Such a picture could not be the portrait of a child-like odalisque, but must be an intimate picture of a middle-aged artist engaged with her unresolvable erotic tensions. Something difficult and intimate. But could he paint such a picture? Did he possess the skill for it? Did he have the vision that would remove such an image from the arena of the merely prurient? Could he hold it together long enough in his mind's eye to get it down on the canvas? And, anyway, would Marina agree to sit for him without her clothes on?

'I like it,' he said.

'You *do* like it,' the older man observed approvingly, and he ran his hand over the back of the cane chaise as if he were wondering if he might have missed something of special interest about it. 'You know what you're looking at. It's a nice piece. We don't get many in this condition.' The man smiled, sure of his verdict. 'You're a collector. I can always pick the collectors.'

'How can I be certain of getting it?'

The man told him to leave a bid of two hundred and he would be sure to get it for him.

Toni left the bid and his telephone number and, with a last backward glance at the chaise, he stepped out into the street. It was another expense that would have to go on Teresa's agency Visa card. But it was a necessity he could not forgo. He stood at the kerb looking across the road. He could see the real Marina sitting at a table behind a red sofa in the window of the café, shadows and reflections of vehicles and pedestrians passing in the street and suggestively interrupting his view of her. She was alone and was reading a book. As he watched her he saw that she was reading the book, indeed, as if she was not expecting someone to join her but was sure of her solitude and was absorbed in the imaginary world of the story; a woman alone in a café reading, the woman of his imaginary painting, her private thoughts concealed within the book. She turned a page then, and as she did so she glanced out the window. He felt a thrill of excitement at the prospect of what he was about to undertake with her. To be a painter again! It had suddenly begun to seem real to him. His preoccupation with their second child, which had persisted throughout the morning, was so thoroughly forgotten now it might never have existed.

He crossed the road and went into the café. Marina looked up and closed the book as he came through the door, as if she had been aware of his approach all the time. She slid the book away from her across the table, leaving her fingers touching it as if she meant to return to it later. She said hello and presented her cheek, and he leaned forward to give her a greeting kiss. He pulled out a chair and sat opposite her. 'So where's Robert?'

'He had to go in to the university for a meeting.'

He was nervous now and was anxious to know whether she had decided to sit for him. He set the two sketchbooks side by side on the table between them. He found that he was already trying to solve the problem of her likeness, searching her features for keys, reaching for her story with the hungry painter's eye. She smiled. Grey-blue eyes, her lids half-closing as she turned away, her fingers going to her blue-striped top and picking at a stray thread, evading the direct scrutiny of his eyes. He considered telling her about the compelling omen of the cane chaise, but instead he reached and turned towards him the book she had been reading. '*The House in the Light*,' he said, reading the book's title aloud.

'You've read it?' She was ready to share her feelings about the book with him.

'Teresa read it,' he said, as if Teresa reading the book made up for his not having read it himself. 'It's been out for years.'

'I never manage to read books when they're first out.' She might have been confessing a forgivable weakness, or admitting something charming about herself.

He decided then that she and Robert must have had a talk last night and reached one of their collaborative decisions; a decision, in other words, that would have been principally Robert's. He felt sure they had decided that Marina would not sit for him. She was too light. There was nothing weighing on her mind. If she were going ahead with the project, she would have been nervous, as he was himself. Now that he was with her, her resolve would have been shaken by anxiety about what she might be getting in to. She would be ambivalent and uneasy. She was, he decided, too relaxed for a woman who was proposing to risk something of herself. He felt angry with Robert for not supporting his project and disappointed with Marina for not having the strength to make her own decision.

'I nearly rang you this morning to put you off,' she said.

'How come?'

'This was all beginning to seem an unnecessary complication in my life just now.'

'So have you decided whether you're going to sit for me or not?' The manner of his question, he realised, was blunt and aggressive.

She smiled at his anxiety. 'Of course. Why wouldn't I?'

He felt a shot of adrenalin in his chest. 'You're saying you're going to do it?'

'If you still want me to.'

'I thought you must have decided not to go ahead with it.'

'Artists always sit for their friends,' she said with an exaggerated mildness, repeating his own words to him. She laughed softly, faintly sardonic. 'Robert thinks it's a wonderful idea. So do I.'

The waitress came to their table and he ordered coffee.

When the waitress had gone Marina said, 'Can I look?'

He pushed his old Macedon sketchbook across the table. So he was to have his project! They believed in him! They were trusting him to come up with something good for their first important show back in Melbourne. He felt, suddenly, the responsibility of what he was about to undertake, his responsibility to them as well as to himself. For something like this, something in the main game, unlike the installations, failure would surely be the only alternative to success. He watched her handling his sketchbook, her long fingers, her skin glossy and pale, as if she had been careful to keep herself away from the sun, a life spent in the unnatural light of her studio, labouring alone in her perfumed gallery to turn Robert's ideas into beautiful paintings that deftly sidestepped the historical banality of their medium. If only he could have touched the pale silk of her fingers, have closed his eyes and visualised an instinctive sense of her; the image of her in his mind shaping itself through touch and avoiding the complications of sight . . . The truth was, he had to find a way to paint her. That was his reality now.

She brushed at the table with the palm of her hand before laying the book flat. She might have been handling a precious object from the archive, incunabula, the earliest text. She examined each drawing with evident interest, turning the book sideways to look at the horizontal then back again when the drawings were vertical. Taking her time, turning back a sheet or two every now and then to look again at a particular drawing. She said nothing.

Watching her, he wondered if she might elude him after all. She was, he decided, an undamaged woman. Unlike the women in the flats with whom he had grown up, and with whose ways he was familiar, Marina seemed to him to have come through unscathed, her dreams intact, even untried, the beliefs of her young womanhood transformed in middle life into a complexity that would escape him. If her inner life remained opaque to him, then his paintings of her would fail. Artists took on projects that proved to be beyond their talents and in the struggle to do something good and great they overreached themselves and became bogged in the quagmires of their own egos. Perhaps he would take some black and white photos of her and work from the simplified tones. Take the direct route. His father would not have approved. For his father, art had been to find *himself* in his subject, to test his own capacity for love, and for that there could be no simplified route, only the endless, assiduous contemplation of a devout. *Without art we are nothing*, his father had once confessed. To pin up a photograph was Robert and Marina's way.

She was looking at the drawing of herself asleep in the conservatory at Plovers, her manner serious and engaged. 'You never showed them to us. We had no idea.'

She was going through the book again. 'Effie, my mother, me, Robert, my father. We're all here. It's extraordinary. There's enough information in this book for a portrait of my family. *The Golding Family*,' she said. It might have been the title of a painting. She held up the book. 'But not yourself? No self-portraits? You kept yourself out of the picture. But it's the house that really astonishes me. It's Plovers. I can't believe you got the house the way you did. I can smell it, something of furniture polish and dogs.' She laughed, as if through his old drawings of her home and her family he had become a puzzle to her, had surprised her. 'I wasn't sure I liked you that holiday,' she said. 'I thought you self-absorbed and arrogant. You didn't seem to be sensitive to anything important. You seemed to be ignorant of all the things I found interesting. But the person I thought you were then couldn't possibly have done these drawings.' She studied him. 'I suppose I must have been mistaken about you, mustn't I? You couldn't have got Plovers like this without falling in love with that house.'

She had discovered what he had only recently discovered himself—that she, her birthplace and her life, had a place in the history of his art. She had in her hands all the proof they needed that his new project really had been written into their lives a long time ago, and was not just some random idea he had come up with on the spur of the moment. It was evidence enough, for himself at any rate, that the project possessed its own necessity. That his old sketchbook linked the three of them and their art to his return to painting in a way he could not have foreseen or contrived was as much a reassurance for him as the coincidence of his discovery of the cane chaise at the auction house. The link of the past to the present in the sketchbook was something his father would have recognised and understood. 'I didn't love your house,' he said truthfully. 'You're bringing your own love of the old place to my drawings.' He could remember feeling no special fondness for her parents' house. All he had cared about in those days had been getting his drawings of people right. An endless striving after the accurate observation of the human presence, that was what he remembered. It had been an obsession. He had laughed at the criticism of his fellow students when they told him he was out of touch and was being merely illustrational. Then, as now, he had never striven after an originality of style. With his father, he had believed style was content. He had looked as hard as he could and had struggled to draw what he saw. That had been problem enough for him without anything else. And that is what Robert had called his gift.

'Thanks for having confidence in me,' he said.

'Don't be so silly, Toni!' she said impatiently. 'Of course we have confidence in you.'

'I want you to know that I do realise how important this island show is for you and Robert. I mean, it's your chance to re-establish a presence in Melbourne, isn't it?'

'It's all right, Toni. Really! Robert and I don't know anyone we'd be more confident about having in the show with us than you.' She frowned and placed her hand flat on the table and leaned to pick up her bag from the floor beside her chair. She took out a sketchbook with marbled boards and handed it to him, a modest formality in her manner. 'My old Macedon sketchbook from that holiday. I'm afraid it's just trees. All I did was trees. It won't interest you.'

He took the book from her and opened it. There was sheet after sheet of dark, heavily worked pencil drawings of trees; studies of trunks, limbs, foliage, shadows, trees alone and bunched together, trees close and distant, silhouettes and entanglements of trees, thick trees and thin trees, tall trees and small trees, solitary trees in the distance and obsessively elaborate studies of interwoven branches. The human presence was absent from her work. 'You're the mistress of trees,' he said and handed the book back to her. 'They're very fine drawings.'

'Thank you.' She took the sketchbook from him and put it back in her bag.

He saw that she was not troubled by the failure of her drawings to engage his interest. It was evidently not her art that was at risk with him.

'Well,' she said, and she set her bag on the table in front of her. 'We'd better make a start, hadn't we? You've only got two months. You'd better come back now and do some studies of me working on *Chaos Rules*.'

Her suggestion took him by surprise. 'I didn't bring any materials. I thought we'd probably just be making a decision with Robert today.'

She observed him coolly, as if she considered an interesting problem presented by the angles and planes of his features. 'You can use my materials. There's everything you'll need in the studio.'

'You're sure?'

'Of course.' She stood up. 'Theo will be there. He still does a bit of drawing and often comes into the studio for a time during the afternoon while I'm working.'

'And does he draw you?'

She smiled. 'Yes, he does. When his tablets are working.'

He paid for their coffee and they went out into the street. He offered to give her a lift.

In the car he said, 'So you're already Theo's model?'

'Theo's been an illustrator all his life. He's very modest about the scope of what he does. He works in pen and ink.

Occasionally watercolour or pastel. I think he's keeping a kind of visual diary of his last days with his son. Something for Robert to remember him by. I'm not sure. He hasn't said as much, but that's my feeling. He's another one who won't let anyone see his drawings.'

He drew up beside the park.

She turned and looked at him and smiled. 'You're nervous. I can tell. That's good. It's always a good sign to be nervous when we're about to attempt something important, don't you think?'

As he stepped out of the car he was suddenly remembering Teresa's need for another child. He realised now that there was not really going to be a serious discussion between them about whether or not they would have this child. They would have it, there was no doubt about that. For although it had not yet even been conceived, it was clear that for Teresa this child already existed; it compelled her imagination and was for her one of her family. He wondered now why he had resisted seeing this. As he followed Marina into the house he promised himself he would reassure Teresa tonight that he wanted their second child just as much as she did. He retained a small private guilt, however, at the thought of his ambivalence; as if the unborn child might detect it in him, his less-than-perfect paternity. What troubled him was the thought that Nada was to be displaced from her unique relation to him. To think of the new child was, for him, to contemplate the end of a particular period in their lives and to look towards the beginning of something new; towards the unknown, in other words, that Teresa feared, though she had not meant the child, but the possibility of his success and the hazards of his place in that other, larger family of the life of art.

2

The Third Hand

seven

Toni was sitting on Robert's library steps in the dining room at Richmond drawing Robert, Marina and Theo. The three of them were seated around the circular table finishing lunch. Robert had worked at home especially for the sitting. He was looking tired. Toni kept thinking to himself that it was not a good day for Robert to be having his likeness taken. Misty was crouched at Theo's feet, gnawing an anchovy the old man had slipped to her. Lying on the table at Theo's right hand was the black sketchbook which no one was allowed to see into, not even Robert. Robert would have loved to have seen what his father was doing in the book but Theo waved him away. *It's just the doodlings of an old man.* The book was held closed with a thick elastic band and a draughtsman's pen was pushed between the band and the cover. It looked more like a ledger for keeping some kind of accounts than an artist's sketchbook.

Toni had no doubt his own likeness had found its way into the book.

There was just the click and scrape of their cutlery on the plates, and the distant murmur of traffic along Bridge Road. Theo leaned and spoke to the cat, his voice a sudden distraction in the elaborate silence. 'We're posing,' he explained to Misty throatily, and he coughed. 'We can't help it. It's the vanity of the self-image. We want to look our best, but we're pretending to Toni we don't care.' He coughed again, or laughed, a throaty catch in his voice.

Robert looked at his father, a brief smile lightening the expression in his eyes, then he looked away.

Toni stopped drawing and began writing in the margin of the paper. His day was going well. A week ago he had been tense and anxious, but now he was enjoying drawing again and good things were starting to happen for him on the page. He wanted to set something of this tone for himself in a kind of diary entry alongside the drawings in the hope that it would inform the oil painting when he came to work on it. He wrote carefully with a sharpened stub of pencil, so that he would be able to read his notes back to himself later. It was a kind of story that he was putting together, something to link him to the continuity of today's rhythm, a lifeline to his present mood in case things ceased to go well once he was back in the studio on his own, faced with the problems of the painting. *Marina has thrust a handful of white daisies with golden centres into the yellow and blue Picasso vase on the small table under the window. The effect is more* confident and relaxed than if she had arranged the flowers with care. This is so like her on certain days. Then, on other days, her confidence deserts her and she spends her time nervously readjusting everything that she has arranged the day before . . . A few lovely white petals and a gilding of pollen have fallen at the feet of Geoff Haine's bronze running man. It is a good piece, and they cherish it. The anonymous bronze figure might be their house deity and the flowers an offering to the fugitive god of art who they worship . . . Marina's painting of the naked man adrift in space leans against the pale wall on the mantelpiece behind the silent diners, the wrinkled soles of the man's feet, the anatomical detail photographic and precise, as if his deathless pallor comments on the mortality of the living . . . The viewer of this painting is drawn to look closely in order to see how it has been done, the illusion of flesh in-depth persisting until the eye is close to the paint surface . . . This is the high craft of the artist's sleight-of-hand and Marina is its master . . . And once the viewer is close enough, he sees with surprise that the appearance of depth has been a trick of the light after all . . . and so the viewer steps back and exclaims, Astonishing! . . . It is the invited response . . . Marina's image is more real than reality . . . It is a realism that is unreal, the realism of dream, so precisely focussed it disconcerts perception and prompts the viewer to turn back and look again, and wonder what it is that eludes and attracts him . . . Marina has achieved the heightened realism of an intense familiarity, which must incite the question in the viewer: What is it I am really seeing? *That is Robert's idea, and she has translated it perfectly, and in the translation the picture has become her own . . . So it is no longer necessary for Robert to paint . . . They are true collaborators, these two . . . The union of their ideas and their practice is seamless . . . This is who they are. And without Robert, Marina cannot be fully visible . . . Nor Robert without his father . . . Nor*

Theo, perhaps, without Misty . . . And so on . . . It is all an arrangement of relationships . . . Light and shade . . . Marina's likeness in isolation from these two is without depth or ambiguity and is an idealisation that is not interesting . . . So why, then, was I able to paint my mother without my father beside her? Surely my mother and father belonged together even more deeply than do these two? . . . These are questions to which I shall never find the answers . . . what is true for one relationship, for one painting, is not true for another . . . Each possesses its own strange inevitability that resists us and we can never finally know what it is we are doing until the work is finished . . . It is as if the picture paints itself through us, and has a larger existence of which we know nothing . . . I don't know anyone who would agree with these observations . . . Only my father, if he had lived.

He stopped writing and started working again on the figure of Robert. He drew quickly, with energy, almost violently, with large sweeping gestures, then suddenly close and with minute touches, the stub and two fingers, the drawing block resting on his knees. In his hand he gripped a rag, with which he occasionally scrubbed at the drawing, as if he were trying to rub through the surface to a shape or figure beneath. *How to see? How to draw?* These were the great questions. It was not, after all, a rational procedure to seek to create on the blank page these figures seated at the table. The three of them. A trinity. *The Holy Family.* The irresistible asymmetry of the triptych. Something like that. His perception of them. Not them, in the end, but himself. Such things could never be matters for precision.

Theo nodded in Robert's direction and confided to the cat, 'My son is tired this afternoon, so we are eating our lunch in silence. This is our penance. This is something he learned from his mother, not from me.'

Robert said, 'Oh, come on, Dad!' and he smiled indulgently. 'Mum and I used to have great conversations.'

'Tell me about them,' Theo said. 'What did you two talk about? The absent father? I've no right to ask of course.'

'We often talked about you, Dad. And you have every right to ask.'

Robert was looking older than his fifty years. Toni was intrigued by the grey patches of slack skin under his eyes, his cheeks tight, his features sucked in around the dome of his skull. He had begun to see that in his drawing Robert was becoming an effigy of his ailing father. The unforseen effect intrigued and excited him. The comparison of father and son was being stated and made apparent on the page with the blunt stub of charcoal. He realised that the drawing was an image of a man who was struggling. And as he drew, Toni was moved by a deep feeling of respect and affection for the older man.

Robert glanced up at Marina, as if he expected her to say something.

She did not speak but smiled and put her hand on his.

Theo observed these silent communications between husband and wife with amusement. He was steady today. His nerves smooth. His drugs doing their job. He had good days and bad days. Today was a good day.

They had forgotten to pose.

'So what happened yesterday?' Marina asked Robert. 'You didn't tell me in the end.' Her tone was gentle, almost coaxing, and she kept her hand on his.

'Here we go,' Theo said softly to the cat at his feet.

'What happened?' Marina repeated, gentle but firm.

Robert breathed and glanced at his father, and rested his knife and fork on the edge of his plate. 'The vice-chancellor reallocated the funding earmarked for my guest lecturer program without bothering to tell me,' he said. 'I've had to cancel the program.'

'But can he do that?' Marina asked.

'It's the vice-chancellor's discretionary fund, darling.'

'But not to tell you? Why would he be so rude?'

'Our vice-chancellor's not a he. Miriam Stewart believes being brutal is an efficient way for her to behave.' He smiled. It was a smile that was without warmth or mirth. 'It's not like the old days at the college. It's not like that anymore. People with only art on their minds getting along with each other. That's all gone.' He picked up his knife and fork. 'Maybe I shall have to become like them.' He resumed dealing with the last fragments of his meal.

'You could never be like that,' Marina said.

Theo asked the cat, 'Who knows what we'll do to save our skins?'

Marina persisted, 'You care too much about people to ever be rude or brutal.'

'That's what I've always believed.'

Theo confided to Misty, 'He's forgetting the critical style he was so proud of. Some of those reviews he sent me! Phew! They were hot. This boy has burnt the pants off a few artists in his day.'

'Why does this woman dislike you?' Marina asked, ignoring Theo.

'It's not personal,' Robert said. 'Her behaviour is routine. Her methods work. And, anyway, she can be very winning. You'd probably find her a charming woman, if you met her. You'd wonder what I'm talking about. She's got power in the system, and within the system people are afraid of her and so they do her bidding.'

'But *you're* not afraid of her?'

He smiled. 'I don't think you quite understand my position, darling.'

Was he accusing her of a lack of sensitivity? Once upon a time he had been resilient in the face of trouble and had flourished under pressure.

Toni was enjoying himself. He was in the zone with his work and only vaguely conscious of the tensions that were surfacing in the conversation. He flipped the sheet and switched from Robert to his unfinished drawing of Theo's head . . . The old man might have been scanning Robert and Marina's interior reactions through the livid blaze under his left eye, the privileged powers of a parental aperture. Seeing through a father's eye what no one else sees. The bright red slash like a wound in the softly weeping tissue of the father's face. A wound that was never going to heal. Not now. It was too late now for healing. It had become a permanent disfigurement, a chronic ulcer written off by his body's overloaded immune system. Almost a badge of old age worn with a certain bravado; *My body may be dying but my mind is still on fire!* Defiant in the face of death. Was that Theo? He liked the mystery of the old man. It intrigued him to think that Theo had made his home in Germany for forty years or more and had now returned to die. Did he feel as if he had come home or had he returned to exile? Clearly Theo did not have much time left to bear witness to his son's life. It seemed unlikely he had decided on something heroic and unselfish at the last minute, *I'll do what I can for the boy*, a near-deathbed conversion to fatherly love after decades of indifference. The last thing on Theo's mind, it seemed to Toni, was to make amends for having abandoned his family when Robert was a boy of seven. What had he expected to find in his son on his return? A man like himself? And wasn't there something of the bully in Theo? A tendency to offer ridicule in the face of his son's present difficulties? Was this a sign of impatience? A failure to appreciate the peculiar achievements of his son? Or was he jealous of Robert's youth and his relationship with Marina and, perhaps, of Robert's inner calm despite the hazards of his present situation—that quiet reassurance one always felt from Robert that, no matter how great the crisis, he would not give up on his private values? Was Theo jealous of his son's strength, or was he impatient with his son's weakness? . . . It was a nice question and Toni was only guessing its answer; putting these few cues together to form his picture of the man. He was aware that his own view was not a fixed or singular truth. Through his art, after all, these three were to become his fictions. He had no choice. They could not remain merely themselves. For in art, and they all knew this, it was the perfect lie that was generative of the perfect meaning, not the literal truth. There was no place in art for the literal truth . . .

A breeze lifted through the open window.

Marina said, 'Shouldn't you be picking up Nada, Toni?'

For an instant he wondered who Nada was: the name intensely familiar. He stopped drawing and looked up. The three of them were watching him. 'Teresa's friend Gina's picking her up with her own daughter these days,' he said. 'Teresa organised it. She calls in at Gina's place on her way home from the office.'

Marina said something, then she stood up and began gathering the dishes.

Toni struggled on for a moment longer with Theo's head. There had been a glimmer, then nothing, the illusion of likeness surfacing then sinking away through the matrix of scumbled charcoal, the ghostly presence of Theo Schwartz a drowned likeness in the depths, elusive and tantalising, a faint message from a dead man: *Here I am!* Then nothing. The reverse likeness of father to son was not working. The son might resemble the father, but the father did not resemble the son. Some things could be made up, others refused to be invented and had to be uncovered, one delicate layer at a time, with great care. And perhaps Theo was enjoying playing a game with him? Cat and mouse. Hide and seek. The old man seeing *him* and getting *his* likeness. He was wondering how he might get a look into Theo's black book. Perhaps the pictures held the key to the man?

Robert took a sip of water then replaced the tumbler on the table. He dabbed his lips with his napkin and sat looking up at Marina. 'You're smiling?' he said. His manner was faintly cross-examining.

Father and son watched her.

'I was just thinking how good it is to be back in Melbourne.'

Robert said nothing to this but stood and began helping her clear away.

Theo confided to the cat, 'As a boy, we can be sure he was never a trouble to his mother.'

Misty miaowed and stood on her hind legs, gripping the table edge with her needle claws.

Robert said mildly, 'You shouldn't feed her at the table, Dad. She'll scratch it.'

That word, *Dad*! Resonating in the lofty room. They all looked at the cat.

'I'm not allowed to feed you at the table,' Theo said, playfully dabbing his hand at the cat. 'Only Marina is allowed to do that.' He suddenly grasped the cat's head and gave it a shake.

Toni rose from the library steps and began packing his drawings and materials away in his folder. He would not show them his work. His drawings were private documents. He would probably show Marina a couple of them next time she was sitting for him alone, but that was all. He fastened the ties on the folder and straightened.

The three of them were watching him, as if they expected him to say something to them after the concentrated silence of his work. He smiled. 'Thanks. That was terrific.' He wondered if he might be beginning to find his fictions of them more interesting than their realities. Something insistent in the way they stood that silenced his imagination. The Schwartz family, he thought, and realised at once it was the title for his painting. He was impatient, suddenly, to get home to his studio and begin work on the picture. He owed them something, at the very least a few minutes of conversation before taking his leave. But he had no energy for talk. Their curiosity would have to wait.

Robert went with him to the front door. 'It's good to see you working,' he said, and stood and watched him go down the street to where his car was parked. At the car, Toni turned and lifted his hand in salute. Robert returned the sign and went back into the house.

eight

A few days later, when Toni arrived for another drawing session with Marina, it was Theo who answered the door to his ring. Theo was clutching his old dressing gown and was trembling and shaking violently. 'She's gone to the post office to pick up the advance copies of Robert's book from the States!' He shouted this information, as if he could not control the volume of his voice. 'She won't be long!' He waited for Toni to come in, holding the door unsteadily and watching him managing his folio and bag. 'You're having a good run,' he said. 'Go on in! Go on in! I'll make us some coffee in a minute. I've got to take my pills.' He slammed the door and ushered Toni ahead of him.

Toni waited in the kitchen. He realised, suddenly, that Theo's black sketchbook was lying on a stool by the benchtop. The rubber band and the draughtsman's red and black pen beside it, as if the old man had been drawing until he could no longer hold steady and had abandoned them there. Toni stepped across to the stool, picked up the notebook and opened it. An exquisitely detailed pen and wash drawing of a naked woman bound to a tree with a rope, one coil of the rope passed loosely beneath her breasts and another coil pinioned her legs below her knees. The woman had one hand raised to her mouth and was evidently calling, perhaps for help or to her captor, her other hand raised above her head in a gesture of entreaty or farewell. The leafless branches of a pollarded tree rose behind the woman like a fan above her head, as if it were an enormous shock of wild hair. The woman had a cat's head, the features an accurate likeness of Misty's. Beneath the figure of the cat-headed woman a caption was inscribed in French in a tight spidery hand that was barely legible. Toni made it out to be, *Le Pécher Mortel*. Perhaps it was not a rope, then, that bound the woman to the tree but the coils of a serpent, indeed *the* serpent. The coils of desire. She was, presumably, bound to the tree of knowledge. The work was highly skilled and of a style and quality that Toni had seen only in reproductions of French and German etchings of the late nineteenth and early twentieth centuries. He did not know what he had expected to find in the sketchbook, but it had not been anything like this. He turned the page. A sheet of nine miniature studies followed the bound woman, almost as if the drawing of the bound woman were the frontispiece to a set of illustrations. Each of the nine small studies depicted a fierce horned satyr of small stature struggling with a powerfully muscled woman of much greater size than he. The satyr and the woman were both naked, and the satyr was aroused. Once again, the woman had Misty's head. Reading the nine drawings from the top left of the page to the bottom right, he saw that the cat's features were subtly altered in each subsequent drawing until, in the final drawing in the bottom right-hand corner, the features of Misty had been replaced by Marina's. The features of the satyr remained Theo's throughout, his expression indicating various degrees of torment, desperation and lust. Each of the nine small studies was set within its own separate frame, so that the whole resembled a page from a comic book. The drawings had been brought to a high finish of intricate detail with pencil shading overlaying delicate pen work. There was a caption in the same spidery hand beneath each, the last bearing the heavily ironic title, *Courtoisie Exagérée*. Looking closely at this tiny picture, which measured no more than two centimetres square, and which was difficult to read not only because of its small size but also because the limbs of the woman and the satyr were so confusingly entwined, he realised that the satyr had at last succeeded in penetrating the woman. She had gained a deadly stranglehold with both her powerful hands around the satyr's neck and was forcing his head and shoulders back, accentuating the anguished thrust of his hips. The muscles of the woman's forearms were corded with strain, the veins raised in sharp relief, her features contorted by fierce emotion signifying either murderous rage or overpowering lust—or, perhaps, both. He held the picture close, examining its extraordinary detail with a feeling of excitement, surprised and impressed by the enormous commitment of energy that must have gone into Theo's execution of this densely erotic fantasy-in-miniature.

A small sound, rather like a suppressed sneeze, made him look around. Misty sat in the doorway, neither quite in the room nor quite outside it, regarding him with the same haughty disdain he'd seen on the features of the cat-headed woman. Toni returned the cat's stare until she blinked and looked away, as if, after all, it was not he who interested her. She began to lick her silvery fur. The house was quiet. He turned once again to the sketchbook. The next drawing was a full-page image of a naked young man lying on his back on a couch, his arms stretched out behind his head, his thighs spread, one knee slightly raised. The young man's wrists were loosely bound by a rope in a careless manner similar to that with which the woman had been bound to the tree. The rope was evidently not so much a physical restraint as an indication of the young man's state of passionate bondage. The young man's head lolled over the lip of the couch, presenting the delicate curve of his throat. Incongruously, his features were Theo's, his spectacles knocked sideways from his nose, hanging comically from one ear. His eyes were closed and his lips parted in an expression of sexual rapture. Marina, wearing the vestal robes of a priestess, knelt on one knee between the young man's parted thighs. She gripped the head of his erect penis in her right hand, and in her left she appeared to clasp his scrotum. The drawing had been devotedly overworked to an exacting finish with a fine hard pencil; here and there, but sparingly, a descriptive touch of delicate pastel colouring indicated the blush of naked flesh. It was only after he had been examining the drawing for a moment or two that Toni realised the woman was not in fact holding the young man's scrotum but was grasping a miniature reaping hook, or sickle, in her right hand, the inner curve of the blade lodged against the base of the man's penis. There was a faintly sardonic smile on her face. The caption read, *Nymphe Mutilant un Satyre*. Toni sensed a movement at his shoulder and caught an oily whiff of Theo's liniment. As he turned from the bench, Theo reached past him and delicately lifted the book from his hands.

'There!' Theo murmured, and he laughed or coughed. 'So what do you think of the innocent pastime of a dirty old man?'

'I'm sorry,' Toni said. 'I couldn't resist taking a look. They're some of the most impressive drawings I've ever seen.'

'Thank you.' Theo was steady again. The formality of his tone not entirely self-mocking. He was wearing his loose robe, which was soiled and smelled of the liniment with which he dressed his ulcers. He stood admiring his drawing of the nymph and the naked young man. 'That's high praise coming from a real artist.'

'Now you're mocking me,' Toni said. 'I guess I deserve it.'

'Not at all. Robert has assured me that you are dedicated to the pursuit of the real thing. These are not the real thing.

Unfortunately, they are not even original.' He tapped the drawing. 'The Master L.D. After several centuries of scholarship we still don't know who he was or even what his real name was. There's magnificent anonymity for you. He concealed himself behind his work, which became his beautiful mask. So we still admire him and wonder about him. He borrowed his subjects from artists far greater than himself, just as I do. If you're going to be a thief, you may as well steal the best. Unlike you young people, I don't attempt originality. It can't be helped. I've been making pictures for German companies for more than thirty years. It's my trade.' He smiled. 'I'm not an artist. I'm a tradesman.'

Toni said, 'They're brilliant.' He waited. 'You knew I was coming over to see Marina and yet you left your sketchbook lying about here. It seemed partly an invitation. I mean, you normally keep it close by you.'

'I'm glad you like my little pictures. I was overdue for my life-saving drugs and was in a hurry. Then you rang the bell. But you're probably right. There are no accidents without intentions.'

'It's kind of you not to be angry.'

'And of you not to be offended.' He looked fondly again at the drawing of Marina as the mutilating nymph. 'I worked with Wolf & Son in Hamburg. They were wonderful days. They were some of the great commercial illustrators of their time. They are all forgotten, except by the collectors, who will preserve their works and their memories for the day when fashions change and the young become eager to rediscover them. I'm very pleased you like my drawings.'

'I do. I like them very much. But I should have asked you all the same.'

'Curiosity's not a crime. Not yet. Tricks. That's all it is. That's all I've got. A bag of tricks. Impressive only if you don't know how it's done. It's better to keep this stuff hidden, however. Perhaps we'd better not speak about it? What do you think?' He chuckled mischievously. 'Now you've seen mine, you must show me yours. That's only fair. We must strike a bargain.'

'I don't show my work till it's finished. Your drawings are finished.'

'Show me anyway,' Theo said playfully. 'Change your rule, it's a silly one. What's ever finished?' He reached and touched the tie on Toni's folio, as if he meant to unslip the knot. He lowered his voice. 'I shan't tell a soul. I promise! No one need ever know. If you show me your drawings,' he lifted his hand from the tie, 'I'll let you see the rest of these. You haven't seen the best yet. I have thirty books like this one. Yes! Thirty. One for each year. More than thirty. I've lost count. They deal with my struggle. My little journey. You know? A lifetime of desires and torments. The usual thing. But not only women. Other things, too. Even things that perhaps you've never thought of. So what do you say? Drawing has been my consolation.'

'My drawings wouldn't interest you,' Toni said. 'They're just private notes compared to these. Yours are real pictures. They're works of art, no matter what you say.'

'So you found them pleasantly disturbing?'

'Impressive more than anything. Yes, I suppose disturbing too, in a way.'

Theo gave a little smile of secret pleasure. 'Marina is pleasantly disturbing, don't you think? But now I *am* offending you. No, you're right. We'll say no more about my son's wife. Anyway, think about my proposition. Robert tells me you're a fine draughtsman.' He waited, then added slyly, 'I may die before you finish your pictures. Then I'll never see your work. Would that be fair?'

Toni laughed. 'I don't think you're going to die that soon.'

'So now you're a doctor? In my condition, believe me, death is already here. These days I'm just an onlooker. Would you like coffee? Life is still a great excitement for Robert and Marina. She wants to have his book waiting for him when he gets home. She knows how much he needs some good news at this moment to bolster his spirits. That's not being in the presence of death, that's being in mid-stride. I, however, just watch. But I still make good coffee. It's the one thing I can still do well.' He stepped across to the bench and looked into the coffee pot.

Toni watched him. 'Your drawings make me realise what a beginner I am. They're really great.'

'Not so! No! Not great. Nothing special. Great is not a word you should splash around.' He spooned coffee grounds. 'I've been living between Paris and Hamburg for the past forty-three years. Since Robert was seven. I suppose he's told you what a cad his old man is?'

'Robert has only ever spoken of you with respect.' It was a lie, Robert had hardly ever referred to his absent father in all the years Toni had known him.

'Well, that's nice, but I don't deserve it from him. Mine's the old story. There's nothing unique about it. I fell in love with a beautiful Polish girl while I was visiting Paris and I couldn't resist her, so I abandoned Robert and his mother and returned to live with her in Hamburg. My beautiful Marguerite!' Theo made a sound somewhere between a throaty chuckle and a sob. He put the coffee pot on and lit the gas. 'She died two years ago. I've been living on my own since. Without her I'm an empty man.' He looked at Toni. 'She would have liked you. You are the young man I should like to have been myself once upon a time. Your situation would have interested her. She was a doctor. A psychiatrist. People and their situations interested her. She understood the transference of the artist and his subject. I told her I would take her to my old home one day. Well here I am! Alone!' He shook his head and turned away. 'Two years is nothing. It's nothing! I have lost time. It's terrible. I'm not going to get over it. They told me it would take a year then I'd be okay again. But they didn't know what they were talking about.'

He turned back to Toni. 'I'm not a great moral example to anyone. This jumping disease is my just deserts. It's a lingering disease. You were right, and unfortunately it's not going to do for me any day soon.'

His dirty white robe swung open as he moved about attending to the coffee and Toni caught glimpses of his chalk-white body, the greenish phosphorescence of decay, the livid patches of ulceration. Theo's body was a scene of carnage and a fascination to his eye.

After a minute the coffee maker began to wheeze, the smell filling the kitchen.

Theo poured coffee into two cups. 'If you want good coffee, don't go to Hamburg, go to Vienna.' He handed a cup to Toni. 'Let's sit down before my knees give way. My hips too. Everything aches. We all get our share of pain before this game's over. I'm not complaining.' He slipped the rubber band over his sketchbook, slid the pen between the band and the cover, and preceded Toni through into the dining room. They sat opposite each other at the round table. 'Marguerite suffered.' He fell silent, gathering his resolve. 'We were never closer than during her last night.' He looked up. There were tears in his eyes. He struggled to continue. 'Then, suddenly, she was gone and I was alone.' He sat a moment. 'The silence is something you can't imagine.' He sat gazing into his coffee. After a while he said, 'They had two teams of rats. One team they fed on caffeine. The equivalent of a hundred cups of coffee a day. The other team they fed with normal rat food but no coffee. They couldn't induce Alzheimer's in the rats to which they fed the caffeine.' He smiled, a boyish smile suddenly, in which there was a ghost of the spirited young man he must once have been. 'We're only complicated rats. So I make it strong. She was a beautiful woman. Without her I've become a garrulous old man.' He laughed and sat looking at Toni over the rim of his cup, the red flash under his left eye gleaming moistly. 'You know why old men talk so much? They don't mind dying, that's not it. They hate seeing their experience go for nothing. It all dies with them. They'd like to pass it on, make it real again, give it a touch of immortality. You're not a big talker yourself.'

'I get going after a few drinks.'

'There's nothing interesting about dying.' He leaned back and regarded Toni, the fingers of his free hand playing over the cover of the sketchbook. 'These are drawings. Don't confuse them with life. Art makes life bearable, not the other way around. Look at the rest of them, if you want to.'

'That's very generous.'

Theo shrugged. 'Promise you won't tell Marina and Robert?'

'Of course not. I was wondering what my father would have thought of your work.'

'Was your father an artist?'

'Yes. I believe he was a very good one.'

'What was his name?'

'He never showed his work. He was unknown.'

'Anonymous, like the Master L.D. I like that. His work might outlive his name. Did anything survive him?'

'My mother collected all his work.'

'Good! Then he has outlived himself.'

'He used to say the purpose of art is to resist the world's ugliness.'

'That is beautiful in itself without the art. All such sayings are true, even when they contradict each other. That is the mystery. Art is instinctive. It's primitive. The learned man sacrifices his instincts to reason. The most dangerous time for an artist is after his work has found favour with the public. Then he is tempted to stop struggling. And that's what finishes him. He stops taking risks. Not Picasso. He knew he was a god. He risked everything to the end. That is divinity. Picasso was the exception. Great art, like great music, comes from struggle. There's no easy way.'

Toni had noticed that Theo's hands had begun to jump and twitch again, his long wispy hair floating around his head as if it were charged with the static of his thoughts.

'If you and I are going to be friends, then I had better tell you the real reason I came back.' He waited a considerable moment, as if he were debating with himself whether to confess his secret to Toni. 'I wondered if over here, where I was born, my old memories of home and my youth might return and overwhelm the pain of losing Marguerite. I came back because I was hoping to distract myself.' He sat staring at Toni for a time. 'It was a futile hope. You won't tell Robert, will you?'

'No. Of course I won't.'

'But he's your friend? Sometimes we tell friends things we didn't mean to tell them. It would hurt him to know I had not returned to spend my last days with him. And I don't wish to hurt him. He calls me Dad. Marguerite would have said that is his denial of the futility of his own hope, the hope of having a real father. But denial is sometimes our only refuge against despair. All our consolations are based on illusions. To the artist, illusion is everything. Illusion is the artist's sacred ground, not religion. Robert is a stranger to me. How could it be otherwise? But he is my son, and I see him struggling to make sense of his life. I've finished with that. That's over for me.'

'I shan't tell Robert what you've said. I promise.'

Theo pushed his sketchbook across the table. 'I want you to have this. I've finished with it.'

Toni hesitated.

'Take it!'

Toni took the book and held it. 'You mean for me to keep it?'

'It's yours. You'll make use of it, I can see that. A little of my experience may be secured with you for a time, eh? To give a gift can be a selfish act.' He laughed and put his hand to the table. 'Now, give me your arm. I'm going back to bed. But I shan't make it without your support.' Toni stood and Theo reached up and took his arm, leaned his weight on him and got up. 'I'm sorry about the unpleasant smell.'

'It's okay.' They went down the passage together and Toni helped him to his bed. Misty came in and stood in the half-light watching them.

He had been alone in the studio copying Theo's head from the sketchbook for more than an hour when he heard Marina come in. He was lost in the work and had more or less forgotten about her. He quickly put Theo's sketchbook away in his bag and looked up as she came into the studio. She was carrying a parcel.

'I met Panos,' she said, coming across the room to him. She put the parcel on the cupboard. 'You remember Panos? He used to do those enormous blue and grey field paintings. He was in the queue in the post office. He had just been told, this morning, an hour ago—he had just come from the hospital. He's got inoperable pancreatic cancer. My god! Apparently there's no cure for it. He's my age. He's devastated. They told him he has a month or two at the most. He looks perfectly healthy. Just a little tired, a little drawn, that's all. I took him for coffee and he wept in my arms. It was terrible and wonderful. I haven't seen him for years, and then there he was in the post office queue, his eyes begging me, and then I suddenly recognised him. He lives alone.' She stood close beside him, her hip resting lightly against his shoulder, looking over his pad with its pencil studies of Theo's head. 'They're extraordinary,' she said. 'Theo's been sitting for you?'

'No.' He remembered Panos as a fierce loner, his vast blue and grey canvases strangely obsessive and dated.

'You're doing them from memory? How incredible.'

'Theo and I were talking for an hour.'

'They've got the look of drawings from life. You really do have an amazing eye. I envy you.' She moved away from him and indicated the parcel. 'Two advance copies of Robert's new book. I'll leave it for him to open later. I don't feel like working. Meeting Panos has upset me. We were never really friends, not close or anything, but what horrible news! Imagine living through a day like today for him ... Then waking up tomorrow morning and finding it is still all true.' She rested her back against the wall and closed her eyes.

He said, 'You'll feel better if we work.'

She opened her eyes. 'I don't think I can.'

He turned the page and began drawing her quickly, the lines of her body, her attitude one of submission to her distress.

'Don't!' she said. 'Please!' She straightened and moved away from the wall.

'It's time to work,' he said severely. 'Get changed and come out and work on your picture. You'll feel better if you do.'

She stood looking at him.

'Caving in won't help Panos,' he said. 'Did I tell you I'd done an oil of you from my old Macedon drawing?'

'I'd love to see it.'

'I also did an oil study from my drawing of you asleep on the island.'

'You didn't say.'

'I don't tell you everything.'

She stood uncertainly a moment. 'I'll change. You're right. We should be working. So you're using oil, not acrylic?'

'You never quite know how oil's going to go on. You're never really in control with it. Acrylic's too predictable.' He watched her leave the studio. He was still seeing Theo's drawings of her; the old man's sketchbook and its contents a kind of confirmation of what he was doing. He liked the feeling. It was intuitive. Theo was right. His father would have agreed. His energy for the project seemed to be inexhaustible. He had never before felt so confident about his choices.

nine

It wasn't long before he had begun painting during the night and sleeping most of the day. He liked the night stillness of the city and the feeling of heightened isolation with his work that it gave him. Then, one night, when he had finished work and it was almost dawn, he did not go across to the house as usual but instead slept on the cane chaise. He told himself he was sleeping in the studio out of consideration for Teresa. She was showing signs of strain and irritation; she was working too hard and worrying about money and he did not want to disturb her sleep once again in the early hours of the morning. But in fact sleeping in the studio was really more of a yielding to the seduction of the night silence, in which he was able to enjoy a sense of unbroken intimacy with his work, than a simple act of consideration for his wife. He lay awake for some time in the pre-dawn thinking of Theo and Marina and Robert, and of how he was mining the intimacies of their lives for his art, and he knew he loved doing it and that it was like a surprising gift that had been brought to him, a trust that had been laid upon him, for which he was grateful and of which he was a little afraid.

He woke mid-afternoon and went over to the house. He cooked eggs and bacon and made coffee and toast and put on the radio. Teresa was long gone with Nada and such was the liberty of his occupation of the empty house that he might have been living the solitary life of a bachelor again. He did feel a touch of guilt at the pleasure he derived from the situation, but it seemed to him that it was inevitable and only right that a certain edge of guilt should mediate a reconciliation between the suggestively transgressive nature of the imaginative life and the daily life of the family, which ideally subsisted within that steady condition of normality so dear to Teresa. Theo had cautioned him not to confuse art with life, but by what means did one achieve such clear-sightedness? Wasn't Theo's advice merely an example of the wisdom of old men? Hindsight, in other words, on a life in which he had himself failed to avoid this very confusion?

.

It was some time after midnight and he was squatting on the floor of the studio working on his ambitious painting, the two metre by two-metre oil, *The Schwartz Family*. The picture was well advanced, but he was having trouble with it. It was not the figures that were giving him trouble but the background.

He was missing something and had yet to understand the problem of the setting for his figures ... He became aware, suddenly, of someone standing in the open doorway to the courtyard and he looked up from the canvas. Teresa was holding her purple dressing-gown closed across her breasts and was gazing at the chaos of drawings and canvases scattered about the studio. She did not say anything or look directly at him and after a moment he resumed working. It was a hot night and he had stripped to his underpants. Sweat was glistening on his back and flecks of paint patterned his arms. He reached and loaded his brush, leaning and dribbling the thin glaze at the fugitive likeness of Theo.

'Why do you have to work in the middle of the night?' Teresa asked, her voice was flat, toneless and unnaturally loud in the stillness, something aggressive in her manner.

'My father painted in the middle of the night,' he said quietly. 'Painting in the night is my family tradition.' He looked up at her, the brush poised in his hand. 'No one interrupts you in the middle of the night.'

'You don't have family traditions,' she said. 'Your people were refugees.'

'They were immigrants, not refugees,' he said levelly.

'What's the difference?'

'There's a difference.'

'Then why do you always tell people your dad was a refugee?'

She was being provocative. He understood that, and he resolved not to get annoyed. 'Dad was a refugee from Poland when he was a boy. But not from England. From England he was a migrant. No different to your own people from Calabria in the fifties.' He sat back on his heels, squinting to see the work in front of him. He did not want to have this conversation. It was a conversation he and Teresa had often had and it settled nothing. It was a difference of view which they never seemed able to finally resolve and which seemed to arise as a point of disagreement whenever there was tension between them. He knew he should just let it go and say no more. And that was what he meant to do. So for some considerable time he kept his thoughts to himself and said nothing. But the question had unsettled his concentration and continued to needle him. Whether his parents were to be viewed as having been refugees or migrants bore upon his sensitivity about their dignity and their precarious social status. He did not wish to think of his mother and father as having been bound by external circumstances in the important decisions of their lives. He did not want to think of them as victims of their fate, but as people who had enjoyed the dignity of personal freedom. The distinction as to whether they had been refugees or migrants was important to him, however, not only for the sake of his parents but also to his sense of who he was himself and why, in particular, he was an Australian and not a Canadian or an American or a New Zealander—

or, for that matter, still a European like his mother's and father's own ancestors.

He stayed silent and Teresa also said nothing more. Then, without thinking, he lifted his brush from the canvas and looked up at her. 'Mum and Dad could have settled permanently in England after the war but they came here instead,' he said. She turned and looked at him. 'They could have gone to the US or to Canada. Or to New Zealand. Coming to Australia was an orderly migration for them. You know that.' She did know it. 'They had a choice. They were migrants, not refugees. Night work is what I learned from Dad. It's my tradition.'

'Whatever you say,' Teresa said without a trace of interest, as if she had forgotten ever having said a word about it in the first place. She looked down at him. 'So how come you're working on the floor?'

He was annoyed with himself for having let himself get annoyed. But why couldn't she just accept his explanation? They were *his* parents and it was *his* story! So he should know! It was simple. He tried to sound relaxed and neutral, but could hear himself sounding aggrieved. 'I like the way the glaze pools in the horizontal.'

'I only asked,' she said mildly. 'There's no need to get angry.'

'I'm not getting angry. I'll work on the easel later when I'm using a thicker glaze.'

After a minute she said, 'You've set up your dad's old suit again.'

He turned and looked at the old three-piece on its rack, standing over against the wall, as if a dark-clad figure observed them from the shadows.

'It's spooky,' she said. Then after a moment, 'I thought she was still out here.'

So that was it! He laughed. 'Marina left *hours* ago.'

'I didn't hear her car.' She looked him over. 'You were working in nothing but your underpants while she was here?' She stepped into the studio and walked over to him.

'I was dressed.' He gestured to his T-shirt and jeans, which were lying on the cane chaise.

Teresa stood above him. 'So what else do you two need the bed for?'

'It's not a bed, it's a chaise.'

'I can see what it is. It's a bed. You've been sleeping on it, haven't you?'

He looked up at her from the floor: she was foreshortened for him, wider than tall, her fists tight in the pockets of her dressing gown, her arms held against her body, pushing her breasts together. He said gently, 'You'll be a wreck in the morning if you don't get some sleep.'

She was silent a moment, her lips compressed. Then she said, 'I want our old life back.' It sounded like an ultimatum, but there were tears in her eyes. 'I'm sitting up there on my own every night watching that box. You come over for your dinner as if you've wandered into someone else's house. When I speak you don't hear me. When do we talk any more? About us? About anything? I'm trying to go along with this project. I'm doing my best to stay with it. I know how important it is to you. But I didn't expect to be sleeping alone. I want to know if you're coming back to our bed, or if you've settled out here for good?'

'Of course I'm coming back. I just need a few undisturbed nights, that's all. I have to get this picture right. It's my first big one. Ever. I have to find it.' He considered the painting and made a slow sweeping pass over its surface with his open hand, as if he were a shaman invoking a spirit. 'It's not right. Something's holding it up.'

'I can't sleep on my own,' she said. 'I've forgotten how to do it. I can't switch off on my own. I need a body next to me. I get up and come out to the kitchen and I look at your light on over here. I'm standing up there just now looking across the courtyard asking myself, *Is she still down there with him?* The *working partnership!*' she said almost violently. 'Jesus!'

'It *is* a working partnership,' he insisted quietly.

'It can't *all* be in my imagination.'

'We're working. That's all that's going on. I finished the sitting with Marina hours ago and she left straightaway.' He turned and indicated a pile of drawings on the plan press. 'Have a look. I did lots of work. It's all there.'

Teresa did not move or look towards the press. 'You're not with *us* anymore,' she said.

He squinted at the likeness of Theo. He had seen something that demanded adjustment. 'Of course I'm with you,' he said absently, as if it were part of an incantation. He loaded his brush and leaned and dabbed at Theo's brow. 'It was too dark there,' he murmured.

'Listen to you! You're talking to yourself! You're not talking to me.'

'I'm talking to you. That's what I'm doing. I'm talking to you.' He touched the brush to the picture again. 'I feel like Dad when I'm painting. It's amazing. The way his hand used to move. I see it.' He moved the brush around, as if he were conducting an orchestra, conjuring a secret music from the air. He looked at the brush with surprise, almost tenderly. 'I've noticed I hold the brush exactly the way he used to hold it. I never realised that before. The brush feels free and light in my hand when I hold it the way he held it. It's incredible how you learn these things and you don't know you're learning them. As if your hand learns them and you just follow along obediently. Then, suddenly, you realise you've been doing it without consciously thinking about it. Somehow that makes it more real. I don't know why. But it does. I paint with Dad's traditions in my hand. I really do. Honestly. It's not an empty boast.'

She watched him painting a while, saying nothing. Eventually she said with grudging admiration, 'I don't know how you do that.'

'Me neither.'

'It was easier when you were doing installations. You didn't need these people then. You only needed Andy. Andy's a real person. He's the best friend you've got.'

'I still need Andy. I'll always need Andy. Nothing's changed.' He fossicked around on the floor among the scatter of drawings and picked up a charcoal of Theo's head. He could see the moulded substance of Theo's living flesh behind the rough likeness on the sheet. It was a visual note, an *aide-memoir*, the drawing like a letter from a friend, not the friend himself but the familiar words of the friend. The drawing represented for him an elusive presence, but a real one; it was a fragment of another, less complicated and truer reality that he believed in with a passionate longing, as if it were something he had lost and needed to recover. There had always been for him a sense of something real having been touched upon in his drawings, no matter how incomplete or sketchy the drawing, a sense of having postponed the decay of the meaning of the experience for himself by drawing it, as if with drawing he encountered a lost or forgotten truth within himself. Even his childhood drawings had possessed this slightly magical quality for him, as if they had referred to another world, a world within which he had once been more at home than he was in the world of the everyday; as if his art were his quest to recover his place in that lost world. He wondered what Theo's Marguerite would have had to say about such an idea. He pictured himself meeting her in Paris. A woman still beautiful and young despite the passing of the years, a woman still filled with the spirit of an eager curiosity about the mysterious inner lives of her fellow human beings. He had never been to Europe, but he could imagine it . . . The cobbles of the street gleaming blackly with rain, the woman greeting him confidently as if they were old friends, *I feel we have always known each other . . .*

Teresa said, 'She's stopped asking where her daddy is.'

He looked up.

'She's started keeping her feelings inside. That's not a good sign. Children should be free to express their feelings.'

'Sometimes we need to keep things inside,' he said. He looked again at the charcoal of Theo. *The problem of Theo Schwartz*—horned beast or fallen angel? Theo's double image of himself. His double image of humankind, mutilated by lust. He set the drawing aside on the floor. Theo would have appealed to his father. He could see the two old men talking art and life. It was a subject for a painting by Rembrandt. 'It's not going to be for long,' he said, examining the figures in the big oil. 'She'll be okay. Children are resilient. You said so yourself.' He liked the way he had dealt with his figures; they were flat, dry, stoic and unreal, not so much likenesses of the actual people as memories of people touched by some unexplained cause for sadness or regret. To see in these figures that he had visualised Robert and Marina and Theo as inhabitants of a nostalgic reality gave him an intense pleasure. He had placed them within the lost world of his own imagination. Some quality of the truth of his drawings had survived the less intimate process of the large painting. But still the background was not right. It was too close to the everyday realities of their Richmond situation.

'She needs you,' Teresa said, shifting her foot closer to the painting, her brown toes intersecting his gaze millimetres from the edge of the canvas. He looked at the broken edges of her alizarin crimson nail gloss, the pale line where her sandal strap covered the dorsal rise of her foot during the day. Her aggression and her vulnerability in her foot. He had an impulse to bend and kiss her feet, *There! All better*, as if she were a child who had hurt herself. 'So why don't you let her come out here with me?' he said. 'You know I don't mind having her around while I'm working. She's happy doing her drawings. She doesn't interrupt me.' He ran the pads of his fingers delicately over her foot. 'You've got beautiful feet.'

'Don't try changing the subject.'

'It's true. I've always thought you had beautiful feet.'

Teresa considered her feet. It *was* true. She was proud of her feet, as if she had had a hand in designing them herself. 'Be realistic. She's a child. She can't sit up all night with you. She has to get her sleep. Once she was out here she'd want to stay out here all night. She needs her regular hours.' She fell silent and stood looking around the studio. 'These materials you're using are costing a fortune. I can just hear Dad when he sees the bills.'

He stood and drew his brush through the rag then swirled it in the jar of turps. 'You said to use the best materials. You said not to worry about the money. *Just buy what you need*, you said.'

'I didn't know it was going to cost this much.'

'I'll make some money with the island show. We'll pay your father back.'

She considered him. 'Why can't you paint my father instead of *his* old man? It would flatter Dad a bit if you did his portrait. That wouldn't hurt, would it? I mean, just because you're an artist, it doesn't mean you can't do something nice for someone now and again, does it?'

'Maybe I will paint your dad,' he said mildly. 'One day.'

'My father's a beautiful man!'

'He is, that's for sure.'

'He's an old god. There's history in Dad's face. And if you don't want to paint dad or me or your daughter for some reason, and I'm not asking you what your reason for that might be, then what about Mum? Mum would secretly love to have her portrait painted. I know she would. Maybe you could do one of her and Dad together? They'd be proud. It would soften their attitude a lot towards you, you know.' She looked at him, alight with her idea. 'Why don't you do it? Really? Put my parents in this show?'

He busied himself putting away his brushes and paints.

'Well?' Teresa said.

'These things have their time. Things happen when they're ready to happen.'

'Things happen when we *make* them happen!' She waved her hand impatiently at the painting on the floor. 'These people aren't even a normal family.'

He laughed. 'There are normal families?'

'Normal is normal! Don't start that! You know what I mean. They decided not to have children! What kind of married couple decides not to have children? It speaks for itself. Why get married, if you're not going to be a family? They don't want what we want. They don't want a normal life like other people. They don't think like us. Neither one of them ever looked me in the eye or listened to anything I ever said or ever asked me a single question about myself. How's that? Think about it. You know where their minds are.'

'They listened to you.'

'For people like them I don't exist. It's you they want to see. When they went to Sydney I thought I was rid of them. Now they're back, taking over your life again as if you owe them something. They're not like the artists we knew at Andy's in the early days. If that crazy lot came here, I wouldn't mind.' She stood glaring at the painting. 'Did you ever see either of these two get drunk or smoke a joint or do anything stupid?'

'Robert and Marina are disciplined people.'

She drew in her breath sharply and glared around. 'God, when I think of my brothers renovating this into a studio for you!'

'I'm grateful. I'm using it as a studio. What am I doing?'

She measured the painting on the floor as if she were thinking of stomping on it. 'His old man deserted his family and lived in Germany for forty years and he's only come home now he's dying of Parkinson's and needs someone to cook for him and do his washing. What kind of a father is that?'

'Theo had a wife in Germany. He had another life there. That's not a crime. His wife died two years ago. Theo came back so he wouldn't have to die alone.'

She pointed at the image of Marina. 'And her old man was a barrister and a member of the Melbourne Club! You're betraying your origins with these people. They've never been our kind of people.'

'They're my friends.'

'They're cold people. You're not a cold person. They only pretend to be who they are.' She turned away from the picture and made a flinging gesture at his small unframed canvas of Marina asleep on the island. 'And what's that doing propped on the plan press I gave you for our wedding? Is it supposed to be an invitation, the way she's lying there making herself helpless?'

He said nothing. The picture still surprised him. The joy of painting again that he had felt while he was doing it. He stood looking at it. It would always remind him of the day on the island.

Teresa looked at him gazing at his picture. She said contemptuously, 'I need a cigarette!'

He turned from the picture and watched her leave. She had not smoked since she had been pregnant with Nada.

As she stepped out the door she said over her shoulder, 'Stand there looking at her all night if you want to.'

He picked up *The Schwartz Family* and leaned it against the plan press. He would take another look at it tomorrow. The background of the pale wall at Richmond and their painting of the naked man drifting above the cold blue sphere of the world had begun to irritate him.

He put on his T-shirt and jeans, switched off the light and stepped out into the courtyard. The summer night smelled of diesel fumes and car exhausts. The smell of his city. The pile of old clothes and racks out in the middle of the open space like a bonfire of personal belongings prepared for the burning: *every last trace of them shall be destroyed!* A yellow half-moon hung in the smoky sky, the same moon that had hung over his father's old town when his father was a boy. One thing that had not changed since then. He thought of the two of them as they had been, himself and his father, painters in the night. It was art that had sustained his father through his years on the moulding line at Dunlop. An artist and an intellectual by nature, required to be a labourer. His heroic silence all those years about the experiences of his childhood. Not wanting to burden his family with those old memories. Never painting his family, only their things, his sense of their vulnerability, his knowledge of the fragility of human happiness. Then the terrible event of his eldest son's imprisonment that had silenced them. It must have seemed like a fragment of past horrors come back to lay its claim on him.

He turned and went into the house. He could not bear to think of his father as having been a man broken by experience.

He paused outside Nada's door and stood looking in at the little girl. Her picture of him with the flaming hair! He must remember to pin it up before it was lost under the junk that was accumulating in the studio. Her belief in him evident in the confident image she had drawn of him, as if she were the bearer of a message of hope to him from his dead father. He stepped into her room and leaned to touch his lips to her cheek. Her delicious smell! If he were blind, he would know his daughter. He straightened and walked out of her room.

In the bedroom he undressed and climbed into bed. Teresa rolled towards him and they held each other without speaking. 'I'm sorry, darling,' he whispered and he kissed her.

'I couldn't bear any longer the suspense of not knowing if she was still down there with you. I was going mad wondering.'

He kissed her cheek, her forehead, her lips.

She lay close against him. 'Did you go in and look at her?'

'She was sleeping.'

'Was she still under the covers?

'I straightened her up.'

'Dad's mum had twelve. Two of them died. How did they live with that?'

'You want twelve?'

'Two would be nice.'

The sound of Teresa's voice entered his dream. The pressure of her head on his chest, the smell of her hair, the weight of her arm across him. In the dream his father had entered a dimly lit room and handed him a small canvas. *Here's your painting, son,* his father had said. He had not been able to see his father's face. There had been a silent companion with his father, as if his father had needed a guide in order to find his way back. Discovering that his father was still alive filled him with remorse; *'They told me you were dead! I never checked! I just accepted what they told me! That's why I haven't been to see you all this time!'* The pure hit of grief at the sound of his father's voice. Disbelief that he had never thought to check that his father really was dead, but had meekly accepted the reports of his father's death as fact. How could he have been so stupid? The companion from the other world led his father to a chair in a dark corner of the room and his father did not speak again. As he was about to look at the painting his father had given him, the murmur of Teresa's voice entered the dream and he was suddenly awake. Their hands had not quite touched! If only he could have felt the touch of his father's hand! The rush of grief and longing of the dream, the weight of his father's gift of the painting in his hands, so real he could still feel it. A certainty the painting existed somewhere. His father's gift to him. What was the subject of the picture? *Here's your painting, son,* his father had said. *Your* painting? His *own* painting? The kind of painting he was trying to paint? Did his father actually say those words, or had he just handed over the painting with that feeling behind it? Toni longed to slip back into the dream.

Teresa whispered, 'I went off the pill. I could be having our next baby.'

The dream had possessed the force of actuality, the emotion of it so strong he was convinced his father had passed to some other life for the dead . . .

'Don't be angry.'

'I'm not angry. I'm just a bit surprised you did it without saying something first.'

'You've been so busy. I was afraid the time might slip by. These things have their moment. Hey? That's what you said, they happen when they're ready.'

'And you said they only happen when we make them happen.'

'I would have told you, but you've been sleeping out there,' she murmured. 'The same way you want your painting, you know, it's the way I want this little brother or sister for Nada. We can't explain these feelings, can we? We just have them. Anyway, I've been feeling we're not a real family with an only child. You remember how gorgeous she was as a baby?'

He kissed her. 'She's still gorgeous. She'll always be gorgeous.' Teresa's cheeks were wet. 'Don't cry!' he said gently, kissing her salty cheeks. 'Why are you crying? I hate it when you cry.' Her tears made him feel accused. As if he had committed a crime against his family. A crime against morality itself, against *normality*. As if he were guilty of a dereliction of his duty towards the family and humanity in general. Her tears always had this completely unsettling effect on him.

She gave a big sniff. 'I'm just crying,' she said. 'Don't worry. I'm not crying about anything. It's just that since you started painting I feel as if I'm drifting with this whole thing on my own.'

He kissed her wet cheeks again.

She sniffed and squirmed around and reached under the pillow for her handkerchief. She blew her nose. 'I'll be ratshit in the morning.' She laughed and lay down again and cuddled up. 'When you're painting I don't know where you are. It's like you've gone somewhere.'

'I'm sorry.'

'I can't follow you in there. That's all. Your painting shuts me out. Even when you're with us you're not with us. I'm not blaming you, but it's lonely.' She hesitated. 'It's not just you and me now. Now it's you and your work.' She was silent. 'And *her*.' She studied him in the half-dark. 'See! You're doing it now! I can feel you still thinking about your work! I should be happy you're working. You're doing what you love to do. You're being a real artist. But you don't share it with me.'

'I just had a dream about Dad. It was as if he's still alive out there somewhere.'

'I have to say this, but your dad's another thing coming between us. Your dad is your work too. It's always been as if you were keeping him in a special secret place, as if you were afraid to share him with me. But I understand now that your dad is with your work. I've only just understood this these past weeks. Your dad and your painting are in the same place for you. It's not something I knew before you started painting again. I'm sorry, but I have to say it. I'm not complaining. I'm just saying that's the way it is. Some things we keep to ourselves. You said that.' After a while she asked in a small voice, 'Do you want our next baby?'

'Of course I want it! How could I not want it?'

'If we were sane, we'd wait until we've got more money.'

'Everything gets ruled by money,' he said. 'The travel business will pick up and Andy will sell my pictures. These things go in cycles. We have to believe in ourselves.'

They lay in the silence in each other's arms.

He had telephoned Marina in the middle of work the other day. He had not told Teresa about the phone call because he was not sure that he understood his motive for making it. He had been working on the figure of Marina when suddenly he was visualising her alone in her studio over at the house in Richmond, seeing her there on her own doing her work, just as he was alone doing his work, and he had felt an urgent need to hear her voice. *'You're working?'* he said when she picked up.

'Yes. And you?'

'Yeah, I'm working.'

Then there was a long uncertain silence.

'What is it, Toni?' she asked. *'Why did you call me?'*

Another silence, only smaller. His awkwardness with having given in to the impulse to telephone her. *'I just called, that's all. I felt like calling.'* He could not say that he missed her. But in a way that was it.

She said, *'It's good to hear your voice.'* As if she understood exactly why he had telephoned her.

Teresa said, 'I never wanted to have children before I met you. It just wasn't there for me.'

In the night silence the bell of the town hall clock struck the hour.

'It's good you want them now,' he said. 'Imagine life without Nada!'

'Don't!' she said.

ten

He had set up *The Schwartz Family* on the easel and had opened the back door to the studio. For the first time he was seeing his painting flooded with natural light. He did not feel he could do any more with it. Either it was finished or he must scrape it back to the bare canvas and begin again. There was an enchanted quality about the three figures, however, which he felt he could not hope to achieve again, for he did not know how he had achieved it this time. The figures had the appearance for him of having been painted not by himself but by an unknown artist, and there was in this a precious sense of the elusive and the mysterious that he did not want to risk losing. It was the background that was the problem. It had remained grounded merely in an illustration of the facts of the setting at the Richmond house and had not been enlivened by the same spirit as the figures. He took the phone from its cradle and dialled the Richmond number.

'The picture's finished,' he said bluntly when Marina picked up. 'Do you and Robert want to come over and have a look at it?'

'You sound a bit grim about it,' she said. 'What's the matter?'

'I'm thinking of scraping it back and starting again.'

'You don't mean that?'

'I mean it.'

'Well for goodness sake don't do anything until I've had a look. I'm coming over.'

He considered telephoning Teresa at the office and letting her know Marina would be with him in the studio again. But in the end he didn't call her. A phone call from him in the middle of the day was more likely to startle her than to reassure her.

When Marina arrived he went out into the lane to meet her. She greeted him and came into the studio. They did not say anything but stood in front of the painting. He was nervous now that she was with him. The three figures seated at the round table gazed fixedly out of the picture plane upon a scene that was evidently of disquieting significance for them. Robert was seated to the left of Marina, his hooded gaze implying a magisterial judgement upon the events he was observing. Theo sat on Marina's right, a familial likeness between the two men, as if father and son might have been the haughty generations of a declining dynasty. The pale fingers of Theo's left hand caressed the silver cat, which sat on the table beside him. Theo's gaze was amused, watchful and interior, the crimson slash beneath his eye arresting the attention. Seated between the two men, Marina was upright and still, as if she waited to hear important news. She occupied the centre of the composition. Something of his original idea had survived. The painting was not what he had proposed when the idea had first occurred to him, but it was still principally her portrait.

'It's very powerful,' Marina said. 'It's beautiful. You mustn't even consider scraping it back.'

He was finding her presence unsettling. The trouble was, the painting had gone beyond them and become something they were unable to sum up or control any longer, an object risen out of their ideas, their experiences and their desires, but larger and more complex than their expectations for it. He lifted his hand to his brow, the reflected sunlight from the floor in his eyes. He sensed Marina react to his movement, as if she too were on edge. 'We should close the door,' he said. 'The sunlight's too harsh.'

Fixed to a wall bracket above the plan press was a new lamp on a fire-engine red swivel. He had set the lamp at an angle so that at night it would light the painting obliquely. He had also hung a drop sheet over the window to the courtyard to control the light from that direction. He stepped up to the painting and brushed at it with his hand. It was an impatient sweeping gesture encompassing the space behind the seated trio, his open palm and the spread fingers of his hand skimming the surface of the paint as if he would solve his problem with a wave of his hand. 'I don't like the background.'

Marina stepped up and stood close beside him.

The tension between them was unexpected and distracting. Something had changed; a remainder of disquiet from his impulsive telephone call to her of the previous week. Something unstated between them now that had not been there before, as if his phone call had established an expectation. He caught her warm breath, the delicate waft of her health, the sweetness of her inner body. Could he paint an internal portrait of her? Would they know her? Pink lungs and purple viscera? Or are we all the same once we pass the barrier of the skin? Our likenesses all alike deep down? Carcasses on the hook? *The brutality of fact*, Francis Bacon's phrase for it. Dismembered by experience. Would we know our beloved's internal organs if we saw them? Spread them with our hands as the Roman augurs spread the vitals of the sacrificial goat; divining the omens, presentiments of one's own fate in the bloodied remains. How deep could one go with a portrait? Where were the limits? *I foresaw my fate in my lover's heart*. Seeing things. Prognostications and tokens of unease. A heady liberation from the daily insistence on the governing norms; an acknowledgement that one's creative decisions and motives were generated in a place of which one possessed no practical knowledge and over which one exercised no conscious control—an imaginary place, in other words, without the morbidity of accumulated responsibilities. He let his gaze rest on her profile, remembering suddenly the optimism of their day together on the island.

She frowned. 'It's always the problem of knowing when something's finished,' she said. She might have been referring to more than the painting. 'I agree with you about the background. You don't suppose it's just too Richmond? The mood, I mean? Having our painting-*within*-the-painting? That sort of thing always reads as such a cliché, don't you think? It's a false note here. I know it's not what you meant. But it's a distraction from the figures and is just the kind of cleverness you don't go in for.' She turned to him. 'I really think you have to do away with this background altogether.'

But he was elsewhere with her: a shift of the light, a sound in the distance, a sudden cool drift of air. It seemed at times the direction of life must be governed by such tokens as these, and one knew one was helpless to resist...

She put her hand on his arm, claiming his attention, offering reassurance. 'You mustn't panic. It's impossible not to believe in the world of these three people. There's something quite eerily intriguing about the way you've represented us. I couldn't possibly have predicted it.' She took her hand from his arm.

He was admiring the curve of her neck below her short hair, the line of her shoulder. He was drawing the line of her in his mind, seeing her differently today. He would do a fresh set of drawings of her. Drawing had always been the most intimate, the most revealing and the most precious aspect of his work. And the most private. The thing he loved most. The naked portrait of her he had thought of when he had first seen the cane chaise in the auction rooms had arisen in his mind as a drawing, a dark, closely worked study in light and shade. But a naked portrait was not something he could suggest to her at this moment. To go from the mundane and the ordinary to a place of magical possibility with another person— one could not adopt a strategy for that. Apart from the naked portrait, however, he had no idea what the arrangement of his next picture would be. He said, 'Why don't we leave it for now? I should put it away and forget about it for a while and start work on my next picture. Come up to the house and I'll make us some coffee.'

She turned to him with interest. 'What's the new picture going to be?'

'I don't want to talk about it just yet.'

She turned back to *The Schwartz Family*. 'I don't think leaving it is an option for you, is it? If you're going to have three paintings ready in time for the island?'

He stood beside her, looking unhappily at his painting, his energies for reconsidering the background blocked and cold.

She said, 'There *is* a solution.' She did not look at him.

'What do you mean?'

She did not speak at once. 'You could let me paint a new background for you.' She turned and looked at him. 'I knew you'd react like that!' she said, her voice filled with disappointment. 'That's exactly how Geoff Haine would react if anyone ever dared suggest they might help him with one of his pictures. You're all the same!' She was angry. 'You think you've got to control every last detail yourselves. You're too precious about it. Everyone gets help at some time. Even the great messiah Picasso accepted help from his friends.'

'I haven't said a word,' he objected, amused by her anger. 'I need a minute to think about it.'

'You don't *have* to say anything. You think collaboration is beneath you. You don't see how childish such an attitude is. We're all collaborators. All of us. None of us does this completely on our own. You need to free up a bit. You're still hanging on to the attitudes you had before your installations. You can't just revert to being who you were then. You were a different person four years ago. We all were. We have to move on. We have to open up to new boundaries in our practice or we just repeat ourselves. When Picasso didn't like the background to his group portrait *The Soler Family*, his friend Junyer Vidal painted a new background for it. It was the figures in that picture Picasso cared about, just as it's the figures in this picture you care about. You're a figure painter, I accept that. We all do. No one's arguing with it. Your figures are wonderful. But you just don't *care* enough about this background to ever give it the magic you've managed with the figures.' She waved her hand impatiently, dismissing his objections as tedious. 'But I think you know all this.'

He did know it. And he knew she was right. Setting was always a problem for the figure painter. He found her argument

compelling. Almost a relief. He stood facing *The Schwartz Family,*
trying to imagine what her backdrop to his figures might look
like. He was intrigued by the sense of possibility in her offer,
a lightness in it that surprised him, almost an inevitability
about it, as if she really had seen the only true solution to his
problem. He turned and looked at her. He was aware that for
the first time he was being seriously challenged by her, and
he felt a new depth of admiration for her. 'So just supposing
I did let you paint a new background for it, what do you think
it might look like?' He knew already that he was going to take
the risk. He had already decided, if being drawn into her
challenge could be called *deciding*. He might be risking
everything. But perhaps that was what he had to do. Perhaps
it was time to risk everything. Perhaps this was what every
artist had to do at some point, to gamble it all at the critical
moment. 'If I do agree, what do you think you'd do?'

'I'd do trees,' she said without hesitation, and she laughed.
'You should have guessed.' She turned to him, excited now.
'Do you really think you might let me do it?'

He was trying to imagine what effect her trees might have
on his figures.

She stood close at his side. 'Robert and I only have one
more picture to do for the show and we know exactly what
that's going to be. So I've got plenty of time. You haven't.'

'What sort of trees?'

'I don't know yet.'

'I think I might. You'd do those trees around your old house at Macedon. Winter trees. Bare and black.' He made shapes in the air with his hands. 'Those big elms against the mountain. A night picture, with the three of you sitting there gazing out from that weird interior light of your lives.' He laughed. 'That's not something I could do. It's something you can do. I can see you doing it.'

She studied him uncertainly. 'Are you sure you can trust me with it?'

The moment was one of intense clarity for him. It was a moment he knew he would look back upon and remember. 'You're the only person I could possibly trust to do this.'

'Toni!' she said with feeling, and she reached and took his hand.

'There isn't anyone else.' The surprising familiarity of her hand in his, her fingers smooth and cool as he had imagined them to be that day in the café. The colour had risen to her cheeks. 'Since that drawing I did of you asleep in the conservatory at Plovers, in a way you've always been a part of what I've been doing with my art. I don't know what I mean by that.' He looked at her hand in his.

'Don't try to explain,' she said softly.

A moment of stillness between them as they stood hand in hand in the sunlit studio . . . Then her gaze shifted, suddenly, to the open door behind him, a warning in her eyes. He let go of her hand and swung around, a guilty flash of Teresa walking in on them. A man was going past along the lane, a pusher ahead of him with a child in it, shopping in plastic bags slung from the handles of the pusher. The man and the child looked in through the open door of the studio as they went by. The man scanning the tableau of the two figures, who might have just drawn apart hurriedly from an embrace; two people observed by the trio in the painting. The man's curious gaze sweeping the interior of the studio. Then he was gone.

Toni did not look at her but reached and lifted the painting down from the easel and laid it on the floor. 'Perhaps we should make a start,' he said.

They mixed a neutral glaze and knelt on the floor and began painting out the man adrift against the black sky with its cold floating world. They worked in silence, conscious of the nearness of the other. It was Robert's vision they were obliterating: the knowing comment of the artist on his image, the self-conscious inquisition of the subject; Robert's restless intelligence forever seeking the means to unlink himself from the images of his imagination, as if he wished to bestow upon them a perfect autonomy of existence. As he worked beside Marina, Toni felt that he was seeing into the secret history of Robert's art; his sense of the three of them linked to each other in ways they would never unravel or fully understand. He wondered what he would have been doing at this moment if they had not returned from Sydney. He could never explain to Teresa in a way that would satisfy her that it was only through Robert and Marina that his work had found a renewal.

They stood and cleaned their brushes. Standing above the altered painting, he realised he could still make out the naked man adrift under the fresh medium, like a body frozen into the ice. The ghostly persistence of Robert's influence interred beneath the neutral glaze. He liked the accidental effect and felt sorry it was to be sacrificed to the trees.

'What is it?' she asked.

He pointed. 'See? It's haunted.'

She looked and said nothing.

'Let's take it over to Richmond.'

She stood considering him. 'You don't think you should take a day or two to think about this?'

'Let's just do it.'

Out in the lane they loaded the picture onto the roof rack of his wagon and she got into her car. He leaned down at her window. 'Theo gave me his sketchbook. Did you know?'

She looked up at him. 'Yes, he told us. He said he was sure you'd make good use of it.'

'He made me promise not to show you and Robert.'

'We'll see it one day.'

There was a question in her eyes, even the moisture of a tear, a need perhaps to be reassured. He might have kissed her then—have kissed her lips and sealed it. 'I'll be right behind you,' he said and straightened. He stood back and waited for her to drive away. He watched until her car turned into the road at the end of the lane and was out of sight. When she had gone he went back into studio and got a brush and a tube of black. He lifted the painting and wrote on the back of the canvas, *The Schwartz Family, 200 × 200cm. March 2003. AP 17. A homage to Pablo Ruiz Picasso's* The Soler Family.

eleven

She was waiting for him on the verandah. As he came up to her carrying his painting she said, 'Oriel's viewing our pictures for the show.' She reached and took hold of the other end of the canvas. 'She brought Geoff Haine with her. It looks as if Andy's here too.'

'The whole family!' he said. He was not delighted by the idea of Haine and the others seeing his unfinished painting.

'It will be all right,' she reassured him. 'They'll be impressed. You'll see.' She set off ahead of him through the house, holding up her end of the painting.

In the studio Robert and Haine were standing talking in front of *Chaos Rules* with Andy Levine and the Bream Island curator, Oriel Liesker. Theo was sitting in isolation on the hard-backed chair over by the wall, a one-man audience to the group around the painting. He had dressed for the occasion and was wearing jeans and a purple silk shirt open at the throat. His feet were bare as usual and his pale hands were jumping and twitching in his lap like freshly landed fish, his fine silver hair shimmering around his skull as if it were not attached but merely accompanied him. Misty was sitting on the cupboard in front of him, solemnly observing the group by the painting. Theo and the cat turned and looked across as Toni and Marina came into the room carrying the painting. Theo inclined his head and raised one hand in solemn greeting, as if he saw himself as some kind of presiding chieftain.

Marina said, 'Sorry, but I've got to hear what Geoff has to say about my picture,' and she abruptly left him standing with his painting and walked over to join the others around *Chaos Rules*. Oriel's physical presence dominated the group around the painting. She was a large woman in her mid-fifties, her abundant flesh modelled around the bones of her Frisian forebears. She was taller than Marina and the three men, and broad in the shoulders, a wild tangle of richly hennaed hair piled on top of her head and held precariously in place with an elaborate arrangement of combs and pins, as if she were perversely determined to make herself appear older and taller than she really was.

Andy left the group and came over to Toni. 'Here's the boy himself,' he said and he stepped up and pinched Toni's cheek, as if he were a familiar aunt greeting a favourite nephew. 'How you doing, old buddy?'

'Yeah, I'm good, mate. How's it going?'

Andy took hold of *The Schwartz Family* and turned it around, squatting to examine it. He called, 'Come over here and look at this, Geoffrey! This is something!' He looked up at Toni. 'You're on to it here, mate. I've got collectors out there queuing for this.' He stood up, one hand steadying the canvas, as if it had already been consigned into his care.

Haine walked over and stood looking at the picture.

'Tell him all about it, Geoffrey.' Andy patted Toni's cheek. 'You keep doing this and you're going to be as rich and famous as our Geoffrey here.'

Marina came over with Oriel and Robert and joined them. Robert stepped in close to the picture and squatted in front of it, adjusting his glasses, his eyes on a level with the eyes of the figures in the picture.

Oriel gave him a steady look.

Andy put his hand on Toni's shoulder, his fingers gripping the back of his neck as if he had caught a thief. 'Toni Powlett, Geoffrey Haine. Have you two met? Painter to painter. You should be friends.'

Toni took Haine's hand. 'Good to see you again.'

'Yeah, likewise.' Haine was a short, heavily built man in his late fifties, his manner cautious and reserved. His bald head was oiled and tanned, his eyes hard and black and attentive.

Andy said, 'What do you say, Geoffrey? Listen to the voice of Geoffrey Phillip Haine, people! We'll quote him in the blurb to your show, Toni. How about it, Geoffrey? Is this what it's all about?'

Robert stood up and turned to Toni. 'I see you've freshly painted out your background?'

'Marina's doing a new background for it,' Toni said. He spoke without thinking.

Marina gave a small smile.

Robert looked surprised but said nothing.

Toni waited for his verdict. His old teacher seeing the build-up of texture, smelling the freshly applied glaze, his practised eye cutting through the surface illusion to the intention behind the artifice—still the master assessing the student's motives and aspirations.

Robert turned to him. 'That's our *Man Adrift* you've painted out.' Robert detecting the ghostly remainder of his own presence under the thin glaze.

Toni felt as if his private thoughts were on display to Robert in the picture. Robert seeing *him* behind his composition.

'It's very good,' Robert said. It was not a wholehearted endorsement of the picture.

There was a steady silence in the big room then, as if a motor had been switched off. They stood looking at the unfinished group portrait. The three members of the Schwartz family gazing out from the strange, inaccessible dimension of the painted image. Robert, Marina and Theo, more real in a way than their realities, something of the truth unmasked in their stony images, something of the inadmissible hinted at in their expectant unease that silenced the onlookers.

Toni feared they might see his picture as merely caricature-in-depth, an exaggeration of the most obvious features of his subjects, and dismiss the work. He had not noticed before that the black frames of Robert's narrow spectacles in the picture resembled the slits of a gun turret. It seemed a crass overstatement to him now, almost a cartoonish effect. He was sorry it was not a more generous portrayal of his friend. The Robert he referred to here could be read as a man lost to himself, a man older than his human counterpart, becoming his own father. The body of the woman seated between father and son was faintly visible through her shirt, a hint of the veiled and the erotic in the manner of Marina's depiction, her slim lips polished jade in the greenish light. It was all there for them to see, every thought that had been in his mind while he had been working alone through the warm summer nights in the privileged silence of his studio. He knew that these people saw through the artist's sleight of hand. That was their job. They were not the bidden public. When they looked at a work they looked at the artist, not at the subject of the picture. He thought with envy of his father, who had never laid his work before strangers.

Oriel was the first to break away, her movement abrupt and impatient. Her shirtfront was open almost to her waist, a necklace of heavy amber beads swinging between her breasts like a slave chain. She flourished a packet of Marlboros. 'I'm stepping out. I need a cigarette. Anybody care to keep me company? Andy, how about it?'

Andy waved her away.

'No? All pure as the driven snow.' She laughed, a big fruity bellow that filled the studio with its overbearing sound. She turned to Toni. 'You haven't got Marina yet, Toni. It's a bloody good picture, mate, but you haven't got her.' She waved her cigarettes at the picture. 'She's your centrepiece, but you haven't got her. Okay? You've got her cat. Stay with it, there's a way to go with this one yet. How many of these are you putting in my show? You and I are going to need to talk. I'll come around to your place in a week or two and have a look at what you're doing for me.'

'It's not finished,' he objected unhappily. He caught Haine's watchful eyes on him. 'It's not finished,' he repeated, a little truculent. The older man turned away, keeping his doubts about the quality of the painting and the newly collaborative situation with Marina to himself. Apart from the fleeing figure of the running man, the human presence was scarcely represented in Haine's work. His paintings were whole, complete, autonomous and entirely his own. Toni was aware that in Haine's classic perception there was almost certainly no such thing as *background*, and that such an idea would undoubtedly offend his sense of the artist's responsibility to the work.

Oriel strode across the clean-swept space of the studio towards the door, calling back over her shoulder, 'For my money you haven't got her, Toni. You've got her cat.' She laughed again as she went out the door, careless and uncompromising, foisting upon them the humiliating perception that Toni had begun painting again merely in order to fulfil her commission for the island.

Andy put his arm around Toni's shoulders and stood close, steadying the painting with his other hand. 'Don't worry about Oriel, old mate. She's always doing that. She doesn't like you guys getting too big-headed. This is brilliant. The punters are going to love it.'

Alongside Andy's small frame and tight curly hair Toni felt large and untidy. There was a disarming innocence about Andy Levine that had often led people to underestimate his toughness and the subtlety of his intelligence. Andy could have been his fight trainer here, his pose saying, *This is my boy!* Toni stepped impatiently out of Andy's protective embrace and retrieved his painting from him. He carried it across the studio and set it with its face to the wall, as if to say, *That's the end of the show for today, folks!*

If only!

On the back of the canvas in his bold black lettering, *The Schwartz Family, 200 × 200 cm. March 2003. AP 17. A homage to Pablo Ruiz Picasso's* The Soler Family.

Haine gave a short explosive laugh.

Toni was dismayed to see how immoderate his dedication must appear to Haine and the others. He caught Marina's eye and she smiled and gave a small lift of her shoulders, acknowledging his predicament. In this formal recording of the work he knew Haine must believe himself to be viewing something more private even than the unfinished painting. And it was true, after all, for Toni had not chosen to paint his picture on a cheap pine stretcher with cotton duck but had used a hand-crafted mitred European cedar stretcher with fine Belgian linen. It was clear, even without the dedication, that he had always seen the picture as a durable artifact, a precious object destined for the permanent archive. The bold black lettering on the back was not only a message to Marina, it was an indication of the reach of his ambition. *In art*, his father had once told him, *there can be no such thing as neutral space. In art, as in dreams, to conceal one motive is to reveal another*. He would have liked to tell Haine that most of these people remembered that his award-winning portrait of his mother had been painted on fifty cents' worth of masonite board from the local hardware store.

Theo's chair was suddenly banging and whacking on the floorboards. They turned and looked. Theo was struggling to get himself upright, the chair teetering on two legs and swivelling precariously under him. Was he endeavouring to come to Toni's aid? Toni was closest and he reached Theo and steadied him before Robert got there. Theo looked up at him and grinned. 'Come and see me. Let's do some talking.' Robert came up. 'Thanks, Toni. I can manage.' Toni watched father and son falter across the studio and go out the door. When they had gone he turned back to the room. Marina was talking with Haine. He thought of joining them but Haine had his hand on her arm and was intent on sharing something of significance with her, no doubt his opinion of *Chaos Rules*. Toni walked across and stood looking at her picture.

Andy came up and stood beside him. 'She's good, eh?'

'She's great.'

'She's doing a new background for you.'

'So why shouldn't she?'

'You're doing it. I just sell pictures.'

The fierce half-naked young man confronted them from the centre foreground of the canvas. The young man's torso soft above tight blue jeans. Something of sex and violence in the image.

Andy said, 'How's our beautiful Teresa?'

'Busy.'

'The travel agency is doing good?'

'So-so. You know?'

'I'll call over and have a peek at what you're doing in that studio of yours. Don't worry about Oriel. I'll keep her off your back. Are you going to have a show ready for me one of these days?'

'I hope so, Andy. I really hope so. Drop in any time. It's been too long.'

They embraced then stepped away.

Andy stabbed a finger towards *The Schwartz Family*. 'Just keep doing it like that.'

Toni walked over to Marina and Haine and said goodbye. In the passage, Theo's door was open. Toni paused and looked in. Theo was lying back on the pillow, his eyes closed, his mouth slack. The dying man returning to his son to distract himself from his grief. *You won't tell Robert?* It was another portrait study. Haine would never see such a modest arrangement of the human form as a suitable subject for his art.

On the front verandah Robert and Oriel were talking. They fell silent when he came out.

He said goodbye to them then stepped off the verandah and walked back along the street to his car. As he turned the key and the VK started with its customary roar, he realised he had his next picture. He laughed. He could *see* it. In his imagination it was already complete. All he had to do was paint it. He did a U-turn and took off with a squeal of tyres, leaving a blue plume of smoke hanging in the air of the quiet street, the VK almost airborne over the speed bump he had forgotten.

twelve

He parked in the lane behind the studio and stepped out of the wagon. He was fired up to begin working on his new picture. He had its title, *The Other Family,* and was visualising himself blocking it in with big confident sweeps of the loaded brush—Oriel's monumental form dominating the centre of the group. He would do studies of them all later; for now, he just wanted to get the strength of the composition down on the canvas before he lost it. He was hungry to be alone and lost in the work.

He opened the back door of the studio.

Teresa was standing over by the red lamp holding up a corner of the drop sheet, as if she had been looking out the window, watching for him to come across from the house. His brother Roy was standing by the plan press, the top drawer pulled out, Marina's island sketchbook by his hand, the small

35 x 60 cm oil of Marina asleep on the island propped on the press in front of him. Roy and Teresa both turned and looked at him as he came through the door from the lane. He noticed Theo's black sketchbook was also lying open on the press.

Teresa let the sheet fall back into place. She was wearing her tailored black suit over a white blouse, the vivid collar of the blouse out over the jacket, her dark hair drifting across her face. After endlessly examining the slight, almost tenuous figures of Marina and Robert and Theo these past weeks, Teresa looked bigger and more robust to him, as if she had grown physically larger. 'Why aren't you at work?' he asked. He saw then that she had been crying and he felt a touch of alarm. 'Where's Nada?'

Teresa said calmly, 'She's at kinder. Roy came over.'

Roy said, 'How's it going, Antoni?'

Toni stepped up to his brother and they embraced.

Teresa watched them. 'I'll get us some lunch,' she said. 'You'll stay for lunch, Roy?'

Roy turned to her. 'Thank you, Terry. I'd like that very much.' He spoke with restraint, an old-fashioned modesty in the manner of his acceptance of Teresa's invitation. A man in his late forties, who had once been handsome, he was now slightly stooped, his appearance that of someone debilitated by chronic pain or prolonged anxiety. There was a trace of a European accent in his soft voice.

'So everything's okay?' Toni said, looking from one to the other. He had not seen his brother since the opening of his last installation at Andy's, an event that seemed so long ago now it might almost never have happened, except for the pile of old clothes and racks still cluttering the courtyard to remind him of it. 'Have you lost weight?' he asked his brother.

'I'm fine.' Roy smiled and put his hand on Toni's shoulder and squeezed. 'You're looking great.'

Teresa said, 'I'll leave you two to have a talk then.' She paused in the doorway, then turned back and stood looking across at Toni. 'So where's your picture?' She was looking into his eyes as if she were determined not to miss anything, determined to detect the lie or the half-truth as it formed and wavered in his mind.

'I took it over to Richmond.'

'So you've finished it, or what?'

'No.'

She waited for his explanation.

'I was having a problem with the background.'

She said nothing, waiting.

He drew a breath. 'Marina offered to do a new background for it.'

Teresa's expression changed and she looked at Roy. Then she turned and went out the door.

Toni said, 'Shit!'

'You do these?' Roy asked. He was holding up Theo's sketchbook.

Toni reached and took the book from him. He closed it and replaced the rubber band and put it away in the drawer of the plan press. 'You think it's okay to come in here and just look at everything?'

'You've got nothing to hide from me, Antoni.'

'The book belonged to Robert's father. The drawings are his. He gave it to me. Did Teresa look at it?'

'She looked at it,' Roy said easily.

'I'm sorry,' Toni said. 'I didn't mean to speak to you like that. Have you been ill or something? You don't look the best.' Roy had always seemed indestructible to Toni. A man of iron or stone who would never grow old or falter. Today he saw something vulnerable, something almost fragile about his brother that alarmed him.

'I had a bit of an operation,' Roy said. 'It was nothing. I'm fine now.'

'What sort of operation? Mum never said anything.'

'I told her not to worry you.'

'Jesus! You didn't tell me about it? Come on, what was this operation? I need to know.'

'It was nothing. Minor surgery.' Roy laughed and gestured around the studio. 'You're doing it!'

'You and Mum still behave as if I'm the baby of the family. I need to know what's going on.'

'Okay. I'm sorry. It won't happen again.'

'So what are you and me supposed to be talking about?'

Roy picked up Marina's island sketchbook. He hefted it and looked questioningly at Toni.

'You can look at anything,' Toni said. 'You know that. I'm sorry. I'm just feeling a bit touchy. I was hoping to get to work. What's all this about anyway?'

Roy opened the book but did not look at it at once, instead he looked around the studio at the drawings and paintings and the paraphernalia of the craft. 'Dad should see this.'

'You mind if I set up a stretcher?'

'No. Go ahead. Do what you were going to do. Don't let me interrupt you.'

Toni did not move. Roy was holding up the drawing of Marina asleep on the island.

'So *this* is *that*?' he said, indicating the oil on the plan press. 'I prefer the drawing. I always preferred your drawings to your paintings. I'm not criticising.'

'It's okay. I feel the same.'

Roy considered the drawing of Marina lying in the shadows of the wattle. 'This I could live with.' He laughed softly, with pleasure. He jogged Toni's arm with his elbow. 'Hey! You're not listening to me! You're way off. What's the matter? You want to work? I'm holding you up? Work if you want to work.'

'No, of course not. It's great to see you. We should see more of each other.' His brother's life was a mystery to him, as remote and sketchy as his father's childhood had been for him.

'Never mind about that. I'm telling you something. This is a beautiful thing. She sat for you like this? This is what you people do? What a life you have!'

Toni said, 'You can have it. I'll get it framed for you.' He had refused to give the drawing to Marina, now he would give it to his brother. He reached for the sketchbook but Roy held it out of his way, turning at the shoulder, a minimal movement that reminded Toni of their father, as if Roy had begun to call upon their father's gestures as he grew older.

'You remember the way Dad used to go on about your gift?' Roy said. '*The gift of the line*, he called it. It would bring tears of pleasure to the old man's eyes to see this stuff. Dad was denied happiness.'

Toni could hear a strengthening of the old accent in Roy's speech, the ethnic scar tissue from his early years alone with their parents emerging again, not erased by the passage of the years but subdued, appearing again now that his brother's strength had begun to erode. Like their mother Lola, Roy had remained a Prochownik at heart and, like her, still carried the indelible marks of the displaced. The name-change to Powlett had not taken with Roy or with their mother. With those two it had been a failed graft. Perhaps one lifetime was not long enough to become an Australian. 'Dad was happy doing his pictures.'

'That wasn't happiness,' Roy said. 'That was keeping up a brave front. Dad never found the freedom to be who he was. You were his chance.'

'I think Dad was happy sometimes,' Toni insisted. It was important for him to believe in his father's happiness. 'I often saw him when he was happy.'

'We knew different people. Dad was careful with you. He never let you see what was really going on with him. He protected you from all that stuff.'

'Like you and Mum not telling me about your operation, you mean?'

'That's it. It's our habit. The family has always protected you.'

Toni looked at Roy. 'Do you remember telling me when you came out of prison that no one's protected?'

Roy looked up from the drawing. 'Did I say that?'

'You said it as if you'd found the key to everything.'

Roy laughed, pleased. 'Maybe I had. You remembered it!'

Toni wondered, suddenly, if their father had broken his silence with Roy. 'Did Dad ever tell you about his childhood in Poland? The war? The labour camp? All that stuff?' He loved his brother achingly, hopelessly, but they had never shared the same reality. He would have liked to say, *My brother!* But it was too deep. Too lost. He knew now there would never be a time when he would know his brother. It was almost as if his brother had been denied a full reality. He would do his portrait. It would be difficult but he would love doing it. He would visit his brother's room in St Kilda and paint him there. They would get to know each other a little. He would do it soon. When the island show was out of the way. He would do portraits of everyone. That was what he would do. He could feel his capacity for it. Teresa's mum and dad too. Why shouldn't they get their picture of themselves?

191

Roy said, 'When Dad used to come out to the prison to see me, we'd spend the whole of visiting time talking about you and your drawing. You were still at Nott Street Primary with Andy in those days.' He stood looking fondly at Toni. 'He'd bring a batch of your drawings and your little watercolours to show me. You were his beacon of hope. You became mine, too. I had your drawings on the walls out there. You had a following with the boys. You were famous. They used to ask me how you were getting on. The truth was never enough for them.' He laughed. 'I invented stuff about you. I invented this other kid who was your rival, so they'd barrack for you against him. They'd ask me, *How's that brother of yours doing these days?* And they'd hang around and wait to hear the next instalment of your life. Dad used to say, *Toni belongs to the new world.* He relied on the fact that you were born here. He felt it made you safe.'

'You were born here too,' Toni reminded him, but he knew it was not the same.

'Yeah. I was born here.' Roy looked into the distance. 'Dad lit up when he was talking about you. He wasn't worried about me. He knew about prisons. He and Mum knew what was happening to me out there. They knew where I was. It wasn't mysterious for them. Dad used to say, *prison is prison, it doesn't matter where you are.* We understood each other. We understood that. It helped me that they knew what was happening to me.' Roy fell silent, thinking back. 'You should get Andy to put on a show of Dad's pictures one of these days.'

'That wasn't what he wanted. Anyway, I don't think Mum would let them out of her sight, would she?'

'He wanted it. We all want it. Don't make out Dad was different from the rest of us. He was a man, like you and me. He wanted what we all want. That big old suitcase under their bed? That's his suitcase from the old days. Did you know that? I'd get home at two in the morning and he'd still be sitting up at the table. I'd see the light on in the kitchen as I was coming across the court. My old man up there doing his painting!' He fell silent. 'That one he did of Mum's ironing board with her teacup sitting on the end of it. You remember that? It looked as if she'd stepped out and would be stepping back in again any second.' Roy studied Toni for a long moment. 'Anyone looks at that picture, they see our mother. We had it pinned to the wall above the sink for years. You remember that picture?'

'Of course I remember it. Dad used to say all art is portraiture.'

'*Self*-portraiture. That's what he said. You can't escape yourself.' Roy set Marina's sketchbook aside and picked up the book that Toni was using. He flipped the pages, studying the drawings. He paused at a drawing of the half-naked old man sitting on a chair. 'Who's this?'

Toni looked over his shoulder. 'Robert's dad. Theo.'

'He sit for you like that?'

'No.'

'You do these from memory?'

'Partly from memory, partly from life. Sometimes photos. Drawings. Whatever. What are we talking about, Roy? Why was Teresa upset?'

Roy stood gazing at the drawing of Theo. 'We're going to look like this. You and me. That's how Dad looked towards the end. He was exhausted. I'd come in and he'd be sitting naked on the edge of the bath with that empty look in his eyes. It would be the end of another shift at the plant. The bath water would have that grey scum around it from the tyre dust. I've seen all kinds of looks in men's eyes, men who'd lost their lives. But nothing ever affected me like that. The way Dad looked.' He fell silent. 'I used to watch his memories moving behind his eyes. Those old nightmares were still living in him and there was nothing I could do to help him. When I was young I used to think you forget things in time. But one life's not long enough to forget some things. Dad *wanted* to tell you. He wanted you to know. But he couldn't. He'd try talking to me about those things sometimes but he'd choke up. He couldn't get the words out. I'd tell him it didn't matter. I'd say I didn't want to hear about it. When I'd walk in on him in the bathroom I always felt shocked and I'd stand a while, then I'd ask him if there was something I could get for him. When I spoke he'd come out of his daze and he'd reach for me and pull me down to him and kiss the top of my head. *No, son*, he'd say. *I've got everything I need. I've got your mother's love and I've got you boys. If there is something else we must have, then tell me what it is.*' Roy looked at Toni steadily.

Toni closed the drawer of the plan press. 'I dreamed about him the other night. Do you ever dream about him?'

'Remember the way he talked? As if our fates had been decided in some other place and time. He told me once he didn't feel betrayed by his old God, he just learned his God was merciless. What a thing to say. Can you imagine saying something like that? What must have been behind that for him to actually come out and say it? *You get the lot that falls to you*, he always said.' He looked again at Toni's drawing of Theo. 'I let them down, Antoni. Badly. I paid for what I did to that guy, but there's no way to ever pay for what I did to Mum and Dad. I should have stepped away that day. It would have been better if I'd taken a beating.'

'But not if you'd let Dad take a beating,' Toni said softly. 'You did it for him. I was there. Remember? It was just bad luck the guy died. Another time he would have got up and walked away.'

Roy closed the sketchbook. He was silent a long while. 'There was an old Spaniard in there with us. Roncales. A little guy with bandy legs. He had a face like a stone that's been used to pound grain for a hundred years. We called him Pony. He was a horseman in a previous life. A real horseman. A horse master. That's all he knew. Horses. He used to paint these enormous blue and red acrylics of rearing horses. He told us the Spaniards had this saying: '*The man who dreams of the perfect horse or the perfect woman never finds contentment in the saddle or in bed.*'

'So you're telling me to be content with what I've got?'

'I don't know what I'm telling you. I just thought of Pony. We hear what we want to hear. Discontent is a disease. That's something I do know. Am I giving you advice on how to live your life? You've got a beautiful wife and a daughter and this house and your gift. You don't need advice from someone like me. That's obvious.'

'In the dream he gave me the go-ahead to be an artist.'

'Don't throw it away. That's what I'm saying. I'd hate to see you throw all this away. I'd give anything to go back and step around that situation now.'

'But you wouldn't step around it if you went back. You'd do the same for Dad today as you did on that day.'

Roy reached out and pulled Toni towards him and kissed the top of his head. 'That's from me and Dad. We love you. Remember that!' There were tears in his eyes. He gestured around at the pictures and drawings. 'Has Mum been over to see this?' He waved at the portrait of their mother. 'You've got her picture up. She's still beautiful, eh? You captured her beauty.'

'I'll invite her to the opening on the island.'

'I'll bring her with me. We'll come together.'

They stood looking at the portrait of their mother leaning on the balcony at the flats, looking out at them.

'I suppose Teresa rang you?' Toni said. 'I don't suppose you just happened to come over?'

'She's worried things are slipping away for you two.'

'I know.'

Roy said, 'I'm not asking you to tell me anything.' He gestured at the oil painting of Marina asleep on the island. 'This picture . . .'

'What about it?'

'Teresa says it's erotic. And she's right. There's nothing crude about it, I'm not saying that, but it's suggestive. Wouldn't you say? It's a great picture. She asked me what I thought of it.' Roy examined him. 'She said it's a picture of a woman lying there waiting for it.'

Toni asked tightly, 'And what did you say?'

'*You see what you want to see*, I said. *Maybe what you're afraid of seeing. It's a picture*, I told her. *Antoni is an artist. This is what he does.*'

Toni looked at his painting of Marina asleep on the island. He had loved doing it. He had painted it from his drawing and from his memory and from the wonderful feeling of their day on the island.

'Teresa believes in family. That's where she sees the strength in things. She believes if families stick together everything comes out all right in the end. She asked me if I thought she was becoming a jealous woman for no reason.'

'So?'

'So she's your wife and I'm your brother. *That* so. Sometimes you behave like the baby of the family. Maybe that's a habit with you too. People treat us the way we want to be treated. I'm not asking you if Teresa has a reason to be jealous. You get one shot. Don't blow it. That's all I'm saying. She asked me to talk to you, so I'm talking to you. She doesn't want to interfere with your work. She's scared she's going to stuff things up for you now that you've finally got going at last.'

'It's not that simple.'

'She's trying to be cool about it, but she's not sure what you're getting up to with this woman and it's driving her crazy.' Roy looked at him. 'She loves you.'

'I know that.'

'I love you too.'

'Yeah, I know.'

'She feels as if you've started keeping your life a secret from her. And for a woman there can only be one reason for her man to be doing that.'

'She said that to you? That's crazy!'

'Is it?'

'You said you're not asking me?'

'I'm asking you.'

'It's difficult to explain this project to her.'

'Have you tried?'

Toni shifted uncomfortably. He resented the interrogation. He just wanted to be working on his new painting.

'Why don't you try explaining it to her? That's all she's looking for. She hates being closed out.'

'Closed out! You two must have had some talk before I got here.' Toni looked at Roy. 'My work's not something I can *explain*. I'd *like* to explain. Okay?' He gestured at the room. 'But you give someone a reason for this and you know that's not what it is. You know that's not the reason. You try to explain this and you start lying. Most of the time I don't *know* what I'm doing.'

Roy said calmly, 'Whatever you say.'

'Did I ever have to explain myself to Dad?'

Roy considered this. 'It's a point.'

'You know it's true. Between me and Dad there was never a need for explanations or reasons or why or whatever about what we were doing. We just did what we did. We loved doing it. We both loved doing it. That was it. That was our reason. Love. Dad was my inspiration. And maybe I was his inspiration. It wasn't just me keeping Dad going. We kept each other going. That's why I stopped painting when he died. I just couldn't do it. For a time I hated it.' He waited for Roy's attention. 'I don't need to explain myself to Marina. Okay?'

'Okay.'

'Marina and Robert know what I'm doing the way Dad knew what I was doing. They are artists too.'

Roy said, 'It's not Robert Teresa's worried about.'

'We all get our energy from somewhere.'

'It's a touchy business.'

'Don't talk like that. Be straight with me.'

Roy pointed to the corner opposite the door. 'Dad's suit. You did something I would never have done. I've always been glad you did it.' He looked at the dark three-piece draped on the rack. 'I can see him walking down Bay Street holding your hand when you were a kid and he's taking you to the beach wearing that suit. Every other kid's dad's wearing a T-shirt and runners.' Roy turned to him. 'What did you mean, he gave you the go-ahead to be an artist?'

'It was as if he wasn't dead. It was like I'd woken up and his death had turned out to be a mistake. In the dream I knew he was still alive somewhere. Not here. But somewhere. He handed me a small canvas. He said, *Here's your painting, son.* It was his voice. I almost felt the touch of his hand.'

They stood silently thinking about their father.

Roy said with feeling, 'I never met anyone with the courage he had.'

'Dad would know why I can't do this without Marina.'

'I guess you'll do what you have to do.'

'It's not what you think between me and Marina.'

'What do I think?'

'I know what you think.'

'She's a beautiful woman. It's what Teresa thinks, not what I think that matters.' Roy stepped across to the window and lifted the drop sheet, holding it up and looking across the courtyard to the house. 'She thinks you put this here to stop her looking in and seeing what you two were getting up to.'

'It's to get some control of the light.'

'Jealous people start seeing hints and clues in everything.' Roy dropped the curtain back into place and turned towards Toni. 'Don't get the idea I'm bitter about my life.'

'Hey! I know you're not bitter.'

'I'm not bitter.'

'I know that. You get more like Dad every time I see you.'

'I know. I've noticed it. I don't mind. Like you, I feel as if he's alive somewhere.' He placed his open palm against his chest. 'He's alive in here. Come on! Let's go and have lunch with your beautiful wife.' He waved his arm, a gesture encompassing the studio. 'You're doing it. He was right to hope for you.'

As they went out the door Toni looked back at the empty canvases propped against the wall.

thirteen

At the front door Toni stood by and watched Teresa kiss Roy goodbye on the cheek, her hand on his brother's arm. 'Thanks for coming over, Roy,' she said. And she left her hand on his arm; being motherly, protective, caring, grateful for his support—and also, no doubt, recruiting him as her ally. 'We mustn't wait so long till next time,' she was saying. 'Come and have dinner with us soon.' She turned to Toni. 'We should make it a regular thing. Once a month. What do you say?'

Roy smiled. 'Thanks, Terry.' He turned to Toni and embraced him, then stepped away and walked down the path to the gate.

They stood at the front door watching him. When he reached the corner he turned and saluted them, his hand lifted, then he was gone.

'He's not looking the best,' Toni said.

'Your brother's a lovely man. It's a tragedy. We should think of someone to invite over with him.'

'You think Roy needs a woman?'

'Roy needs to meet the right woman,' Teresa said confidently.

'People have always been suggesting ways of running Roy's life for him. Setting him up. Straightening him out. Seeing ways of putting him on a level with themselves. Everyone thinks they've got the answer for Roy. But none of it ever made any difference. He is who he is.'

Teresa said calmly, 'He needs the right woman.'

It had always been a belief in Toni's family that Roy had been handed his task for life and had recognised that task when he saw it. As if his steady masculinity had been given him for that one occasion, and nothing could have prevented or altered the outcome of that day. Things foregone. As unalterable as the night Nada was born and Toni had seen that she already possessed her own personality—even while she was lying on the sheet in the hospital, just separated from Teresa, almost before she had taken her first breath; a little person who was not just *them* but was already somebody else. 'We're already ourselves when we're born,' he said.

'What's that supposed to mean? Who else would we be? The right woman would recognise Roy for who he is. The funny thing is, with his past and all that, he's the one man apart from you who I'd trust with Nada. You know what I mean?'

'Roy didn't go to prison for doing something wrong,' he said. 'He went for doing the right thing. There's no reason why you shouldn't trust him.'

'Well I do trust him. That's what I'm saying. I'm *saying* I trust him.'

They were silent, a brittleness between them. They stood looking out at the empty street.

'Roy's lived a life that's been a lot like Dad's,' he said. 'It's been a broken life. I don't know why that is. It's almost as if one of us had to repeat something. To pay for something in the past.'

'You love him.'

'He's my brother.'

'You should paint his portrait while you've still got the chance.'

He looked at her and laughed. 'I will paint his portrait. What do you mean, *still got the chance*? Roy's going to be around for a long time yet. Did he tell you something about his operation?'

'I just meant it would give him a reason to come over and see us. He could sit for you then stay and have dinner with us afterwards. He needs a family.'

'Family's not the answer for everyone.'

'That's a ridiculous thing to say and you know it is. Everyone needs a family.'

Two young men and a young woman came along the other side of the street. The men were carrying slabs of beer and laughing. They turned in at the house opposite and went up to the front door and let themselves in.

Teresa said, 'Party time again over there. Do you want to get her while I clean up the lunch things?'

'Sure. Okay.'

'You don't have to.'

'No. I want to.'

'You don't want to. I can see you just want to go back down there and work. You hardly said a word all through lunch. Why can't you say you want to be working instead of pretending you want to pick up your daughter?'

'But I do want to pick her up.'

'Her seat's in the Honda. The keys are on the bench.' Teresa turned and went back inside the house.

He followed her. It was true. He had been seeing it all through lunch with Roy, the big new painting waiting for him. He could *smell* it, the faint enticing odour of the new cedar stretcher like the guilty smell of a lover's skin. He paused in the passage and stood looking at his father's framed gouache. It was a tonal image of a straight-backed chair and a corner of their old kitchen table at the flats, one of his mother's jugs and a blue-striped bowl. The domestic vision he had inherited. The gentle melancholy of the low-toned mood suggestive of a vanished Central European light. The scene speaking to him of his father's silence. Outside the flats the night and the howling city, but in these objects of his father's contemplation an eternal stillness. The still lives of his father's inner world.

The absence of the rattle and clatter of the moulding line. Calm. Familiarity. Simplicity. These three things, and his father's certainty of their universal value. It was an image that bore witness to the tranquillity of Moniek Prochownik's endurance and had not been intended for public display. Toni knew what was expected of him. It had always been his father's noble vision of art's place in life, and his fear that he would fall short of it, against which he had measured his own art and his life. No one but himself would ever know this little picture as he knew it. He had watched his father paint it. No one else would ever see in it the beauty and the achievement he saw in it.

He turned away and continued along the passage. In the living area Teresa was clearing away the lunch things, scraping their plates and piling them on the bench. He stood watching her a moment as if he was going to say something, then he walked across to the bench and picked up her keys.

She brushed by him, banging down plates and cutlery on the draining board, leaning and flinging open the door of the dishwasher. She did not put the dirty dishes into the machine, but straightened and considered him. 'You come out of there glassy-eyed with that lost look on your face. I said to Roy it's as if you've wandered into someone else's house.'

'I know. I'm sorry,' he said quietly. He waited for her hostility, for the suspicion that was burning in her to come out. Perhaps he *had* wandered into another man's house. Another man's life. Another man's family. How to know if the life we are living is authentically our own? How to measure the degrees of our own truth against the daily events of our existence? Against the sliding scale of reality and illusion? How to check the drift from one to the other? Perhaps he had crossed a line back when his father died, and had not noticed that he was crossing a line but had blundered on, impelled by his blind grief and his loss, moving away from the painful reality of who he was. Not that terrible line that Roy had crossed, but another line, some kind of shifting demarcation of borders between imagination and reality. Perhaps, after all, he really did not belong here with Teresa and Nada. What had Teresa said about Robert and Marina? That they were only pretending to be who they were? As if she could not believe in their reality. As if they possessed for her no depth, no warmth, no humanity, but were only the drifting figures in their own landscapes, artful depictions of themselves, constructed with care, with great skill, and even with love, but figurations only, lacking the one essential of her own reality: a family.

'You're not even listening to me now!' Teresa said, her anger coming out. 'You sit over there at that table chewing your food in silence! There's no getting through to you! I could serve you a plate of cardboard and you'd eat it.' She stood confronting him; large, determined, angry, bewildered, demanding his attention. 'So you're not going to ask me how come your brother came over to see us? You're not curious to know why Roy suddenly turns up on our doorstep out of the blue?'

'You called him and asked him to come over.'

'Yes, I called him and asked him to come over. And it looks as if it's just as well I did. I can't believe you're letting that woman solve your problems for you.'

There it was, in the open. 'I know it must look that way to you. But that's not the way it is.'

'That *is* the way it is, for Christ's sake! Just be fucking honest with yourself for once!' Her anger flaring and beaming in her dark eyes. The incontestable logic of her case. The justice of her indignation. 'She's painting a background to your picture! You're going to *her* for your answers! That's the way it is!' She began to slam the plates into the dishwasher one at a time. 'Either have the guts to be fucking honest, Toni Powlett, or fuck off!'

He more than half-expected her to slam a plate into his face. He was seeing her looking at Theo's boldly erotic nymph mutilating the satyr, looking at the pictures of the bound woman under the tree, the fierce naked wrestlers, and his own suggestive painting of Marina asleep under the wattle. He wanted to explain to her the essential innocence of these images, but he knew there was no way to do that. What were the words, the tone that would carry that story? He wanted to tell her as Theo had told him, *Don't confuse art with life*. He said nothing.

Teresa straightened and closed the door of the dishwasher. 'Just go and *get* her, for God's sake!'

He drove Teresa's Honda to the kinder and picked up Nada. On the way back he parked at the corner shop and bought a latté in a polystyrene cup for himself and a chocolate Freddo Frog for Nada. He carried her across the main road and they sat on a bench by the swings. They had their treat then spent a while on the swings before going home. He resisted going down to the studio. Later, the three of them had an early tea sitting around the television. The news came on at seven and he watched the first couple of minutes of it. Teresa was on the couch clipping items out of the travel section of the previous weekend's paper. Nada was playing with Snoopy Dog on the rug.

He eased himself out of his chair. 'I might go down and do an hour's work.'

Teresa did not look up from her clipping. 'You wouldn't like to read her a story before you go?'

'Sure.'

Teresa gave Nada a cuddle and told her, 'I'll come in and kiss you after Daddy's read you a story.'

He and Nada went down the passage and he helped her undress and get into her pyjamas. She wanted *Mog's Mumps*. The book was on her bedside table. She handed it to him and lay down and waited for him to begin, her eyes on him, one arm around Snoopy Dog, the toy tucked in beside her.

He sat on the bed, holding the book so she and Snoopy Dog could see the pictures of the witch and the cat. He read, 'Baked, boiled, grilled or fried, show me what's in Mog's inside.' There was an X-ray of Mog's insides. A large fish was lodged sideways in the cat's stomach.

Nada said, 'Snoopy Dog said why is Mog sick?' She asked the question as if she had never asked it before.

'Tell Snoopy Dog because Mog ate too much.' He did not enjoy the privilege of communicating directly with Snoopy Dog. Only Nada knew the language. He waited while she turned aside and whispered the explanation to Snoopy Dog. It sounded like English, but he knew better. When she was ready he continued reading.

He read the story four times. And each time he read it, Nada asked for an explanation of each of the pictures on Snoopy Dog's behalf, and each time she asked he gave her the same answers, as if he were giving the answers for the first time. It was a familiar ritual. Nada had heard the story maybe a hundred times. When he had first begun to read to her he had been surprised to find that she did not want the novelty of variation, but wanted the reassurance of familiarity. He had eventually seen how, with repeated readings, the stories he read to her became her own territory. Evidently there was, in her perfect foreknowledge of the story's details, a powerful magic that she did not discuss or share with anyone except Snoopy Dog. In the early days he had introduced new twists of his own to the stories for a bit of variety, but she had been upset and had angrily accused him of not telling the truth. Hearing a familiar story repeated last thing at night before she went to sleep was a reassurance for her that, while she slept, the boundaries of her world would not change, and when she woke in the morning all would be as it had been when she had gone to sleep. Her inner world was posted with the landmarks of these familiar, unchanging stories. It fascinated him to encounter the fierceness of her distrust of innovation and to witness her implacable resistance to it. And yet her deep conservatism did not inhibit her imagination— it had been through their shared drawing sessions that he had remembered that the landscape of his own childhood had been just such a dangerous place of enchanted borderlands as was hers.

He closed the book after the fourth reading and sat stroking her silky hair, waiting for her eyes to droop. He accepted nowadays that what she needed from him was certainty—that state of mind most deeply distrusted by artists, who nevertheless long to reconnect with the spontaneous candour of childhood. The paradox fascinated him. Nada would scarcely have benefited from Robert's experience of the disappearing father. A parent there one minute and gone the next. And perhaps, with Robert's background, he and Marina had been right to resist partnering their art with the demands of a family. *We decided it is enough that we are artists*, Marina had once said. *We realised we couldn't have everything, and we chose art*. He looked down at Nada. She was wide awake, watching him. 'It's time you went to sleep, darling. Daddy's got to work tonight.'

She looked up at him steadily from the pillow, as if she were considering a question of great moment.

He stroked her hair. Was she lonely, he wondered, as Teresa feared? Did she need a brother or a sister by her side to complete her world? 'Go to sleep now. Mummy will come in and kiss you goodnight in a minute.'

She asked seriously, 'Can I come and do a picture with you, Dad?'

'It's too late now, darling. You'll be tired in the morning. On the weekend. You can come down and work with me in the studio on the weekend. Okay? I promise.'

Her eyes remained fixed on his face and she waited for the gravity of her request to register with him.

Her eyes were mirrors of his father's eyes, dark and filled with emotion and with hope and belief. Her beauty and her vulnerability moved him and he felt again the familiar tightening in his chest, his fear for her, his longing that she have a good life and that no harm ever befall her, the same longing his father had known for him and for his brother, that his children would never know the monstrous desolation that had devoured his own childhood. 'I'm not going to be doing a lot tonight,' he explained. 'I just want to lay down a rough grid of this picture that I've got in my head. If I don't make a note of it tonight, I might lose it. Pictures are like that. You and I both know they can disappear into their own world without saying anything to us and never come back.'

She listened seriously, watching his features, as if she possessed a full understanding of everything he said, everything that was in his mind, the importance to him of his work. As he talked to her he was remembering waking in the night when he was a boy and seeing the light under the bedroom door, getting out of bed and going into the kitchen. His dad's arm slipping around him. His dad sharing his precious night hours with him, as if he had been waiting for him. Feeling his dad's pleasure at having him beside him in the night while he worked. The two of them together. Privileged beings. No longer dwellers in the rat flats, but painting their dreams. Absorbing the arcane language of his father's art. Drawing and painting the same familiar objects night after night and seeing something different each night in their figurations. There had been no limit to what they had visualised in those household utensils and cheap pieces of furniture, repeating their studies of them again and again. It had been for him the unveiling of an enchanted landscape that had lain concealed from his sight until then beneath the banal familiarity of the everyday appearance of things. *You can never paint the same picture twice.* It was Nada and Snoopy Dog and *Meg and Mog*. You can't hear the same story twice. How often had she ordered, *Read it again, Dad!* . . .

'Please, Dad,' she said. She was anxious but calm. She was not going to panic. She was observing the play of his thoughts in his eyes. She was not pleading with him, but was asking him seriously to have her request understood by him for what it was, asking him whether he wanted her at his side while he worked or whether he would rather be alone and without her. For that had become the pattern of the past weeks, since he had begun the project with Marina. She had been shut out from his company. Exiled from the magic zone of their art. It was as if she were to refuse Snoopy Dog admittance to her bed. Was she not asking herself at this very minute, *Is this the way it is to be with my father from now on? Or am I to be readmitted?*

He tucked the bedclothes around her and kissed her forehead, inhaling the smell of her warmth.

He knew she was not going to insist.

It would have made it easier to refuse her if she had insisted. If she had cried and ranted and thrown a tantrum. There might have been a case against giving in to that kind of thing. But she did not insist. And then, suddenly, he knew that she was not going to ask him again. If he said no to her request this time, she would let him go without further protest and would turn over and face the wall and confide her disappointment to Snoopy Dog and wait for her mother to come and kiss her goodnight. She was not going to throw a tantrum. That was not her style. He set *Mog's Mumps* aside on the night table and got off the bed and stood looking down at her.

She lay there watching him. Waiting for his verdict . . .

What if she never again asked to join him in the studio? The thought chilled him. What if this became the moment in her life when she turned away from her father and began to follow a new and solitary direction of her own? Accepting, in the way of her certainty, that he no longer wished to share with her the privileged world of art?

'Come on then!' He leaned down and helped her out of bed. 'Just one picture. Your mother's not going to be impressed with this idea.'

She did not show any reaction. She did not jump up and clap her hands. It was not a triumph. It was not a moment for exuberance, but was a reaffirmation of the way things ought to be between her and her dad. Composed, she got up out of bed and turned and knelt on the covers to tuck Snoopy Dog in. 'You can come on the weekend,' she told the toy dog as she kissed him and patted the bedclothes into place around him.

In a former time, Snoopy Dog would have been included. Now he was to be left behind. It was her sole concession to the necessity for change. Her acknowledgement that not everything could be quite as it had been before. Innovation had become a necessity and in one stroke she had made it her own.

He took her dressing-gown from the hook behind the door and helped her put it on. It was not a cold night, but all the same he helped her fasten the four pink buttons down the front of her dressing-gown, for he was sensitive to her need for a certain formality at this moment.

'There!' He stood up.

She took his hand in hers.

In the living area, Teresa was leaning on the bench talking on the telephone.

He held up one finger and mouthed, 'One picture. Okay? Then I'll bring her back to bed.'

Teresa asked the person on the other end of the line to hold on and she set the phone aside on the bench. 'This is not on!' she said firmly and she stepped up and reached for Nada.

Nada drew away, gripping his hand, her little body pressing against his leg.

'Just one,' Toni pleaded quietly. 'Please!'

Teresa stood between them and the back door. In this matter, her daughter and her husband were united against her.

They were silent, the three of them, waiting.

Teresa said, 'I just hope you don't think you can make a habit of this.' It was surely a phrase from her mother's book of good mothering, dug from her memory to meet the occasion. 'She needs her sleep.'

'Half an hour,' he said. 'I promise.'

'Half an hour.' It was an important concession. Teresa stepped aside and went back to the bench and picked up the telephone. She watched them.

He and Nada did not look back or speak. They were alert, like refugees who have tricked the guard into letting them slip across the border, aware of the guard's suspicious gaze following them, tense in case his voice suddenly calls them back.

He pointed to the far corner of the studio. Nada's drawing of him with flaming hair was pinned to the wall above her grandfather's old suit.

She looked up at her old drawing of him, then sat at her little table and got her pencils out and began to draw at once; as if for her, also, an image already existed in her imagination and had been waiting to be brought into the light of the page.

He set up a new canvas on the easel and sat on his stool gazing at the blankness of the prepared ground, struggling to reconnect with his image of *The Other Family*. Nada's unself-conscious clarity of vision was not available to him. He sat there looking at the pale field of the empty canvas for many minutes, then he stood and took a large brush, loaded it with a thin grey medium and began to draw the shape of his group with long, looping, confident strokes, reaching and bending and standing back, then up close washing over the negative spaces. He was painting with energy . . . During the next hour a grey ghost of the sculptural group emerged on the prepared ground of the large canvas. It might have been a granite monument approached through dawn light. A massively portentous work of civic sculpture, a memorial to some long forgotten occasion, or a ruin. An illusion of solidity and presence. A first state. Oriel Liesker's large limbs and monumental head providing focus and substance. They were there, there was no doubt of that, these ghostly presences, figures of memory and imagination, anonymous, seeming to embrace or to struggle with one another. A viewer might already have begun to read their story; something human, tangible, and reluctant. They were as yet still akin to the figures of his installations and without the grace of individuality, without the distinction of personality. Not portraits, but effigies in stone or bronze, closer to Haine's fugitive figure than to real people. He did not attempt a placement of Marina. In his sense of this picture Marina stood apart from the group and he was unsure of her relation to them.

When he at last broke off he saw that Nada was asleep at her desk, her head resting on her arms. He put down his brush and his palette and wiped his hands and walked over to her. He leaned and eased his arms under her and carried her to the cane chaise, her warm body close to his face. He laid her on the chaise and covered her with the rug. She stirred and murmured but did not wake. He stood looking down at her.

He left her sleeping and went over to her desk and looked at what she had drawn. A triangular little girl with red hair held Snoopy Dog's hand and looked out of the frame of square paper at the viewer, as if the two of them stood before a mirror, contemplating themselves.

He lifted his canvas from the easel and on the reverse wrote in black, *The Other Family*. He leaned the canvas against the wall and took a sketching block from the drawer of the press and sat on the stool and began a drawing of Nada sleeping. As he drew he thought of Marina sleeping on the chaise at her parents' home in the conservatory all those years ago, himself crouched in the shadows taking her youthful likeness . . .

At a sound behind him he turned.

Teresa stepped through the door. She walked across and gathered Nada in her arms and lifted her from the chaise. She stood in front of him, angry and reproachful, the child cradled against her breasts. 'You said half an hour. You promised.'

'I didn't think it would hurt to let her sleep.'

'You promised,' she accused him. 'I left you just to see how long you'd keep her. You'd obviously have kept her out here with you all night!' She turned and left the studio.

He rested his sketching block on his knees. Standing defiantly in the doorway with Nada in her arms, Teresa had presented to him a strong composition, an image that was both archaic and monumental, the timeless subject of mother and child. The great passion of the artists. The greatest. One day soon he would paint them. Something of strength and devotion and ageless determination . . . He sat on the stool staring vacantly across the studio at his father's old suit where it clothed the wooden frame he had built for it, a presence in the shadows of the dark corner. It suddenly came to him then that for the Bream Island show he must call himself Prochownik. He stood up. It was as if something had woken up in him. Prochownik would be his painting name from now on! It was obvious. Why had he never thought of it before? He must phone Andy in the morning and make sure the advertising material for the show carried his new name—his new name, his old name. The name of his father. It was a feeling of reclaiming something more than the name, a feeling of opening himself up to his capacity to make art. The decision excited him and he set the sketching block aside and started working again on *The Other Family*. It was to be the first work of the painter Prochownik...

It was four in the morning when he at last draped the sheet over the picture and left the studio. He was hungry and his head was buzzing with the intensity of the session. The image of the emerging painting swam about before his vision. He crept into the house, not putting the light on but relying on the night glow of the city through the tall windows. He opened the fridge and stood looking into its interior.

The room light came on and he turned.

Teresa stood by the entrance to the passage. 'I'll make you something,' she said and she came into the room. 'What do you want? How about coffee and scrambled eggs?'

'I can get it,' he said. 'You need your sleep.'

'I wasn't sleeping.'

Her eyes were swollen and her cheeks blotchy. She had been crying.

'When you're working you've got to eat.' She said this as if he were a builder like her brothers and she was doing her wifely duty—the good woman feeding her man.

He sat and watched her cook and they did not speak.

She brought the plate of food and the coffee and set them in front of him and pulled out a chair and sat and watched him eat.

'How's the new picture coming along?'

He did not want to talk about *The Other Family*. His connection to it was still too tenuous and he feared he might lose it. It was a private thing and he did not yet understand it; the exploration of its human landscape was still a place of uncertainty and struggle. It was a thing composed half of desire and half of dream. It was nothing. It was an illusion. It was not yet a painting. It might not be there when he looked again. 'This is great!' he said. 'Thanks.'

She watched him eat in silence for a while. 'It's like something has hatched in you.'

He looked up at her, chewing.

'You're like a man in a trance. Like a man in love, if you ask me.'

He ate the scrambled eggs.

'I'm wondering if you're going to stay like this? Or are you going to turn back into the Toni Powlett I married? I have to say this. I have to say something.'

'I'm still the same person,' he said. He looked at her and smiled.

'So what is it now?' she asked. 'I can see you're going to tell me something.'

'I've decided to show as Prochownik.' He pronounced it softly, Pro-shov-nik.

'So you're telling me you're changing your name?'

'Not for everything. Just for my work.' He wanted to hear himself telling her in full. 'From now on, I'm the painter Prochownik,' he said, and he felt the rightness of it going right down into the root of his being.

'Just for the painting?' she said doubtfully.

'Just for the painting.'

'It was her idea, wasn't it?'

'It was my own idea.'

She stared at him. 'So if I said I'm talking to a stranger through a glass door it wouldn't be so far from the truth?' She waited and, when he did not react, she made an exasperated sound and got up and went over to where her bag was sitting on the lounge. She took out her cigarettes and lit up.

He stopped eating.

She came back and sat down again, taking the smoke into her lungs then letting it out slowly, lifting her chin towards the ceiling and closing her eyes.

'You've taken up smoking again?'

'You noticed!' She waved the smoke away from his food. 'Do you think you can live with someone for years and share everything with them and have their child and still be a stranger to them?'

'You haven't smoked since you were pregnant with Nada. What about the new baby? Are you going to be smoking while you're pregnant?'

'We're having a new baby? Listen! I'm trying to talk to you. Are you and me strangers? That's what I'm asking you.'

'You're exaggerating things.'

'I'm lying in our bed on my own while you're down there painting and this feeling comes over me that I should face the truth. The truth is, things are falling apart for us, Toni. That's the truth.'

He pushed the plate away and drank the last of the coffee. 'Things are changing for us. That's true. But they're not falling apart. Change is always difficult.'

'Listen to him! Change is always difficult! What is this, the wisdom of the male? There's more coffee. You want some?'

'No thanks.'

'Am I making this up?'

He reached across the table for her hand but she pulled it away.

'No! Don't grab me. Look at me! You have to talk to me.'

He looked at her.

'Are you having an affair with her?'

'With who?'

'With *her*! With her! With Marina-fucking-Golding! Who the fuck else do you think I fucking mean? With *her*! Jesus Christ!'

'Take it easy.'

'*Are* you?'

'Don't shout, you'll wake Nada! No. Definitely no. Of course not. It's crazy to even think it.'

'You used to want sex every night.'

'And you often didn't want it.'

'That's different.'

'It's not different.'

'It's different!'

He would not argue with her. When pushed, Teresa did not back down. She did not know how to back down. He had learnt early in their relationship that backing down was not a possibility for Teresa. She had that in common with his brother. Once they were stirred up, those two just went for it. It was something in their natures. He was not going to fight her. In a fight with Teresa he knew he would lose because she was prepared to go the extreme and he was not prepared to go to the extreme.

The last enchantment of his work had gone.

Across the road the party was reaching full throttle, the bass thumping of the sub woofers penetrating the walls of the house, penetrating the walls of his chest, causing his heart to doubt its own rhythm. He was exhausted. He pushed his chair back and stood. 'Let's go to bed.'

She got up. 'You're not sleeping down there tonight? I never know if you're sleeping down there or coming over.'

He put his arm around her and held her.

She stubbed out her cigarette in his empty coffee cup.

'You want me to stop doing this?' he asked.

'You don't mean that!'

If she asked him to give up the project, would he give it up? Giving up the project would be giving up his art. That was the truth. How to live without it? What else could he do? Get a real job? Doing what? Become his father and work on the Dunlop moulding line? Only Dunlop had long since gone from Port Melbourne, the vast manufacturing plant replaced by expensive city apartments. His dad would not know the place today. His dad would be even more a stranger there today than he had been then. The lines of weary blackened migrant workers had disappeared from Port Melbourne's streets long ago. It was another age now. Another place. History had swallowed the lives and the dreams of those men and left no trace of them.

Teresa rested her head on his shoulder. 'I married an artist. I know what I did. I've always secretly dreaded the day you'd become successful.'

They went across the room and he switched off the light. They went down the passage and got into bed and held each other.

'Don't ever just suddenly quit, will you?' she said.

'Shh! Go to sleep.'

She relaxed against him. 'I need you here in our bed with me. When I'm here alone, the night disfigures everything.'

fourteen

Someone was banging on the window and yelling. He was coming out of a deep sleep with the feeling that it must be the people from the party across the road, who had reached the fighting stage and had come over to have it out with him, over whatever it was he had done to provoke them, something he could not fathom. He opened his eyes. It was daylight. Teresa's side of the bed was empty. The banging on the window and the yelling was renewed. He got up and went over and pulled the blind aside. On the verandah, Andy play-acted a shocked expression at him, holding his wrist out and pointing to his watch.

Toni dropped the blind and pulled on his underpants, then went out along the passage and opened the front door. 'What's happening?'

'I'm looking at your pictures.'

'What time is it?'

'Two.'

Andy followed him into the bedroom and stood watching him pull on his clothes.

'You know what?'

'What?'

'You don't show.' Andy waited for his reaction.

But Toni was not listening.

'You don't get into that circus. You stay out of it. It takes too long that way. On the show circuit you're just another performing bear. You don't need to build up that kind of CV. Bream Island's the last time you show. We sell your three pictures before the opening. When they come to the island your stuff's all got red stickers on it. Nothing's available. The day they discover you, they find they're too late already. We don't pass up a chance like this one. The first thing they think is, *Hey, this guy must be good, everything's sold, so how do we acquire one of his pictures?* Then I tell them. *Listen, it's not so easy with this guy. Be patient. He's sensitive to deal with. He likes his privacy. He never shows. Leave it with me and I'll see what I can do for you*, that's what I tell them. And I've got some good news for you, too. You're going to like this.'

Toni was hearing Andy's voice but he was not registering the details of what his friend was saying. Andy talked all the time, that was the way it was. Andy's dad had been the same. In the backstreet car yard in Port Melbourne, Andy's dad telling them his dream of running a new Ford dealership out on Burwood Highway with the big shots. Andy growing up in the yard developing an instinct for closing a sale. Now his business was selling art. Andy Levine was the dealer who, in his early twenties, had transformed the old Port Melbourne biscuit factory into one of Australia's most successful contemporary private art dealerships. Andy would have made more money selling cars. As he said, everyone needs a car. But he preferred selling art, which no one needs. Andy preferred artists to cars. He liked the way they took risks trying to make sense of their precarious lives. Artists fascinated him. He used to say it was like watching a movie, seeing someone's story unfolding, and you knew they could fall. And they *did* fall. And when they were on his books, and sometimes even when they were not on his books, Andy picked them up and dusted them off and gave them some money and sent them away to repair the damage. And he liked the people in the art business who were like himself, the dealers and promoters. He was one of them. These people were his other family too. He loved the strange intimate association of it, the rivalries and the shared hopes and the comradeship when someone took a fall or when they suddenly began to fly.

There was a wayward instinct in Andy that Toni loved. They both knew there was nothing objective going on in the art business. *Selling is not the ennobling art*, Andy was fond of telling anyone who was willing to listen to him. *Selling is the enabling art. Without sales*, he would tell them, *everything goes cold and the world comes to a standstill. Without sales no one has any fun.* Andy enjoyed making money, but that was not the whole story with him. He loved his artists. He was their champion. He was on their side. He was in awe of what they did.

Andy had been waiting a long time for his old friend to come good. *You can never tell*, he would say. *Sometimes they come good and sometimes they die away and never do it. It's touch and go. No one can give you the reasons for those who produce and those who don't produce.* Andy had known Toni even before they went to school together. Andy's gift was an instinct for reality. He did not claim infallibility but, as some horse trainers have an instinct for speed and stamina in a horse, he had developed this sense about art. He did not need someone to tell him what was what about contemporary art. Andy could not have dealt in old masters. *For the old stuff, the decisions have all been made, the risks have all been taken.* There was no need for Andy's gift of divination with old masters. As far as he was concerned, the old stuff belonged in the auction houses. That's what the auction houses were for. Dead artists did not interest him. He loved to see and touch and be with the living artists, to be surprised by them, the weird and wonderful things they came up with. That was where it was at for Andy Levine. With the living. A hand on the shoulder when they needed it. A kiss. A little hug. Buy them a drink. A meal. Coax them back up out of the trough until he got a smile.

Andy followed Toni out into the living area, talking his enthusiasm.

'I think we might get Harvey to take *The Schwartz Family* for the National. We'll see. We'll see. Now hear this. After you left Richmond the other day, Geoffrey goes over with Marina and he turns your picture around and he talks admiration for your work for the next half-hour.'

Toni looked at him. 'That's hard to believe. He dismissed it and me with it.'

'Not so. That's just Geoffrey. He gives people the impression he's aloof. He's not, he's shy. Oriel and Robert came in and stood listening to him. Geoffrey makes a serious business of collecting the work of his contemporaries. He always has. He's very choosy. *Get me one of Toni's pictures*, he says to me when he's done. *While I can still afford him*, he says. So how's that? You don't get a better start than Geoffrey Haine putting one of your pictures into his collection. He won't keep it a secret. It's going to make them sit up and take notice in Sydney. Believe me. You're on your way with this. Geoffrey's been on his own with this figurative stuff for twenty years. He's the one who persisted through the bad times with it. He did the hard yards when it was a sin to use paint and canvas. He went hungry. He was suspect with the critics for years. Some of his best early shows were never reviewed. Like your beautiful installations. It's true. The public curators didn't want to know him. But he stuck at it. Now he sees you coming in and it looks to him like he's having a voice with the new generation. Which thrills him. You're the young bull and he likes what he sees. He can see you're dangerous. Geoffrey is your first serious admirer. This is how all the best love affairs begin.' Andy laughed. 'You and Teresa should consider moving to Sydney. Geoffrey would open your show. You'd be on a boom in that town. They know how to celebrate their artists. Did I tell you I'm opening a new gallery in Paddington in the spring?'

Toni was standing at the big windows looking out into the courtyard. The living area and kitchen were flooded with sunlight. Teresa had switched on the wall fountain in the courtyard before leaving for the office, and the water was spraying and sparkling in the sun. The blackbird was taking a bath. Then he noticed the obvious. She had had his pile of installation stuff removed. There was nothing left of it. The heap of old clothes and timber racks was no longer there. He felt a touch of nostalgia. There was going to be no reinstalling his old life now. No going back along that road. It was finished.

He turned from the window and went into the kitchen, where he picked up the coffee pot and held it up for Andy, who was still talking. There was a note from Teresa on the bench. *Dearest, I let you sleep. I hope the work goes well today. Give me a ring if you get a chance. Love you!*

Andy was sitting on the couch fiddling with the television remote. 'I take a couple of your smaller oil studies and maybe a couple of the bigger drawings and I give an exclusive look to one or two of my Sydney collectors. Geoffrey's getting too dear for them these days. I make it special for them to be looking at previously unseen Toni Powletts.'

Toni called, 'I'm signing my work Prochownik from now on.'

'Hey, that's good! You've got it there, old mate. That's beautiful, Toni. You're doing it for your old dad. Brilliant. I love it. Prochownik. That's it.' Andy watched the television for a couple of seconds then switched channels, as if he were searching for his own wavelength. 'Prochownik,' he said admiringly. 'I wish I'd thought of that. Wait till we get you into a couple of the big collections, then the word's going to travel around. *Look, I got myself a Prochownik!* They don't keep it a secret, either. *You got a Prochownik? What the hell's a Prochownik? How come I haven't got a Prochownik? What am I missing here? Maybe I'm slipping.* Next thing you know the only question they're asking each other is, *How big's your Prochownik?* They don't know art from horseshit. They know money and they know size. They don't need to know art. They know everything else.'

Toni stepped across and handed him a mug of coffee. He was not listening to Andy's spiel. He was preoccupied with how *The Other Family* was going to look to him this morning. He was working at visualising the picture in his mind's eye. It was an obsessive exercise in anxiety, coloured at the edges by his waking apprehension of violence from across the road. How to be alone with his work was beginning to be a serious problem for him. He was missing Marina's support, missing her confident assurance about what he was doing. He felt in danger of losing a vital connection.

Andy yelled, 'Hey you! Prochownik! You listening to me? I'm not doing this with anyone else, okay? Pay attention. It's a special. A one-off for Moniek Prochownik's boy. It's him

I'm doing this for. Me and Geoffrey are coming in behind you on this. Prochownik's *the one who doesn't show*. That's this new guy as he's coming onto the market. The one whose work is hard to get hold of. He's not showing his tits to everyone. I can't do this with two or three artists. It's an exclusive situation. Okay? You getting this?'

Andy got up off the couch and walked across and stood beside Toni and put a hand to his shoulder. 'You're an innocent, brother. They'll eat you alive out there. I'm doing this for you and me and your old dad. You got that? For his belief in your gift. For Lola, too. You understand? For *us* when we were kids in the rat flats. I can't do this for someone I don't know.' He tapped Toni's skull with his forefinger. 'You in there, buddy? You hearing what I'm saying? This is the style for you. *Prochownik, the one who never shows*. What's your old dad thinking about this? It's your moment. Take it. We only get one moment. Hesitate and we lose it. No one recovers from bad timing.'

Andy walked back and sat on the couch again and sipped his coffee. He picked up the remote but did not put the television on. 'And get yourself a good accountant. There's only so much one man can do for another.'

Toni drank his coffee standing at the bench. Andy was always talking. So what? That was Andy's business. The piped music of continuous enthusiasm. Keeping the spirit strong. Creating the buzz. No one looked for long reflective silences from Andy Levine. *Silence is for the next life*, Andy always said whenever someone told him to shut up. *In this life I'm talking*.

Andy was sitting there looking at him now. A rare pause in the flow here. Andy sitting forward on the couch with his elbows on his knees looking thoughtfully across the room at him as if he was making a diagnosis. Toni smiled. He loved his old friend. They went back so far they were family.

'Prochownik's studio is out of bounds,' Andy said, thoughtful and slow, as if he were telling a story. 'But for the director of the National, for Harvey, we make an exception. Harvey will like Prochownik. Harvey is Irish. Prochownik doesn't know Harvey. It's better Prochownik doesn't know him. There's no prejudice with him there. And Prochownik's not Irish. Harvey is about to discover Prochownik. I let him discover him. I give Harvey the right of discovery of Prochownik. Critically, Prochownik is virgin soil. He's unspoiled and he's got a touch of the ethnic. Which is a handy flag to have on the mast these days. Prochownik is nobody's darling. He is terra incognita. The prestige of discovery is all Harvey's. And Harvey is a man with a serious budget. I'm not asking him to go out on his own either. These people don't like going out on their own. I show Harvey *The Schwartz Family* and tell him to talk to Geoffrey Haine. Then I leave the two of them to get on with it. Geoffrey is buying a Prochownik and he won't be able to hide his admiration for that picture. He won't even try hiding it. Geoffey Haine is not a mean-spirited man. Believe me. I know the guy. Obstinate he may be, but not mean. I could tell you some stories about our Geoffrey. So it'll be Harvey's call after that. After Geoffrey speaks to him, Harvey's got the choice of going down in history as the curator who passed up Prochownik or being the genius who discovered him. Don't worry, there's going to be a waiting list for Prochowniks if Harvey takes *The Schwartz Family*. You want a Prochownik? Join the queue! We're talking the words here. Committed. Innovative. Challenging. Prestigious. These are the words, Toni. The trade words. They don't mean a piece of shit but without these words you're nowhere in the market. Work of the highest standard. A new benchmark. Prochownik and Haine are the forefront of the contemporary neo-figurative school. That's the way this operates. Trade words coming out of the right mouths and going into the right ears with the right timing. Smart. They like the idea of smart, it reassures them that they're smart. But first they've got to be told. If you don't tell them they're buying a work of genius, they'd never guess. They can go and tell their friends, *This is a work of genius I just bought. It's a Prochownik.* Owning the Prochownik almost makes *them* the genius. That's the whole idea. These are the people who collected Aboriginal dot and line thirty years ago and are unloading it in New York today and making a bucket of money. This is not about love. This is about money. Don't forget that. Art, shmart! Forget it! Prochownik is the next spin of the wheel for these people. They'll see with him it's cool to celebrate being white Australian male and figurative again. That's going to be a big relief to them.' Andy drew breath and put down his coffee mug. 'Well, let's go and do it! Show me what you've been up to. What are we sitting around here listening to me for?'

They crossed the courtyard and Toni opened the studio.

Andy made an exclamation and went straight over to the corner and put his hand on the old suit, as if he were putting his hand on the shoulder of an old friend. 'You kept it!' He stood looking at the suit, touching it respectfully with his fingers. 'Your old man was the one who made us believe. Now we know. Did we know then? *He* knew! We knew nothing. We believed him. Remember the day you brought this into the space? Your dad had been gone less than twenty-four hours. You were still finding it hard to breathe without him.' He bent and read the sign. '*Moniek Prochownik's Outsize Sunday Suit*. That's it! He was a beautiful man, Toni. A beautiful man. Jesus, I loved that man. I can still see this suit sitting out there in the middle of the gallery all on its own. That was raw stuff, mate. You were the only one who could have done it. You didn't even have a clue what you were doing. You just did it and we saw what a massive thing you'd done. It stopped us cold in our tracks.'

'No one knew what to make of it.'

'*We* knew what to make of it.'

Toni went over to the easel and flipped up the drop sheet. He stood looking at *The Other Family*.

Andy came over and stood beside him. 'Now we're here doing this. Your dad should see us today. Would you and me have been thinking about art if it hadn't been for him?' He looked around at the clutter in the studio. 'Boy, you've been working! Look at all this stuff!' He stepped across and picked up the canvas of Marina asleep on the island and stood with it in his hands, admiring it. 'This is the one for our Geoffrey.' He looked some more at the painting. 'So, you and Marina Golding, eh? These things come around.'

'We're just friends.'

'Friendship's a great thing.'

'I mean it.'

'You mean everything, Toni boy. I never heard you say anything yet you didn't mean. You're a rabbit for sincerity. Meaning something doesn't make it true. Don't confuse the two things. Meaning and truth. They're not the same thing. Your old dad knew that.' Andy was silent. 'So, she's doing a new background for you?'

'We'll see. Maybe. Who knows.'

'Yeah, what do we know? I never had the hots for those two, I have to tell you. Who are they showing with these days? What brought them back from Sydney? I heard they were doing okay with Number 8 up there. Robert Schwartz is like a guy with two glass eyes.'

'They're my friends.'

'Sure.'

Toni was standing in front of *The Other Family*. He was seeing himself in the empty space to the left of the big group; a figure looking on, an onlooker. The voyeur. That was him! For the first time ever he was seeing himself in his work. The imaginary image of himself in the picture was not so much a likeness as an enigmatic male presence, erotic and naked, a presence bearing a dangerous power to disrupt reality. There was no doubt this self-image owed something to the fantastic intensities of Theo's drawings, levering a crack in his defences. He was pleased. He liked the idea.

Andy said, 'Hey! You've still got your mother. I can sell Lola this afternoon.'

'Mum's not for sale.'

'Prochownik's mother's not for sale! You hear that, folks?' Andy held up the portrait of Toni's mother. 'You should be in my business. Tell them it's not for sale and you double the price. It's not for sale, it's the only one they want.' Andy set the painting down with care. 'It's all for sale, old buddy.' Andy talking to himself now. 'Your house. Teresa's underwear. Your mother. Find the price, that's all.'

'Mum's not for sale.'

'That's what they said about London Bridge. You're making it a serious enterprise for them. You've almost got me believing you. Mum's not for sale!'

Toni was squinting at the imaginary figure of himself in the painting, seeing in it a confirmation, a move into his own space. So there really was to be no escape for him from art? It was a good feeling. And it was true. Had he ever doubted it? Had there ever really been a choice for him? 'Maybe Dad was right,' he said. 'Maybe it *has* all been decided and we're just here filling in between the dots.'

'What happened to his pictures?'

'Mum's got them.'

'You and I ought to take a look at them one of these days. I should give your dad the show he never had. *Prochownik I*. We could make him famous too.'

'Dad didn't want to be famous.'

'Everyone wants to be famous. You ever do a portrait of him?'

'No.'

'I'm taking these two. Okay?' Andy had the 35 x 60 of Marina asleep on the island and the 50 x 30 of Theo Schwartz sitting on the library steps reading in the corner by the bookshelves at Richmond, looking like the tragic bust of Seneca.

Toni was mixing a glaze. He was working. He was putting himself in the picture. 'Take whatever you like,' he said.

Andy stood watching him for a while. 'I'm leaving. I'll be in touch.'

As Andy was going out the door, Toni called, 'Nothing's for sale yet.'

'Listen to the voice of Prochownik, folks! Nothing's for sale!' Andy was gone.

Toni did not look up. He was working at the problem of himself. It was not Haine's monumental works, after all, but Theo Schwartz's illicit intimacies that he was drawing upon. It was a delicious surprise for him . . .

fifteen

A week later *The Other Family* was going nowhere for him. He found to his dismay, after the initial euphoria of beginning work on the problem of himself, that he was unable to translate his imaginary presence convincingly onto the canvas. He made no attempt at the figure of Marina, but painted himself into the composition and scraped himself back to the canvas a dozen times. Always, however, there was the feeling that something essential to the success of the figure was absent. It was a great disappointment to him that this image of himself remained so unresponsive, so without light and life; so without, in fact, the conviction of that elusive sense of presence that is necessary in all successful representations of the human figure in art, even if the representation is no more than an entirely impersonal depiction such as the fugitive figure of Haine's running man. He was finally forced to admit, with a faint feeling of self-disgust, that he was blocked. His visual sense of himself was inadequate to the task he had set himself. He could not deal with it. For days he did not know what to do, and he had begun to despair when, late one night, he thought of the book he had been holding in his hand the day Marina had telephoned out of the blue and told him that she and Robert had returned from Sydney—that day when he had not had the heart to do anything.

Glad of this distraction from the frustrating and enervating task at the easel, he got off the stool and went over to the pile of books by the door. The book was still on top where he had left it. He picked it up and examined it. It was his father's old Penguin Classics edition of Sartre's *Nausea*, the familiar and very beautiful greens and yellows of Dali's painting, *The Triangular Hour,* on the front cover. He had been holding the book in his hand that day, not exactly reading it but looking at it, his eye touching down at a sentence here and there while he had posed for Nada. He could not remember what it was that he had read then that had made him think of the book now, but holding it he nevertheless felt a comforting sense of connection with it that provided him with a certain feeling of reassurance. He did not search randomly through the book's pages for the line that had arrested his attention that day, but sat on the stool and began to read the book from the beginning. It was a welcome relief from struggling fruitlessly with the attempt to paint his own image ... Then, suddenly, when he had forgotten the impulse that had made him seek out the book in the first place and was already lost in the world of its story, the phrase that had arrested his attention that day was before his eyes: *I should like to understand myself properly before it is too late.* He read the sentence over several times, feeling strangely comforted by it, as if he shared with its author, or at least with the character to whom the author had given this thought, the feeling of being lost within himself, and of being unable to solve a conundrum about his own existence that demanded a solution before he could move forward with his work. It was true, after all; as an artist he was, like the character in the book, a stranger to himself. Although the estrangement of the character in the book was of a more dramatic kind than his own, it nevertheless corresponded to his own in his imagination, which was where the realities of the book took shape for him. He felt an enormous gratitude to the book and, instead of going back to the arduous struggle of his work, he sat on the cane chaise and continued to read until he had finished the story. By then it was daylight outside his window and he could hear Teresa's voice calling to Nada and the sound of the morning cartoons on the television. He had been deeply absorbed for several hours in this strangely beautiful story of a man in search of an image of himself that would satisfy his sense of his own moral worth and would, indeed, justify his existence—and even, possibly, give him a certain pleasure in his life. The fact that the story had not ended happily with the fulfilment of this man's dream had the strange effect of uplifting Toni's mood and of making him feel more optimistic than if the story *had* ended happily. It felt good to have been reminded that the complete fulfilment of such a dream of perfect sanity as the character in the book possessed was unrealistic, and that it was the possession of such a dream, and not its realisation, that had prevented his otherwise inevitable descent into despair. He read the final sentence again before laying the book aside. *The yard of the New Station smells strongly of damp wood: tomorrow it will rain over Bouville.* Then, with a feeling of regret at having to leave the familiar enchanted world of the story, he closed the book and set it aside on the chaise, promising himself that one day soon he would return to it and read it again, as if not to do so would be in some way a betrayal of what he had gained from it. He stood up and stretched the stiffness from his limbs, then went over and opened the door to the courtyard and stood looking out at the sunlit morning. He not only knew now exactly what he had to do, but he also believed that he would possess the will and the capacity to do it. Somehow his dilemma had resolved itself while he was reading, as if he had gone to sleep and dreamed away the block that had stood implacably before him only a few hours ago.

He went across to the house and joined Teresa and Nada, who were having their breakfast in front of the television. He was tired but anxious to get on with his work and so, instead of going to bed after Teresa and Nada had left, he drove to the local hardware store and purchased a cheap full-length mirror of the kind used on the doors of built-in wardrobes.

He brought the mirror home and set it up at the back of the studio. Then he took off his clothes and sat on the stool.

There he was. A naked stranger.

He might not have been looking at himself but at another man who, until this moment, through a kind of mental blindness, he had been unable to see. Looking at his naked body as a subject for his art was a novel experience for him, and was quite unlike looking at himself in the mirror in the normal narcissistic and semi-critical way that he did every day while he was having a shower or shaving. Now his eye was detached from his vanity and he was at liberty to search in the mirror for the truth of the visual form of the naked man reflected there. As he sat gazing at himself it was as if he had become two people.

During the following nights he worked up dozens of studies of his naked torso and limbs in pencil, charcoal, gouache and oil. The studio was soon filled with these intimate images of himself. As he worked on a large freehand charcoal drawing of his shoulders and chest, he was aware that all this self-research, the newness of it and the promise it seemed to hold for him of a real and substantial future as an artist, was linked in some way to his having accepted his identity as the artist Prochownik and to having cast off the old false identity of Powlett—a name which had been given to his father before his own birth by the foreman at the Dunlop plant, who had told his father on his first morning at the factory, *Prochownik is not a name in Australia*. In what precise way this relinquishing of the falseness of his past name was linked to the revolution of his view of himself and his art, he did not know, and perhaps he never would know. All he knew for certain was the feeling of rightness about it. Belief in himself was the key to it, not understanding. As he worked he wanted very much to tell Marina everything that had happened to him since they had taken *The Schwartz Family* to Richmond. But he resisted the desire to telephone her. He was not sure why he resisted, but was aware that there were probably a number of good reasons to resist. So instead of speaking to her over the telephone, or even in the flesh, he made do with imaginary conversations with her in his head. He was at liberty, in these very real but imaginary conversations, to say whatever occurred to him without censoring his thoughts, and so during this time alone with himself and his own reflection, Marina became the ideal companion of his hours and seemed to share with him a perfect intuitive understanding of his situation.

He did not attempt to depict his facial features in any of the studies of himself. Seated on the stool in a variety of poses, and sometimes standing close up to the mirror, he examined his body hour after hour, and as the days and nights passed he gradually became his own familiar. When he closed his eyes before going to sleep beside Teresa in the early hours of each morning, the intricate details of his body remained imprinted on his inner eye . . .

Teresa said very little to him during this time either about his art or about the absence of Marina from his studio. She was being watchful and careful. She was crafting the situation along and was hoping for the best, like a woman in a war zone waiting for the resumption of normality and praying her family would emerge intact. Nada had all but disappeared from his days and in his moments of lucidity away from his studio he regretted this intensely, but he did nothing to change it. He had not heard from Marina on the progress of her new background for *The Schwartz Family*. But this no longer seemed an urgent matter to him.

One night he was playing around with Theo's head on a drawing of his own torso when he realised there was something about the composition that greatly intrigued him. He set up a small canvas on the easel and painted an oil study of the subject. When he had finished it he titled the painting *The Eye of Tiresias*. The bizarre, but beguiling, image came to him not only from Theo's drawing of the youthful satyr with the head of an old man, but also from the passing glimpse of Theo's head on the pillow, framed by the doorjamb, as he went by his bedroom that day; imagining the old man's sorrow at the loss of his beloved Marguerite, and seeing his features hollowed by misery behind his closed eyelids. There was something beautiful and poignant in the perversity of this image for Toni, the dying man's head on his own youthful torso. He was aware of dealing not with strict likeness but with the repressed, the inarticulate, the unconscious, the as-yet-unrealised, and knew himself to be in touch at last with that dimension of himself that had always eluded him, a place only revealed by a trick of the light at night when he was tired and his mind was no longer clear but was open to the bright, sudden, uncanny energies of fatigue. He could scarcely bear to leave his work and his studio even to eat or to sleep and he did so only reluctantly and briefly, anxious all the time he was away to get back as soon as possible. As he worked he was conscious of touching upon something concealed that he would only be able to recognise when the work was finished. He did a larger painting of Theo's head on his own naked body, working for hours without a break, lost in the process and unaware of the passing of time. It was an image that seemed to hold for him the key to something of great importance . . .

He smelled the cigarette smoke and looked up from the canvas. She was standing in the doorway. She took the cigarette from between her lips and let the smoke drift from her mouth. The way she stood—loose and careless, the cigarette held close to her lips, her other hand propping her elbow, her eyes squinting at him through the smoke—he realised she had been drinking. She was wearing her dressing-gown, her weight resting on one leg, the gown held closed as carelessly as her attitude, her hip thrust out, giving in to the heaviness of her body. Looking slowly over the scene, seeing the interior of his studio as if it were at the bottom of a lake.

'I can heat something up if you're hungry.' She spoke in a lazy tone, as if she could scarcely muster the energy to speak at all, or addressed him from some other place, a place where these events were of no consequence, her gaze going over his naked body, lingering on his glistening skin.

'What do you think of it?' he said.

She looked at his painting, considering the head of the old man, alone with himself at the end, in the secret, sacred place of the dying. The naked body of the young man, smooth, cool, charged with energy and expectation. She gave a small lift of her shoulders and took a drag on her cigarette, her expression indifferent. 'You're not painting her anymore then?'

He got off the stool and pulled on his underpants and his jeans and put on his T-shirt. 'It's a way of approaching myself,' he said, standing looking at his picture and making a futile effort to include Teresa. It sounded, however, as if he were offering her an excuse. 'It's a way of taking myself by surprise,' he said and he turned from the painting and looked at her. It sounded silly, *taking myself by surprise*. It would have been better to have kept silent than to have attempted to explain himself. He loved the painting and knew she saw it as something weird and inexplicable. 'My problem is to get myself into that picture.' He pointed. 'That big one. There!'

She looked without interest at *The Other Family,* unveiled and leaning against the press.

He noticed how a drooping of the flesh at the corners of her mouth had begun to interrupt the clean youthful line of her jaw. He felt guilty, as if the signs of her ageing were the result of his neglect. She was tired and was beginning to give way a little. Tired of work. Tired of waiting for *him*. Tired of their money problems. Tired of dealing with it all on her own. He said gently, 'We should take a holiday after the show. Go to Tassie for a couple of weeks. Or over to Perth. We've never crossed the Nullarbor together.' Once again, as soon as he had spoken, he realised it would have been better if he had remained silent.

She turned towards him, cool, sardonic, removed, the wine of disbelief in her eyes. 'You want me to heat something up for you before I go to bed?'

'No. It's okay. I can do it. You go on. I'll clean up down here.'

'I made a lasagna and opened a bottle of Dad's red earlier.' She watched him. 'I was hoping you might have come up and shared it with us.' She did not wait for him to respond but turned abruptly, faltered, a hand to the doorframe, steadying herself, then left.

He should have followed her at once and comforted her. But he did not move. Instead he stood looking into the darkness after her . . . Then he turned from the doorway and examined the bizarre fiction of himself. It was, of course, the image of himself that he had been looking for to include in *The Other Family*; a young man's body with the head of a grieving monster. The fascination of the paradox. The artist, in other words. Himself! It was the most important thing he had ever done. He was sure of it. One day Nada would forgive him his neglect of her. But would Teresa ever be able to forgive him? Tomorrow he would begin transferring the image to *The Other Family*. Marina would know it the moment she saw it. There would be no need to explain or to excuse it to her, or to Theo or Robert, or to Andy either. Whatever the opinions of these people about the painting's success or failure might be, none of them would require an explanation from him. It would not distress them or threaten them in any way that he had chosen to stay up night after night neglecting his family in order to do such a thing.

Reluctantly he turned away from his painting and went over to the door and stood a moment, his hand to the light switch, looking back at the *The Other Family*. He loved the painting, and he feared it. His life as an artist! He switched off the light and closed the door. The house was in darkness and there was the stale smell of cigarettes and the heated lasagna. He turned the oven off. He was too distracted to eat. He stood in the darkened room at the window looking across the courtyard toward the studio. Teresa's fountain was still on, the glint of water spouting from the wall in the tinkling silence, splashing into the stone bowl . . .

3

Prochownik's Dream

sixteen

As he stood at the tall window in the house gazing across the darkened courtyard towards the studio, he was trying to decide whether to return to the studio and begin work at once on the image of himself in *The Other Family*—for it felt to him that its moment had arrived—or whether to go and get into bed beside Teresa and give her the comfort and reassurance that she needed and which was the very least she might expect from him at this moment. He stood at the window for some minutes before he turned and went out to the studio. He felt bad about abandoning Teresa, indeed he felt like a miserable traitor for doing it; but he did it, nevertheless.

He set up *The Other Family* and mixed a glaze and, within a few minutes of beginning work, Teresa and the rest of the world had gone out of his mind—the rest of the world, that is, except for Marina, with whom every now and then he enjoyed a brief imaginary exchange; the perfect companion of his solitary hours. He worked without a break through what was left of the night and on through the dawn and into the day, until the naked male figure stood boldly to the left of the principal group in the big painting, poised side on to the viewer. It was a figure that was strangely familiar to Toni, one which in some essential way represented himself, even though its features—or such of them as could be made out, for it stood within a puzzling array of shadows—were those of an old man. As he stood in front of the painting, seeing the figure with a feeling of surprise, he had little recollection of the hours he had spent painting it. He felt that he had at last taken root in his own work, and the possibilities for his art seemed to him to be endless. With the inclusion of himself, he had stepped through a doorway and the field of his future endeavour lay open to him. He would paint them all. Teresa and Nada and Teresa's family and Andy. All of them. Repeatedly. Naked and clothed. He would depict their vulnerability and their humanity. That is what he would do. *Paint what you love,* his father had told him, and at last he seemed to understand what his father had meant.

He cleaned his brushes and lowered the drop sheet over the canvas. As he emerged from the studio the bright sunlight seemed to bite into the interior of his skull. He winced and put out his hand to the fountain to steady himself. His outline seemed no longer fixed but wavered around him as he moved, a charged and luminous corona of fatigue and hallucination.

In the kitchen he leaned against the bench, the shining outlines of the telephone and the refrigerator beside it blurring and shifting, as though with an effort of will he might summon the power to dissolve their volumes into abstract patterns of light and shade . . . He closed his eyes.

The doorbell pealed twice then someone banged on the front door.

He stood staring down the passage. The banging was repeated. He went out along the passage and opened the door. It was Marina.

'I've done it!' she said breathlessly. She was obviously agitated and emotional, her eyes glistening with tears. She stepped towards him and embraced him. They held each other tightly. They might have been lovers who had been separated and had found one another again after a long and dangerous return. She was laughing softly, or perhaps she was weeping, her body pressed against his, her warm cheek against his cheek. 'I've done it!' she whispered. He could smell her sweat mixed with the paint extender. After a while she lifted her head and looked at him, her grey eyes alight with a kind of wonderment. 'You're trembling.'

He kissed her on the lips and she did not resist but responded to him eagerly. They stood embraced in the doorway for a long moment, uncaring that they were in full view of passers by in the street. The pressure of her belly and thighs against him, the irresistible pulse of his blood arcing in his thighs, the intensity of the moment so great he thought he might faint. He took both her hands in his and drew her into the house and closed the door. She was barefoot and was wearing a loose, grimy black T-shirt with a tear in it over a paint-stained denim skirt. She resembled a figure stepped out of his op-shop installation, her short hair spiky and going every way, as if she had been sleeping on the street or was Haine's fugitive figure emerged from the freeway undercroft. They kissed again, Toni's father's modest gouache on the wall behind them, their desire for each other was urgent now and he knew it had been decided and that they would not resist.

'Not here,' he said, taking her by the hand and leading her through the house and across the courtyard to the studio. They made love on the cane chaise; tenderly, slowly and passionately, like two people who knew something of which they had been forbidden to speak.

Afterwards they stood hand-in-hand in front of his painting of *The Other Family*. They looked at the monumental group and the solitary naked figure of the man, and they wondered what it was that had brought them to this point in their lives. And they each knew that no one else would ever understand this moment as they understood it themselves.

She broke the silence. 'Are you afraid?'

'Yes.'

'Hold me again,' she said. 'Just for a little while.'

He took her in his arms and she rested against him. From the top of the plan press the portrait of his mother gazed back at him across the studio.

.

She drove fast, zig-zagging in and out of the traffic. They might have been fugitives fleeing the scene of a crime. At a set of traffic lights she turned to him, her eyes seeking his. 'I reached the point where I hated your picture,' she said. 'I believed I wasn't going to be able to do it.'

He said, 'You've got a green light.'

She drove on.

He listened to her talking and said nothing. Her cheeks were pale, her lips dry and without lipstick, fatigue lines etched around her mouth, and those familiar purple shadows under her eyes. She looked older than her years and he felt a rush of tenderness for her; the hours he had spent since that day on the island, looking and looking at her, and now to have been surprised by her in this way! Suddenly everything had changed.

'You might hate me when you see what I've done to your picture,' she said.

'I won't hate you.'

'God, I just want to cry or laugh!' she said. 'How can we be so sane about it? What have we done, Toni?'

She pulled up outside the Richmond house and switched off the motor. She did not get out of the car but sat behind the wheel looking down the street. After a moment she turned to him and she leaned and kissed him on the mouth.

Did he feel he had betrayed Teresa? He was not sure. Surely it had been something beyond those ordinary things, betrayal and trust, something belonging to another realm, to another dimension altogether. Or had it been merely betrayal after all? Was this what betrayal was, something sudden, something disturbing and extreme that was not planned, but which interrupted one's life, one's reality violently set aside, so that the extraordinary might take place? He said, 'Let's go and look at the picture.' He saw then how vulnerable she was, how vulnerable perhaps to everything; to life, to growing old, to dying, to being forgotten; touched by an instant of brilliant excitement then darkness and silence for ever. Vulnerable to all that. He saw it in her eyes and he felt her solitariness and her fear. He reached and touched her wet cheek tenderly.

She walked ahead of him through the rooms of the house to the studio.

Theo was sitting with his back to them on the hard-backed chair facing *The Schwartz Family*, which was mounted on the easel. Misty was sitting on the floor beside his chair. Theo turned and watched them cross the floor towards him, a knowing smile gathering in his eyes. 'You two!' he said. 'You look as if you've walked ashore from a shipwreck.' He laughed and waved an unsteady hand at the painting.

Toni felt a touch of excitement to see his painting. He said hello to Theo and took the hand he offered, and he and Marina stood beside him and looked at the painting.

The three pale unsmiling figures and the silver cat seated at the round table gazed mutely back at them; as if they were blind and had seen only the past and could see nothing beyond their own brief day. The features of the three figures were strangely unshadowed now, awaiting completion, figures waiting for a word of explanation: *Why are we here?* It surprised him to see how they shared something with the featureless figures of his installations. They were his all right, there was no doubting it. The source of their illumination puzzling and interior and belonging to the past. The silver-haired cat, detached, observant and knowing, by Theo's hand—the cat-headed deity for whom no mystery was too deep. Oriel had been right, at least about that. He had got the cat.

Behind the seated figures at the round table a diminishing perspective of leafless European trees now. A powerful quality of innocence and of dream and of something private and undisclosed in the heavy perspective of trees in the windless air; an enormous stillness imposed on the three figures by the great trees; trees that were not trees but were dreams of other worlds. The ghostly remainder of Robert's naked man adrift had gone, sunk too deep under Marina's medium to be visible any longer. But there all the same. He knew it. An invisible truth, returned to the unconscious. Through the intricate latticework of the leafless branches her parents' enormous red-brick house, Plovers. And rising above the house and above the trees, commanding the painting's visible weight as if it were the sky, the great dark bulk of Mount Macedon, the magic mountain of Marina's innocent childhood, her solitary years, her fears and her dreams and, at last, her loss of belief. Why did he think this? What made him see such an encompassing sadness in her painting of her old home? Did Theo see it? Did Robert see it?

'Well, what do you say, Prochownik?' Theo laughed, and turned and looked up at Toni.

Marina waited beside him.

So Andy had passed the word around. They all knew now. 'It's wonderful,' he said. 'It's beautiful. I love it.'

Marina touched his fingers and looked at him and she said nothing.

He turned to her. 'I love it.'

Theo said hoarsely, 'The shipwrecked fools!' He reached and dragged at Toni's arm. 'Help me get to bed, Toni. I was hoping to stay up and drink coffee with you and do some talking. But I can't. I expected you sooner.' He laughed. 'Now I'm running out of steam. Help me up.'

In Theo's bedroom Toni helped the stricken man into his bed. The warm, pungent smell of liniment rising from his open gown, a glimpse of scarlet ulcers, like sword wounds in his chest and abdomen. A rigidity in Theo's smile, a freezing of his expression and a clenching of the muscles of his face and neck and shoulders; an effect of the drugs he was taking to dampen the explosive firing of his nerves. When Toni had made him comfortable, Theo reached and took his hand and smiled up at him. There was a youthfulness in his smile, a desire to share something yet of the beauty and the madness; a smile in which there was the acceptance of his own departure from life, looking at Toni from that place of the sick and the dying, which is not the place where the living spend their days.

'I've got a lot to tell you,' Toni said.

Theo said, 'I knew it that day she brought you into the house and introduced you. There's nothing we can do. These things! We'll talk soon. There's no hurry.' He closed his eyes and relinquished Toni's hand. He was in some distress. He called as Toni was at the door, 'We always confuse life and art in the end. It can't be helped.' He laughed, his dry, ironic cough of a laugh, as if something was caught in his throat. He waved Toni away.

.

They sat across from each other at a table in the window of the Red Hat café and she nursed her coffee and watched him. 'It's wonderful,' she said quietly and waited for him, and when he didn't speak she said, 'What will you do if Teresa finds out?'

He didn't want to talk about realities with her. 'Theo's right,' he said. 'This was with us from day one. From the day you rang and then I came over for lunch and you two asked me to join you in the island show. I wasn't sure then, but when we went to the island, after that I was sure.'

'I was too.'

'I didn't plan it.'

'I know. Neither did I.'

'I didn't *expect* it would ever happen.'

'I hoped it would happen. Now I'm glad it has happened.'

'Sometimes we can know too much about another person. We become too familiar with someone and it prevents us from seeing them properly.'

'I don't think we can ever really know anyone,' she said and looked past him out the window at the busy street. 'Even ourselves. I don't think we should expect to. Most of all not ourselves.'

She was watching the people going by in the street, the flash and the colour of the traffic reflected in her eyes, the light playing across her features. He did not want to think about the real world with her. He wanted their friendship to be encompassed by the world of their art. There it would be safe. He did not want to admit it into the everyday. Theo was right, art was not life. How to keep them apart? Was there a severe and monkish discipline for it? A superhuman detachment? He thought of Theo's torment, the frozen rigidity of his gaze, the terrible grip of his muscles, a man no longer able to be himself.

She said, 'I don't believe we really want to understand other people, or ourselves. Not really. We say we do, but we like to be among strangers.' She looked out the window. 'To be anonymous is what we most want, not to be known. Secretly we want to be solitary. We can't stand having people know who we are. It terrifies us.' She turned from contemplating the street. 'I love feeling lost and alone in the city. The city is our natural place. We need it. I fear more than anything being lost and alone in the bush. Out there we're confronted with ourselves. In the bush there's no escape from who we are or from each other. We pretend to love the wilderness, but we hate the thought of it, really.' She fell silent, then after a moment she said, 'When I couldn't work out what to do with your picture I resurrected all my old work. Except for that Macedon sketchbook I found for you, I hadn't looked at any of my old drawings for years. I got out all my folders and spread everything over the floor of the studio. And there it was. It was obvious. You were right. It was trees. Trees and the mountain! Plovers. Home. Me and my work! I'd forgotten how much I'd done on my own before I met Robert. My old work covered half the floor of the studio. Theo came and looked at it. He encouraged me. He helped me to see what I had to do.'

'Theo's been our secret collaborator,' he said, and smiled.

'Yes, he has. The idea of doing a new background paralysed me for days. I thought I was solving *your* problem for you, and I was scared to touch the picture in case I ruined it. Then when we saw my old work spread out on the floor, Theo told me not to paint a background for you, but to paint one for myself. Now your wonderful picture is like our day on the island. Other people will see one thing, but we'll know it's really our special secret.' She reached and took his hand. 'I feel better, suddenly. With some people we're able to be more ourselves than we are with others. That's just the way it is, isn't it? There's no point trying to understand this.' She sat looking at him. 'You're worrying about Teresa now, aren't you?'

'She'll be wondering where I am.'

'I'll give you a lift. What will you do?'

'I may just tell her and get it over with. I'm a hopeless liar. I hate deceit. I can't carry it off.' The idea of Teresa's reaction appalled him. It was what she had feared and predicted. She would believe he had been lying to her all along. Her confidence in him would be shattered forever. Things would never be the same between them. 'I envy Theo in a way,' he said with a laugh. 'He seems to have earned the right to belong to his own world.'

'Robert and his mother paid the price for Theo's freedom.'

'Theo has what I've always thought of as an artist's freedom. It's a pity someone has to pay.'

'He's horribly lonely. I don't think he really wanted to go on living after Marguerite died. How utterly unpredictable these things are. He's always talking about you in front of Robert. It's not fair to Robert. He's incredibly insensitive with Robert. He behaves as if it were somehow Robert's fault that he left them when Robert was a little boy. He's tough and unforgiving with his own son and with you he's charming. Robert is forgiving. He's generous. Despite everything Theo has done, he loves him and excuses him. He says, *Dad's an artist*, as if that explains everything. People used to believe it was their duty to understand these things, now no one bothers anymore.'

They drove across town in silence. When they got to the corner of his street he asked her to let him out. 'Drop me here.'

'You're sure?'

'It's fine here.'

She pulled in to the kerb and leaned across and they kissed. 'Take care. Ring me.' Her hand on his arm. 'Remember, whatever happens, you matter to me enormously.'

He got out of the car and stood watching her drive away. *You matter to me enormously . . .* He turned into his street. Teresa's Honda was parked outside the house. If he really were a coward, he would go around by the lane and sneak into the studio by the back door. He walked down the road towards the red Honda.

seventeen

As he walked towards Teresa's car he noticed for the first time, as if it were something that had suddenly become important to him, that each of the tiny front gardens in the row of uniform weatherboard houses was planted differently from its neighbour. A miniature parterre of rose bushes was followed by a solitary gum tree, then came an arrangement of neatly clipped English box hedges, which was followed by a cluster of old-fashioned sweet peas growing on chicken wire. It had never occurred to him before that these gardens so strongly advertised the private dreams of the owners of the houses to which they belonged. Were these people oblivious to the existence of each other, or were they eager not to be influenced by the tastes of their neighbours, but determined to cling to a private idea of themselves and their property that, in the grandeur of its associations, far outstripped the modest reality?

He wondered if he had ever really been a true citizen of this place. The great black circles of dried sunflower blooms in a neglected garden swayed towards him in the hot wind and seemed to menace the air. The long night feverishly working on his figure in *The Other Family* and the vertiginous unreality of his day with Marina had left him spent. He calculated that he had not slept for thirty-six hours. He did not know what to think any longer, and he felt himself to be dangerously exposed to any random or bizarre idea that might take hold of him and influence his behaviour. He was exhausted.

He turned in at the front gate and saw, with a rush of nostalgia, the low hedge of lavender bushes on either side of the path that Teresa had planted shortly after they arrived. This house to which they had brought Nada home from the hospital two days after she was born, swept up then in the excitement of being parents and becoming a family. He stood on the path staring at the front door. How could he still call this place his home or ever again take for granted Teresa's love and support? He felt like a man who had been stripped of his liberty, and for the first time he knew something of what it must have been like for his brother, Roy, when he was removed from the family and sent to prison. How could he ever again speak confidently to Teresa? The whispered intimacies and private confessions they shared in bed at night before they went to sleep! His *wife*! As soon as he walked through that door Teresa would look into his eyes and she would know, and he would see the pain and the anger wash through her.

He would be the one to bring Teresa's reality down and to destroy it. He felt sick with the inevitability of it. And yet, in a secret place within himself that he could imagine disclosing to no one, he believed that what he had done possessed its own truth and its own necessity. He would admit his guilt to Teresa and would accept the consequences, no matter what they were, but secretly he would not relinquish his belief in the necessity of his friendship with Marina to himself as an artist. If only there were a way to make Teresa see the situation as he saw it himself! To recount to her calmly, and in all its detail, the true story of how events had unfolded for him from the moment of Marina's telephone call that day when he was posing for Nada. Show her how these events had not been part of a conscious plan but had surprised him and had lifted him onto a wave of energy and confidence that had made the renewal of his work possible. He did not feel any more guilty for what he had done than Roy must have felt for defending their father from his persistent tormentor that day. Guilt, after all, was not concerned with consequences but with intentions.

He stepped on to the verandah. Teresa was not going to forgive him. He knew that. He had betrayed her, and for Teresa that would be the end of it. He thought of how his father had created art as a haven, had refused the hazards of the human likeness and of public reputation, and had searched within the familiar objects of their lives for a morality that had sustained himself and his family; a morality that sustained Toni even now, and which had in it something that was essential to his belief in himself as a man and as an artist. That would always be the case. He would always know himself through his father's vision of art. And perhaps what Marina had said in the Red Hat was true, and there was no point in trying to explain or to understand such things. He opened the front door and stepped into the passage.

Nada ran towards him from the living area calling excitedly, 'Daddy! Daddy! We've been waiting for you!'

Teresa stood at the far end of the passage silhouetted against the light from the courtyard windows. He lifted Nada into his arms and hugged her to him.

She struggled to loosen his grip. 'Uncle Andy sold your pictures, Daddy!' she cried breathlessly. 'He said we're going to be rich!' She chanted, 'We're going to be rich! We're going to be rich!'

Teresa came up and she laughed and put her arm through his. 'There's a message for you from Andy. Listen to it while I open the champagne. We've been waiting for you.' She turned and kissed him, cupping her hand to the back of his head and pressing her lips firmly against his mouth. 'God, I love you, Toni Powlett!'

'We're going to have a party!' Nada cried, forcing her head between them.

In the kitchen he held Nada in his arms and the three of them listened in silence to Andy's message, Teresa watching him, the bottle of champagne in her hand, her eyes smiling, her pleasure for him. Andy's voice, loud and confident, coming into the kitchen. *I'm in Sydney, mate. They love your stuff up here. Geoffrey bought* Marina Golding Asleep on the Island. *You like the title? He's showing it to his friends. It's his latest coup. I knew that was the picture for Geoffrey. Five thousand. Okay? How do you like that? He's set the starting price for you.* Theo Schwartz Reading Paul Klee's Diaries *went for three and a half. Don't worry, that's a terrific price for an old man reading a book. We'll put twenty-five on* The Schwartz Family. *We'll test them. I think they're ready to get serious. How's that other big one coming along? I've told them up here you're on a roll. Sydney's got the hots for you, mate. You can tell Terry you guys are going to be rich. Just keep painting, buddy!*

Andy talked until the machine ran out of tape.

Teresa handed him a glass of champagne. 'It's happened, darling!' She touched his glass with hers, watching for his reaction.

Nada reached for his glass and he let her have a sip. 'I told Andy those pictures weren't for sale yet.'

'You know Andy. With Andy everything's for sale. He'd just think you were trying to push up the price saying a thing like that.'

'I wouldn't do that.'

'I know you wouldn't do it.' She gazed steadily at him, measuring his response. 'Isn't it fantastic, though? I knew you'd do it. I knew from the minute I saw you at Andy's party that you were the only real artist in the place. Don't you feel like yelling and dancing? Do you really think he'll get twenty-five thousand for that picture? Has Marina done a background for

it? Has she still got it? You won't have to give her half will you?
How much will Andy's commission be?'

'I don't know.'

'Didn't you ask him?'

'Andy will look after us. I don't need to ask him.'

'You'll have to start being businesslike about it. There's no
point giving money away.' She refilled their glasses.

He carried Nada over to the couch and sat and rested his
head against the back of the cushion. He closed his eyes.

Teresa brought the bottle over and sat close up beside him,
studying him. 'You look worn out. There's nothing the matter,
is there? You're happy, aren't you? You're selling your pictures.
It's happening at last. You're a real artist. You're being who
you've always wanted to be. This is what you've worked for.
It's the beginning, isn't it?' She reached for Nada and took
her from him. 'Let Daddy have a rest for a minute, darling.
Don't give her too much of that, it'll make her sick. We'll be
able to repay Dad. God, you've got no idea how good this
makes me feel. Can I ring Mum and tell her yet? I can't wait
to hear their reaction.'

They drank the wine and Teresa talked about the money
they were going to make and what they would do with it.

He lay back against the couch, struggling against the
whirling in his head, struggling to keep his eyes open.

Later he read *Mog's Mumps* to Nada and fell asleep beside her
on the bed. His sleep was deep, soundless, dreamless; a sleep

of exhaustion. He woke with Nada's arm over his neck. They were both sweating; her head thrown back and her mouth open, dark strands of hair sticking to her forehead, the sweet, intimate smell of her child's breath in his face. He held her close, then eased himself free of her encircling arm. He got up and straightened her on the bed and stood looking down at her ... The telephone began to ring. He went down the passage to the kitchen. The clock on the refrigerator showed two a.m. He picked up the telephone. 'Hello,' he said cautiously. He already had the feeling it was going to be Robert.

Robert said, 'I'm sorry to wake you, Toni.'

'I wasn't asleep.'

'Dad's had a stroke. We're at the Alfred. I thought you'd want to know at once.'

'Is he going to be all right?'

There was a short silence. Toni could hear voices and noises in the background, an echoing space, a siren wailing. Robert said, 'No. I don't think they expect him to survive the night.'

That word, *Dad*! 'I'll come over,' Toni said.

Teresa came into the kitchen and walked across to put her hand on his arm. She whispered, 'Who is it?'

'There's no need for you to come over,' Robert said. 'There's nothing we can do. He's not aware of us.'

He held the phone away. 'It's Robert. His dad's had a stroke.' He put his mouth to the phone again. 'I'm coming over. I'm sorry, Robert. I'm terribly sorry.'

'You were fond of him. He thought a lot of you. He was glad of your friendship.'

'I meant, I'm sorry for you.'

'Thanks. I know you did.'

'I'll see you in half an hour.'

Robert said, 'We're not in intensive care. Come to casualty. They're not giving him any treatment. They're just making sure he's comfortable.'

Teresa went to the front door with him. 'I came in to look at you,' she said and she kissed him. 'I couldn't bear to wake you. You both looked so beautiful sleeping in each other's arms.' She kissed him again. 'Drive carefully!' It might have been that the sudden grip of death on Theo had rendered them all vulnerable.

As he pulled out from the kerb he turned and waved. She lifted her hand.

He drove along the empty streets of the city and thought of Theo asking him not to tell Robert his real reason for coming back; *I came back because I was hoping to distract myself . . . You won't tell Robert, will you?*

The hospital was a blaze of light and activity, a hub of life and death in the sleeping city. He found Robert and Marina in a curtained cubicle in the casualty department. Robert stepped up and embraced him, taking Toni by surprise and holding him strongly in his arms. He began to cry.

Toni put his hand to the back of Robert's head and held him against his shoulder.

273

Robert yielded to his friend's embrace for a moment, then he drew in a big breath and stepped away. 'Sorry!' he said, and he laughed; he was an emotional, almost boyish version of himself, suddenly. He reached into his pocket and pulled out a handkerchief and blew his nose. He looked at Toni and grinned. 'I don't know why, but seeing you made me cry. I saw you come through that curtain and it caught me in the throat.'

'I can have that effect on people.' He thought Robert seemed younger and lighter with his grief, almost as if he had shrugged off a burdensome inhibition.

They laughed and both reached at the same instant and touched each other's fingers, then let their hands fall away, something of pleasure, shyness, surprise and embarrassment at this sudden intimacy, the unaccustomed openness of their emotion with each other.

Robert said, 'You walked in just then and I remembered the way it used to be with us. The old days. You know? The way it was for us? I've got to ease up.' He stood looking at his father lying in the bed, tubes and drip lines and pulse meters coming out of him.

Marina came up and she and Toni held each other lightly, their eyes meeting, then they stepped apart.

Theo lay on his side with his mouth open, a clear plastic tube going down the black hole of his throat, an oxygen mask clamped over his nose with an obscene pink garter around the back of his head, his wispy hair waving back and forth in the cold stream of the airconditioning. Theo's eyes were closed and his skin was the colour of stone, one skinny arm out of the covers, a drip insert coming out of the back of his hand. Except for the noise of his breathing he looked dead.

Robert stood at his shoulder. 'We might go and get a coffee. You want a few minutes alone with him?' He looked at Toni, giving him an awkward sideways grin. 'You might like to say goodbye.' He shrugged and turned quickly and walked across to where Marina was waiting for him, and they went out through the curtain.

Toni took Theo's hand and held it. The hand was cold and still. No sign of the jumping nerves. 'I'm sorry to see you go, Theo.' But his voice sounded insincere and he was self-conscious with it, as if he were acting the role of saying goodbye to a dying friend. It was easier to speak his thoughts silently. But what if Theo could still hear? As if in response to this thought, Theo gave a shudder and his hand closed around Toni's fingers. For a brief second it was unnerving, as if Theo were taking hold of him, then Toni realised it was probably a final contraction of the nerves, a lifetime of nervous reactions echoed in this last mockery of friendship's clasp. He thought of saying something about Theo rejoining his Marguerite, but the thought was too sentimental to utter. Remembering Theo telling him old men talk too much not because they fear to die, but because they hate knowing their experiences and their knowledge are going to die with them, the fruits of their struggles going for nothing. He leaned and touched his lips to Theo's forehead. The skin was cold and slightly damp. He straightened. Theo's blatant borrowing, his bold plagiarism of the French printmakers, an example that had broken a deadlock in him and made him see that he had to become the familiar of his own nakedness if he were to be an authentic painter of the human likeness. He turned away and went in search of Robert and Marina and a coffee.

eighteen

Theo died the following night. The funeral was held on a day of grass fires and hot winds from the desert, a final vicious blast of summer before the tempering of the seasons. As he stood with Robert and Marina in the chapel at the crematorium, the heat storm seemed to Toni an unfitting send off for Theo, whom he had thought of as having been a Central European by election, and as having shared something of the cool, grey, indeterminate tones of that mythical ancestral place with his own father, each of them an artist and an exile from his native country for most of a lifetime.

During the first week or so following Theo's funeral an unreal stillness settled over his work and over his life with Teresa and Nada. He tried working during the day again and sleeping with Teresa at night in their bed, for this seemed to him a necessary concession to Teresa's cherished normality.

Nothing difficult was discussed. It seemed events had sobered them, and they had both eased back on their demands and expectations. Robert telephoned one evening while they were watching a show on the television and offered to give Toni his father's collection of sketchbooks. 'He wanted you to have them,' Robert said. But Toni could not accept them. Robert's gesture was far too generous. And, anyway, Theo had cherished hopes for his work that had reached beyond the grave, and Toni did not want to be the gatekeeper of the dead man's dreams.

Each weekday morning at seven forty-five he kissed Teresa and Nada goodbye at the front door and watched them drive off to the kindergarten and the agency. After they had gone he made coffee and went down to the studio. But his work did not advance and he failed repeatedly to place the figure of Marina convincingly in *The Other Family*. He had lost touch with the picture. Without Marina the project had stalled, and he began to realise that he was not going to have three major works finished in time for the island show. In frustration he telephoned Andy and asked him to borrow back his painting of Marina asleep on the island from Haine. 'That picture was my main reference and I need to look at it.' But Haine had gone to New York and Andy was unable to get hold of the painting. Toni needed more life studies of Marina, but he did not feel at liberty to call her and ask her to sit for him. It was a baffling situation, and he began to resent the compromise that it represented for him. The storm had not broken over his head and destroyed him and his family; but the manner of his survival scarcely seemed to have made the escape worthwhile.

·

He stepped away from the canvas and stood looking with disgust at the failed figure of Marina. He didn't have the will to scrape the image back yet again and he left the painting and stood at the window. The blackbird was back, taking a bath in the fountain. The faint hum of the city out there. He turned away from the window. In the studio everything had come to a standstill for him. He picked up a book at random from the pile by the door and took it over to the chaise. *I came to Warley on a wet September morning with the sky the grey of Guiseley sandstone. I was alone in the compartment. I remember saying to myself: 'No more zombies, Joe, no more zombies.'* He had soon developed a loathing for the book and its principal character, the miserable Joe Lampton, but he kept reading as a kind of punishment for not having the courage to face up to *The Other Family*. His own craven attitude was mirrored in the weak personality of the book's hero, and his loathing for the man was, he knew, partly self-loathing. He could not imagine his father enjoying such a book, but the old Penguin paperback was well-thumbed and had obviously been read a number of times. He had been reading for an hour or more, slumped miserably on the chaise resenting the power of the story to keep him there, when he heard a car pull up in the lane and the slamming of its doors. He tossed the book aside and got up and went over and opened the back door of the studio. Marina was straightening from the back of her car. She turned, a carton hugged to her chest.

'I brought Theo's notebooks,' she said. 'Robert insists you take them.'

They stood looking at each other.

She looked down helplessly into the carton in her arms. 'There are thirty of them. One for each year. I haven't counted them.' She looked up. 'Please, Toni! Don't look at me like that! Where shall I put these?'

He stepped up to her and took the carton from her and they went into the studio and she closed the door. The black notebooks each had a year blind-stamped on its spine. 'They belong to Robert,' he said. 'I can't take them.' He could smell the familiar perfume of her.

'You're working,' she said, and she walked across and stood in front of *The Other Family*. 'You and Robert can sort out the notebooks. He's not going to take them back.'

He set down the carton. 'You and I are not finished with this yet.'

'The male figure is wonderful,' she said. 'It's even stronger than I remember it.' She did not mention the new figure of the solitary woman.

'I was working with the right information for that one.' He watched her turn from the painting and move restlessly about the studio, as if she were afraid of being still or of standing too close to him. She went over to the window and lifted the sheet and looked across at the house. He picked up his sketching block and began making a rapid drawing of her.

She turned from the window and watched him. 'It's no good,' she said. 'I have to go.'

'Do you want to see the notebook Theo gave me?' He gestured towards the plan press. 'It's there. Have a look at it before you go.'

She walked over and picked up Theo's book and stood leafing through it, making little exclamations of amusement.

He drew quickly, finishing one sketch then doing another, hungrily gathering as much information as he could. 'So what do you think?'

She said, 'It's very Theo.'

'Not exactly a memoir for his son of his last days.'

She said gently, 'I do miss him.'

'So do I.' He waved his stub of charcoal at *The Other Family*. 'He gave me the key to that figure.'

'Robert seems to have been liberated by his father's death,' she said. 'It's as if it's all been resolved for him, and now he can get on with his life without having to deal with it any more. He seems happier.' She looked across at Toni. 'How do you mean, Theo gave you the key to it?'

'I got down to the reality of it with Theo's stuff. That painting there against the press, it's me with Theo's head. It's where I got the male figure for *The Other Family* from. The idea was straight out of his youthful satyr with his own head. A straight lift. Theo's idea, not mine. It wasn't until I began

to draw myself naked that I understood what I was doing.'
He stopped drawing. She was bending down, examining the
picture. 'Pose for me naked,' he said.

She turned and looked at him over her shoulder. 'I don't
think I should.'

'Without you this picture's nothing. Look at it! I've scraped
you back fifty times. It's hopeless. I can't *see* you! I don't *know*
you! Without you it's never going to be finished. This whole
thing is still your portrait. *The Marina Suite!* Remember?'

She stood up and glanced towards the window. 'What about
Teresa?'

'She's at the office.'

'I probably shouldn't have come,' she said. She stood looking
at him uncertainly. 'I wanted to see you.'

'Pose for me,' he said. 'Stand there by the window against
the light. Just for a few minutes.' He began to draw her. 'If
you don't pose for me, I'm not going to be ready for the
island show.'

'That's blackmail.'

'It's the truth.'

'Half an hour, then,' she said.

'Half an hour.'

'Turn away while I get undressed.'

'No. I need to see you moving. I need to see everything.'

She sighed and drew her T-shirt over her head and took
her jeans and underwear off, placing the clothes on the pile
of his father's books. She stood naked against the light, looking

at him, her arms hanging awkwardly at her sides. 'I feel ridiculous standing here like this in front of you. Suppose Teresa comes home and sees me.'

'She'll kill us both.' He was surprised and touched to see how old she looked in the hard light, without make-up or her clothes. 'You're beautiful.' He drew rapidly.

'Don't say that. Please! I know I'm not beautiful. You don't need to say things like that to me.'

'You are beautiful to me,' he said seriously.

'You are to me, too.'

They both laughed helplessly.

'What a ridiculous conversation to be having,' she said.

'Stay like that! Just the way you are. Your outline's disappearing into the light on your right side and it's sharp and beautifully cut on your left side.' A minute later he said, 'You can move if you want to. Turn around. Sit down. Whatever. I'll tell you when to hold it.'

Suddenly they were working.

She stayed an hour and when she was leaving he went out to the car with her. 'Will you come again tomorrow? Will Robert mind?'

'No, of course he won't mind.' She smiled. 'That was hell.'

'It was brilliant. It's like being let out of prison to be working again.' He leaned down to the car window and they kissed, and she touched his hand quickly. He stood and watched her drive away, waiting until she turned at the end of the lane, then he went back inside. He lifted *The Other Family* down from the easel and picked up a new canvas, 74 x 100 cm. He set it on the horizontal and prepared a medium. He drew straight onto the canvas with the medium. He could see the finished work: Marina lying naked on her stomach on the cane chaise, her forearms resting on cushions, her chin on her hands; a woman alone in the privacy of her own thoughts. Not a girl. Not a young woman. Not a pale odalisque to tease the eye of the voyeur, but an older woman, naked and alone; an artist, vulnerable and preoccupied with the complexities of her own creativity and anxieties, the uncertainties of her life. It was the painting he had visualised that day at the auction rooms when he had first seen the cane chaise. It had surprised him. Like an unexpected visitor.

He worked quickly, with the energy of having abandoned caution.

While she had been posing for him she had told him, 'I used to think that one day I'd go out on my own with Robert's blessing. It was an event that stood in the future of our lives. My eventual independence always seemed to have been implied in his recognition of my work when I was his student. We both believed it would happen one day.' She had fallen silent then, and when he had asked her why she had never gone out on her own, she said, 'Eventually we just stopped talking about it and I began to see that my work was with him. That my work was *our* work.'

He decided to title his new picture *Nymphe*, as a homage to Theo. He was working again and didn't care about anything else. There was, he suspected, something of Theo's selfish freedom in his attitude now. He wasn't altogether comfortable with this, but perhaps it was necessary. He could not work cautiously. That was not the way he could do it. Caution blocked his energies. He did not inspect Theo's books. One was enough. When he finished work for the day, he pushed the carton into a corner and covered it with a cloth.

nineteen

For the rest of that week Marina came to the studio each afternoon and posed naked on the chaise. After they had finished work they went up to the house and he made coffee. He did not let her see the new painting but covered it with a drop sheet after each session. He was cleaning his hands on a rag and she was already dressed and sitting on the edge of the chaise fastening her sandal.

She smiled. 'You look happy.'

'I'll finish it tomorrow.'

'Then you won't need me to pose for you again? Is that it?'

'That's it.'

'Our last session then?' She sat looking at him. 'It's a little sad. What about the figure for *The Other Family*?'

'I've got the information I need for it now. I'll do it when I'm alone. I don't think I'd be able to do it with you here.'

'I'd get in the way of the fiction?'

'Something like that.'

'What will you do with this one? You can hardly put it in the show.'

He had not decided what he would do with the new painting. He doubted if he would ever be able to persuade Teresa of its innocence. He had not told her that Marina had been posing for him naked. He thought, however, that she might have guessed. It had just seemed too difficult a subject to be direct about. The evasion was all part of their new pact of silence. It made for enormous tensions between them and he hated it. But there didn't seem to be an alternative. It would be over soon and then there would be no need for it. Perhaps he would remove the canvas from its stretcher when it was dry and put it away, lay it on its face in the bottom drawer of his plan press and conceal it under a pile of drawings, let it lie in the dark for years like his father's pictures, until it no longer possessed the power to arouse jealousies and dangerous emotions and could be viewed for what it was, just another piece of art. He thought how much simpler it would have been if, instead of hazarding the human likeness, he had become a painter of still lifes like his father.

'I can't wait to see it,' Marina said. She got off the chaise and looked around the studio. 'I'll always remember these days working together. It's been wonderful.' She fell silent. 'Your dad's old suit, Nada's drawing, all your drawings and your private things. It's very precious to me.' She looked at him. 'We've really got to know each other at last, haven't we?'

He looked up from cleaning his brushes. 'Time for coffee before you go?'

'It had better be quick. I should have gone ages ago.'

They went up to the house and he made coffee. She sat at the table leafing through one of Teresa's magazines, not reading the magazine but flipping the pages, glancing at the ads for perfume, the photographs of celebrities partying.

He set a mug on the table by her hand.

She pushed the magazine aside, her action reminding him of the way she had pushed the book aside in the Red Hat.

She smiled, regretful. 'I love you,' she said simply. 'I just wanted to say it. It seems important to have actually said it.'

He looked at her. In a few minutes she would be gone, and the chair she was sitting in would be the chair she had sat in at this moment—how to capture the strange, beautiful, surprising, dangerous unreality of such a moment? Hold a person preciously within that moment against the rush of time? Hold oneself within the image of the other? He reached and touched her fingers where they lay touching the magazine. His father telling him, *The artist is the only one to ever know how great his failure is. Other people see only what he achieves. Not what he has attempted.* 'Before you went to Sydney you used to stand back and watch us,' he said.

'Did I?'

'I didn't see you in those days, except in that drawing I did of you at Plovers. I saw you then, just at that moment, and I was caught up in you lying there in the shadows for a few hours that day. It was a secret truth for me, that drawing. But then I forgot it. When you came back from Sydney it was as if you'd stepped into the light and wanted to be seen. And then I began to remember you and to see you for the first time.'

'I wanted you to see me.'

He sat considering what she had said. 'Why?'

She shrugged. 'Does it matter? Do we need to understand these things? I don't know why. I just *felt* it. I wanted you to see me.'

'You seduced me that day I came over to Richmond for lunch.'

She laughed.

'You stood beside *Chaos Rules*. And the way you stood insisted I look at you.'

She got up. 'I'd better be going.'

He stood beside her, conscious suddenly that this was the moment when it was to come to an end. They would go on being friends, of course, but it would never again be as it was at this moment, this place they had made of their own and the precious sharing of the work.

'Don't say anything, please!' she said. She put her arms around him and kissed him firmly on the mouth.

He held her, his eyes closed, the pressure of her belly against him, her lips. Now he could *see* her. He knew he would get the figure of the woman for his picture . . .

There was the sound of the front door slamming. The crash of the front door was followed by the rapid click-clack of Teresa's heels as she hurried down the passage towards them.

Marina and Toni pulled away from each other, shocked and off balance.

Teresa stood in the doorway looking at them, her briefcase in her hand, her black suit crushed at the button line where she had been sitting in the car, the white V of her blouse vivid against her tanned throat, her big dark eyes filled with fierceness and pain.

Marina said breathlessly, 'Teresa. Toni and I were just saying goodbye.'

Teresa stepped forward and dumped her bag on the settee, then she turned and looked at Marina as a killer might look at her victim, calculating how she will do it, where she will bury the knife.

'I'd better be going,' Marina said. Her voice husky, her words catching in her throat.

Toni came out of his frozen pose. 'Yeah. I'll see you out.'

Marina turned to him, her hand to his arm. 'No, it's okay!' Her hand on his arm the touch of an intimate.

Teresa registering the touch.

Marina hesitated as if she were going to say something more, but she said nothing and turned and left.

Through the window they watched her cross the courtyard. 'It wasn't the way it looked,' he said.

'Gina's picking up Nada,' Teresa said, as if he had not spoken. Her tone was unreal, calm, menacing, tight, a voice in an empty space. 'I thought, well it's Friday and we're going to be having some entertainment money soon, so I'll go home early and me and Toni will go out for a meal and a movie later.' She looked at him. 'I thought we might make love before we went out.' She spoke in a flat monotone, as if she were saying, *I thought we might burn the house down*. 'Like we used to, in the afternoon. Before Nada. That was my idea.' Her black eyes were filled with contempt.

A passing truck's engine brakes rattled the windows.

She said, 'So you've really been fucking her all this time, then?' She turned away. 'You disgust me!' She turned again and faced him, threatening suddenly. 'I'm not taking any more of this shit. I want my life back in one piece.'

'It wasn't the way it looked,' he repeated. 'As Marina said, we were just saying goodbye.' He stepped towards her and would have touched her, but she thrust him away with her forearm. She was a big woman and she was strong. She was proud of her Calabrian stock. She relied on it. Teresa knew who she was. She was *certain* of who she was and was calling upon those certainties now without even thinking about them. She was wife, mother, businesswoman, dutiful daughter, a beautiful woman, and a loyal friend. 'Just have the guts to tell me straight,' she said.

'Marina and I are not lovers.'

'I don't believe you.'

'What can I do then?'

'Convince me.'

'How, if you won't believe me?'

She brought both hands down hard on the table and shouted, 'Convince me! Fuck you! Fucking convince me!'

'I love you,' he said, shocked by her pent-up violence and her pain. 'You know that. We're a family. You're tired. We're both tired. We're strung out.'

She gave a sob and flailed wildly at the air. 'I'm not being convinced by this shit!'

'If I was cheating on you, you'd know. You know you would. You'd feel it in your guts.'

'I didn't ask you if you were cheating on me, I asked you if you were fucking that skinny old bitch.'

'No, I'm not.'

She wiped at the table with her palm. 'I'm in an important meeting with clients and suddenly I get this feeling. It's like I'm waking from a dream. I'm giving everything to the business and nothing to Toni, I think. That's what this pain I'm feeling is. I'm neglecting my husband. That's the real problem, not his art. His art's not the problem, it's me! This is what I suddenly think. I stop hearing what they're saying in the meeting and I'm thinking about this feeling that I should be more attentive to you, to us, to you and me. I never have any energy left at night after working in that place all day. So I close the meeting and I close the office and I call Gina to pick up Nada and I come home early. I choose my freedom. That's what I do. Just for once. I choose *us*, you and me against all the pressure, and to hell with the rest of it. Why am I stuck in this meeting with these people on a Friday afternoon when I could be home with my man? That's what I say to myself, and the answer is clear. In the car on the way home I'm thinking of us getting it together. I'm laughing out loud in the middle of the traffic at the thought of us making love in daylight the way we used to. When we couldn't help ourselves. Then we go out and we see a grown-up movie in the Europa as if we're singles and we have a drink and a meal and we hold hands and watch the people on the street.' She fell silent. 'I get home and you're fondling that slut. Why do I feel jealous if you're not fucking her?'

'I don't know. I wasn't fondling her. You tell me.' He realised as the words were coming out of his mouth that it was a mistake to have added, *You tell me*.

She closed her eyes. She was struggling to hold it together, her fingers gripping the table edge as if she was trying to snap a piece off. 'I just work. And then I work and then I fucking work some fucking more.' She opened her eyes. 'The business is going to shit. I've told you this? How much I owe Dad and the bank? When's Andy going to pay you the money he owes you? What are you doing about it?' She crumpled suddenly against the table. 'I can't take it anymore!'

She let him take her in his arms, unresponsive and limp. He cradled her head against his chest.

After a minute she lifted her head and stepped out of his embrace, pushing her hair back and wiping at her eyes. 'I'm not one of those women who can live with this kind of thing.' She pointed towards the kitchen bench. 'I'd grab one of those kitchen knives over there and drive it through you. I'd do it! We've never been down this road. We've never been anywhere near it. I couldn't bear it.'

He said steadily, 'Nothing improper is happening between me and Marina.'

'*Improper!*' she laughed wildly. 'I'm trying to stay reasonable. Why do I hate her? I hate her! You know that? You ever feel hate for someone? *Improper*, for Christ's sake! Do you even know what I'm talking about? I've never liked those people, her and that weird fucking husband of hers. But I never hated them. Now I hate her. You know what this is? Hating someone? It eats you up. It sucks your energy. It's all you think about. You lie awake at night with it. You see it everywhere. Everyone I look at reminds me of it. You get the feeling they know and you don't. I tell myself we don't hate without a reason to hate.' She looked at him. 'I want to kill her,' she said seriously. 'I think about killing her.' She was staring at him, a suffused intensity in her expression, as if she might suddenly let out a great howl of pain and hatred.

He could see her holding Marina to the floor, driving the big Victorinox carver into her back with powerful strokes of her arm. It was an image from a horror movie, but it was real to him; the sweat dripping off Teresa as she held Marina's neck in a death grip, straddling her with her big thighs and driving the knife into her body again and again. And Marina struggling, but pinned. No hope. Teresa too big and too strong for her. The violence of the image was so real he went dry in the mouth. 'It's true,' he said. 'You work day and night. We never see each other except when we're both tired.'

'The business will fold if I don't work day and night. So what am I supposed to do? What do you know about it? You're down there with her. Or over at Richmond. Or on that fucking island, for all I know. While I'm working day and fucking night and looking after Nada and doing everything.' She stood gazing at him. 'You've never done a portrait of me. You've never even done a decent drawing of me or your daughter.'

'I will. Soon. I intend to. I haven't been doing portraits since you and I met. I haven't *been* drawing. I've been doing installations till now. This project is something different. It's a new beginning. Now I'm painting again I'll be doing portraits of you and Nada. And I'll do your mum and dad and your brothers. I'll do everyone. There's a life's work in it. Roy and Mum and Andy and everyone. I'll do lots of portraits of you all. It's all in front of me. I know what I have to do. I'm ready for it.'

She may as well not have heard him. 'You've never once asked me to sit for you. I would have. You could have done a nude of me for our bedroom wall. You used to say my body was the ideal woman's body. Why did you never want to do a nude of me? Artists paint nudes of their wives and lovers. That's all those guys over at Andy's ever wanted to do. Every time they saw me, *Pose for me, Teresa!*'

'You always said you didn't want me to paint you in the nude.'

'I never said that.'

'You said it.'

A small, intense silence gathered between them.

'So, have you done a nude of her?' she asked.

He could think of no way of answering her question without igniting her fury.

Teresa took one look at him and made a strangled noise in her throat. She pushed him aside, flinging herself past him and going through the door, taking the courtyard in a couple of strides.

He caught up with her at the studio door.

She stood inside the door breathing hard. Beside her the shrouded naked portrait of Marina on the chaise. 'Where is it?'

'Where's what?'

'The painting you're doing of her?'

'I'm doing paintings of all of them.'

'Show me the ones you're doing of her.'

He eased himself between Teresa and the shrouded portrait and opened the top drawer of the plan press. He took out a sheaf of charcoal and pencil drawings and gouaches and put them on top of the press. There were several nude studies of Marina among them.

Teresa stood at the press looking through the drawings and small studies, pausing for a considerable time at each drawing or coloured wash of Marina's anatomy, going methodically through the pile. When she had finished she stood looking at a small gouache of Marina lying on the cane chaise. 'She's beautiful,' she said. 'She's got perfect skin. I've noticed her hands and her neck. She's smooth and slim. She's a smooth sexy woman. Wouldn't you say?'

'I wouldn't describe her like that.'

She gestured at him with the drawing. 'She lies there for you like this with nothing on?'

'We had models at art school doing this every day. It's normal. It's part of the job. With figure painting you have to work with the model naked before you can understand what you're doing. You have to know what's under the clothes or nothing ever looks right. It's part of the process. It's work.'

'Just the two of you down here? Does she go behind a screen to undress? Or does she slip her panties off with you watching her?'

'It's my work,' he pleaded. 'This is my studio. It's the way it is. It's the only way to see the vulnerability of people. You have to see them naked. All artists know that.'

Teresa said with a kind of resolute sadness, 'Whenever we're making love these days I feel you thinking about her.'

'That's not true.'

'It's what I feel.'

'Why don't we go out and have a meal? You're right. We need time together to sort this out.'

She sat abruptly on his painting stool and held her head in her hands. 'Jesus! I'm fucking exhausted with all this. I feel as if I'm going to scream or burst. There's a pipe in me that's going to explode if I don't let it out. I know if I let go and start screaming I won't be able to stop. I'm scared. I never felt like this before.' She lifted her head and looked up at him. 'I'm frightened. I'm living the nightmare of not being able to get yourself out of a small space that gets smaller the harder you struggle to get out of it. Everything seems to go calm and normal, then this stuff starts up again. I know what I saw when I came through the door just now. I know what I saw. I can't take this stuff any more. My head's full of it. I don't know what to believe anymore. I can't talk to you. I can't talk to Mum. Mum would have a fit. There's no one to talk to. I talked to your brother. I talked to Roy. I trust Roy, but I can't tell him what I'm thinking. You don't talk to me anymore. You talk to her. I hear you in my head talking to her day and night.'

He stood beside her, his hand to her shoulder. She was trembling.

'I don't know. I just don't know.' She stood up suddenly, pushing him aside, not violent now but determined, wiping at her eyes. 'Don't touch me. Please! I need a minute.' She stood looking around the studio. 'I don't want to overreact.' She registered the shrouded easel next to her and flipped up the drop sheet. She reached and pulled the sheet all the way off the painting and stood looking at it in silence. The image of Marina naked on the cane chaise, lying on her stomach.

A stillness settled over the studio.

The distant rushing of traffic along High Street like the sound of an industrial fluid injecting into a pressure vessel ...

Teresa gave a strangled cry and snatched the painting from the easel, driving it to the floor and dropping on it with one knee, as if she expected to punch through the canvas. But the expensive Belgian linen held and did not rip. There was the delicate aroma of cedar as the stretcher splintered, the sharp crack of the fine-grained wood opening up under Teresa's weight. But the close weave of the linen resisted her. Teresa was panting and letting out moans, wrestling with the canvas as if she had a grip on the flesh-and-blood Marina at last, making contact with her demon.

Toni grabbed at her from behind but she elbowed him in the eye. The blow was hard, vicious and without restraint. He cried out and backed off, his hands pressed to the pulse of agony in his eye. He moved in again more cautiously, ready this time. He was remembering the playground. He got her in a headlock, pushing her over and bending her double, tears streaming from his eye.

She snatched at his testicles, getting a grip and ripping at him through his pants.

He howled with pain and released her, stumbling back and going down.

She struggled to her feet and snatched the red lamp from its bracket and smashed down at him.

He saw her eyes above him through the gleaming bracket of the lamp, his vision blurred through the pain, the big lamp coming down. She made a low sound of deep physical effort as she smashed at him with the heavy red lamp base. He held his crotch with his left hand and fended off the blow of the lamp with his right arm. If the weighted lamp base hit him on the head he was a dead man. It struck his lifted forearm and he cried out, the pain flashing into his shoulder. Teresa lifted the lamp and brought it down again. It struck him on the shoulder this time and he yelled again. He knew, suddenly, that she was going to kill him. He saw, calmly, beyond this moment to the appalling aftermath, watching the red lamp arcing elegantly through the air above his head . . . At the third blow he managed to grab the lamp by its shank. He ripped it violently out of her hands and got one arm around her. She was strong but he was stronger now. He had found the strength of desperation; Roy telling him years ago, *Every fight is a fight for your life, Toni.* He wrestled her to the floor, ripping her arm up behind her back and forcing her face into the twisted image of naked Marina, the wet oil paint smearing onto her hair and her suit jacket, the close familiar stench of it in his nostrils. He heard himself laugh hysterically. His heart was thundering . . .

He held her, pinning her to the floor, her fierce eye staring up at him like a feral cat in a trap, not Teresa now but this other woman, her mouth open, drool coming out of the side of her lips, her mad eye looking up sideways at him, primed to go berserk the instant he let the pressure off, a run of sweat and snot oozing out of her nostrils, a pink streak of blood. He wondered, suddenly, if he had hit her. He realised he was crying. He would swear he had not hit her. He had never hit anyone. He was not a violent man. He was pinning his wife to the floor and twisting her arm behind her back like a mad rapist or a killer, but he knew he was not a violent man. His heart was racing out of control. He dragged in several gulps of air. When he spoke it was with the unfamiliar voice of a stranger. 'I'll let you up if you promise not to destroy my picture!' The insane comedy of it! *Let* her destroy the picture! The two of them like school kids wrestling on the floor. *I'll let you up if you promise* . . .

She did not answer.

She was not speaking to him.

'Promise!' he pleaded. It was the only language he knew.

Her eye wide and fierce, waiting her chance. If he let her up, she would make no mistake this time.

He could hear children's voices in the lane outside. Kids coming home from school rattling a stick along the tin of someone's shed and yelling to each other. Normality just beyond the wall . . .

The tension went out of Teresa. She closed her eyes and a shudder went through her.

He eased his grip.

She did not move.

He released her and got to his feet.

She lay on the floor on her side, like the victim of a road accident, her suit and blouse smeared with the viscous medium of the paint, her pantyhose torn. She was sucking great gulps of air and sobbing noisily.

He stood over her, appalled. He bent and touched her arm. 'Get up!' he urged her gently. 'Please, darling!' He tried to help her. She did not resist but she was a dead weight, and he could not raise her with his one good arm. He crouched beside her, a terrible fear and remorse in him. Minutes went by and her terrible sobbing gradually subsided. Eventually she struggled into a sitting position, wiping at her face with the sleeve of her jacket, then examining her sleeve, like a kid who had been in a fight in the schoolyard.

He stood waiting.

Slowly she got to her feet. Carefully she straightened her clothes, wiping uselessly at the paint stains on her skirt. She did not look at him.

He moved to help her and she turned on him viciously. 'I'll burn all this! All of it!'

He stood and watched her leave the studio.

She made her way across the courtyard. She was weeping. That was the word for it; a *weeping* woman. She went into the house and closed the door behind her. She did not look back. He was trembling, the pain throbbing deeply in his chest, his hand numb and tight. Why hadn't he just let her rip the painting apart? Why had he stepped in? He said aloud to the empty studio, 'No one's dead. No one is dead.' It seemed a forlorn consolation. He examined his arm, extending his fingers and grimacing, the numbness spreading, the pain burning in his shoulder and his chest. *Thank god Nada wasn't here to see us!* He sat on the stool, bent over, cradling his arm as if it were his wounded child.

twenty

He lifted a corner of the broken stretcher with his left hand, carefully unfolding the canvas then flattening it against the floor with his foot. In the peculiar stillness of the studio, he stood gazing down at the damaged painting. The paint was slewed and creamed across Marina's likeness, streaked across her features and twisted into a vivid carmine and yellow candy spiral down her back. The thing she was lying on no longer resembled a genteel chaise longue from leisurely afternoons of tea and toast in the conservatory at Plovers, but appeared to be some kind of shiny metallic contraption, a trolley, its purpose institutional and sinister. The woman on the trolley might have been eviscerated through the back, her organs brutally exposed to a hard clear light without cast shadows. It was an image from the internal narrative. Was she on the butcher's slab? Or in the mortuary? Perhaps interrogators had finished with her? Was that her story? Maybe they had thrown her out of a building, or had torn her apart in a frenzy of senseless cruelty and madness, driven by an obscure need for revenge. But as to who had done this to her, or what the motive for it may have been, the painting offered no clue.

Whatever the story of this twisted and broken woman, the viewer must be led to ask from what experience such a violated depiction of the human body had arisen. Her Raphael mouth was stretched into a thin wire grin, the expression in her eyes ironic and doleful, a last resistance of the human spirit lingering after the body had been broken. The leering naked woman was not a corpse, but gazed out of the painting with her one good eye, accusing and interrogating. His painting had become a Rorschach ink blot; an invitation to associate, to see whatever his unconscious predisposed him to see, himself mirrored in the thing perceived . . . He stood looking at his broken picture thinking of his father's Sunday suit, seeing the old black three-piece not as it was now, behind him in the corner of his studio, his mute witness, but hanging off its rack alone in the emptiness of Andy's space; the beautiful, poignant thing that worn-out old suit became after his father's death. It had ceased to be what it started out being, and had become a new thing, a thing more durable than its old self, its story deep in the weave, deep in the smell of his father's sweat, its story not in the violence and the suffering of his father's childhood, a story about which his father had kept silent, but the story of his father's enduring love. His father's old suit had become a sign of the way all men falter and break at the end, but do not abandon love. An object attracting the speculations of mind and memory. The claim standing over his life after his death: the artist Moniek Prochownik, *The one who made us believe*.

He turned around and looked at the suit in the corner. Nada's drawing of him with flaming hair looking out above it. He turned from his father's suit and looked at the picture on the floor again. It could no longer be mistaken for an erotic nude. It was no longer the banal image dictated to his expectations, but had become something else, something he could not have seen or foreseen. Despite his conscious intention, it had become an interior portrait, something closer to the question of living flesh. *Chance is not random,* his father had claimed. *Chance is personal. Each of us has our own kind of accident.*

The pain in his arm was a hot tide moving into his bowels. He had begun to feel dizzy and nauseous. He sat bent over on the stool, nursing his arm, waiting for the nausea to pass. After a couple of minutes he gave a groan and got to his feet. He had to do something. What was Teresa doing? Was she still in the house, or had she gone to her mother's? Or to Gina's to pick up Nada? They had never been convinced by him, now they would be appalled. Or was she waiting for him to come out, the carving knife in her hand, ready to plunge it into his belly and finish the job? He could still see the insanity in her eyes as she swung the lamp over his head. Was the situation going to get worse yet or had the peak of it passed? How could he tell? Carefully he moved the red lamp aside with his foot and stepped across to the window. He lifted the sheet and looked over towards the house. There was no movement in the kitchen. The house was uninhabited. He knew it. He was too alone with what had happened. He needed to talk to someone. He took the telephone from the wall bracket and dialled his brother's number. Roy knew about this kind of thing. Roy had dealt with it. Violence had been Roy's home territory. Roy was the one among them who would not panic at the sight of blood. Hadn't they always turned to Roy whenever one of them had been threatened? *Call Roy, he'll know what to do.*

Roy picked up and said hello.

'What are you doing?' Toni asked shakily.

'Sitting at my window watching traffic,' Roy said. 'Why, what are you doing?'

'I had a fight with Teresa.'

'You okay?'

'I think I might have a broken arm.'

There was a silence while Roy took in the seriousness of the situation. 'Is Terry okay?'

'Don't worry, I didn't kill her if that's what you're thinking. Physically she's fine.' Remembering the man Roy had killed all those years ago, not meaning to kill him, only to fight him, to warn him off, to force him to cease his senseless persecution of their father—but the man's heel catching the concrete kerb of the yard out the front of the flats as he backed away from Roy's fierce advance. Roy's fist taking him in the throat and the man going down. The crack of his skull on the concrete like the crack of the cedar stretcher. So easy. And it was all over. Everything changed. Their lives were silenced for years.

'Did you hit her?' Roy asked, no change in his tone.

'No. I don't think so. No! I'm sure I didn't hit her. I wrestled her to the ground but I didn't hit her.' It was a fine distinction—*wrestled, but did not strike his wife with a closed fist.* Did the law recognise the significance of such a distinction? In the end, the law had not acknowledged Roy's lack of intention to kill. 'She was hitting me with the lamp,' Toni explained. 'She could have killed me. I had to do something. She says she's going to burn my work.' His story sounded melodramatic and exaggerated and as if he were talking about someone else.

'You can never tell what people will do when they're hurting badly enough,' Roy said. He spoke as if he were making a general observation about people's behaviour. 'They step out of themselves. You want me to come over? I could talk to her.'

'I don't think she's here. What do you reckon?'

'Maybe you should ring your mate Andy and get him to come over there and take your pictures to his place for safekeeping. That'll be one problem off your mind. Then see someone about your arm.'

There was a long silence.

'Call me back if you want me to come over and talk to Terry.' When Toni did not say anything, Roy said, 'Give her a bit of space. She's going to need some space from you. Terry's not a woman to lay down and take it.'

'I know. I know that.' Toni was silent. 'Don't you want to know what the fight was about?'

'I think I might have a pretty good idea.'

He waited but Roy offered no more. 'That's it?'

'You do what you do, Toni. No one's telling you how to run your life.'

He was taken aback by his brother's lack of engagement with his situation. 'I suppose you think I deserved it.'

'I didn't say that. You're my brother. Call me if you want me to come over.'

'Don't say anything to Mum about it, will you?'

After Roy had hung up, Toni stood at the window looking across at the house. So he was on his own with it. But Roy was right, he should secure the paintings. Give Teresa a bit of space. Deal with things one at a time. See a doctor. He stepped over the broken image of Marina and went out the door and crossed the courtyard.

He stood in the living room listening. He had an image of Teresa lying on their bed in the front room, curled up waiting for him. It was a fiction, of course, he knew that, but he still went to the bedroom and looked all the same, seeing her there in his imagination until he saw the empty bed. He went to the window and pulled aside the blind. Her car was not in the street. He knew, suddenly, that the violent phase of this thing was over. It was finished. Whatever was to follow, there would be no more violence.

He went through to the kitchen and called Teresa's parents. No one picked up and there was no answering machine at the Grecos. He rang Andy and left a message. Then he called Andy's mobile. The diversion was on and he left another message. He had a growing dread that he had stepped over the line like his brother and there would be no going back to being the person he had been before this. A feeling of having slipped over the edge into something else, something unforeseen, something to do with being the artist Prochownik that he had not anticipated. Out there from now on, in no-man's-land with his brother. Was that the fate that had been lying in wait for him? Struck sideways by the real storm when he was no longer expecting it. Theo's kind of freedom, an existence loaded with anxiety and loneliness. He hesitated, then telephoned Marina. She picked up on the first ring.

'Are you all right?' she asked worriedly. 'I've been sitting here waiting for you to call.'

He told her.

When he had finished she was silent for a while, then she said, 'What are you going to do?'

'No one's dead. That's what I keep telling myself.'

'Where's Teresa?'

'I don't know. I'd say she's gone to her parents' place. Roy was probably right. I should give her a bit of space. I shouldn't have jumped in and wrestled her. I should have stood back and let her have a go at the painting. I don't know why I jumped in like that.'

'I shouldn't have abandoned you the way I did. It was cowardly of me. I should have stayed and faced things with you. Together we might have had some hope of explaining.'

'No! It was better this way. This is bad enough, but it's a million times better than Teresa killing you.'

'I'll come over and give you a lift to casualty,' Marina said resolutely.

He could hear that she didn't really want to do it. 'No. Don't do that. I can get there.'

'I'm coming over.'

'No! Please don't come over.'

'How will you get to the hospital?'

'I'll call a cab. Look, I don't think we should meet right away. Okay? I think we should let this thing settle for a while.' He waited. 'Are you still there?'

'I feel responsible. I feel I ought to be doing something to help.'

'You're not responsible.'

'I *am* responsible. We can't just decide not to be responsible when things go wrong.'

'Another minute and you wouldn't have been here,' he said.

'If only I'd left when I should have!'

'Teresa's always going to believe I've been lying to her ever since the day on the island.'

There was a long silence, then Marina said, 'I suppose in a way you have been. Or at least not sharing the whole truth with her. I'm not saying you could have. But I can imagine how she's feeling.'

This was not what he wanted to hear.

'So the painting's ruined?'

'It's changed. I'm not rejecting the change.'

'What do you mean?'

'I don't know.'

'Promise me you'll let me know what's happening. I need to know or I'll be imagining the worst.'

'Have you said anything to Robert?'

'Robert's not home yet.

'Will you tell him?'

'He'll hear anyway. It'll be better if I tell him myself. Don't worry, he'll be fine with it. He'll just hate the way it is between you and Teresa.' When he did not say anything to this she added, 'Call me as soon as you've seen the doctor.'

After he had hung up, he stood at the kitchen bench; the peculiar stillness of the house, as if he and Teresa and Nada had never lived there. Outside, the city, the streets. The sirens that never stopped wailing along High Street. People killing and yelling and dying. He had become one of them. He had entered another reality. He was in pain and he was afraid. He hated being alone in the house. He looked across to the studio. That was where he wanted to be right now.

twenty-one

Teresa had taken Nada and vanished. The agency was closed and the Grecos were not talking to him. His right arm was in plaster to the elbow, the weight of it held in a sling. The X-ray had shown that the blow from the lamp had caused a hairline fracture of one of the slender bones in his forearm. The young woman doctor who explained the injury to him and set the arm in the casualty department of the hospital—in a curtained cubicle no more than three metres from the cubicle in which Theo had died—assured him that the injury would cause him no lasting problems. He had become a night worker again, like his father. In the night with his work he did not miss Teresa and Nada as acutely as he did during the day, and while he worked he could even imagine that they were sleeping peacefully in the house, as if everything was going along as usual for the three of them, and they would meet at breakfast and talk and laugh and tell each other their dreams, before going their separate ways into the day. Under its shroud of silence and darkness the night was not reality.

He was sleeping on the chaise again and had set up the coffee maker and the toaster on the plan press. Whenever he needed food he walked down the back lane to the corner shop and bought bread and tins of baked beans and cheese. The house remained dark and uninhabited on the other side of the courtyard and he rarely visited it.

Cold autumn rain slid down the windows of the studio. He was working on the figure of Marina in *The Other Family*. Andy had been around and paid him the money from the sale of the two paintings. Toni had kept on working while he told Andy the story, and for once Andy did not interrupt but sat on the stool in silence, his elbows on his knees, gazing steadily at the floor between his legs. Once or twice, particularly during Toni's recounting of the fight, he made a small noise, denoting his disbelief or his dismay. But, when Toni had finished, he stopped working and turned around from the canvas and stood waiting to hear the verdict of his friend; the only one, in the end, with whom he had felt able to share his feelings of guilt and the strange ambivalent acceptance of his new liberty.

Andy looked up at him. 'And you've heard nothing from Teresa since she walked out of the studio that day?'

'Not a word.'

'Do you have any idea where she is?'

'For all I know she could be staying with her mother and father or with one of her brothers. But they're refusing to speak to me.'

'And what about her friend, Gina?'

'I got nothing out of her. When I telephoned she just abused me and hung up.'

'So,' Andy said, he was matter of fact, as if he were saying something ordinary and of no greater consequence than anything else he might say, 'What if she doesn't come back?'

It was too vast. The implications too devastating to consider.

Andy was silent for some time. 'I never want to have to choose between you and Teresa. I love you both. Nada too. But if it comes to it, and I have to choose between you, then I am going to choose you.' He looked steadily at Toni. 'I'm telling you this now so you'll know. It's not something that makes me happy or gives me any satisfaction to say. In fact, it saddens me more than I can tell you. It seems to me the most obvious thing is that you need Teresa and Nada and they need you. I love them too. Don't forget that. This is not just you and your family and your art, it's us, your friends. It's me, Toni. And it's your mother. And it's Roy. And it's Robert and Marina. Don't forget that. You're not on your own with this. I'm saying this stuff about choosing between you and them because it's what I'm thinking. And if *I'm* thinking it, *you* will be thinking it later, and Teresa will be thinking it, and whoever else. And we don't want to leave a question like that sitting in the dark between us. I'm saying it now so it's out in the open. But there is nothing good here.' He considered Toni, his manner concerned and sorrowful. 'Tell me one thing,' he said eventually. 'To me it's the key to this business, and I need to know it. What would your dad have made of all this?'

Toni stood looking at the big canvas, the figure of Marina on the left margin of the picture, her figure deeper within the picture than his own enigmatic presence, her back to the viewer; her figure, surprisingly in the end, draped and evidently in the act of leaving the space of the large central arrangement of the composition, the group with Andy and Haine and Robert, dominated by the tall, imposing, presence of Oriel Liesker and her great pile of hair, which suddenly he was seeing as a predatory bird in the act of alighting on its prey. A stranger would not have imagined the picture to be a portrait of Marina Golding . . . His father, who had been a gentle man, would of course have been deeply hurt by the violence and the infidelity. He would have been shocked and saddened beyond words and must surely have seen it as a failure in his son to deal with the demands of art in a decent way. He may even have found in these events an echo of the violence of his own young life. Seeing the violence breaking in upon them again, despite his care, as if it were an inevitable part of his family's destiny to suffer such things. After his father's sudden death, when his grief had been fresh and at its most acute, he had often lain awake at night wondering about the young man who might have been himself if history had been different.

And it had seemed to him then that his fate was no more than an accident, and carried no larger significance in the course of things than the momentary satisfaction of his own paltry and insignificant desires. If he had been standing in front of his father now, instead of Andy, would he have been as frank in telling his story, or would he have censored his account, and have left out the more difficult parts? He looked at Andy. 'I don't know what Dad would have thought about it,' he said in answer to his friend's question. But it was a less than honest reply. Andy's question was too difficult for him at this moment, and he could not answer it, not even in the privacy of his own mind. He knew that if he should ever believe that he no longer deserved the respect of his father, then it would not be possible for him to continue with his art. The meaning of his art and his life were inseparable from his love and respect for his father.

'Well you think about it until you *do* know, old buddy!' Andy said, something of impatience and even of a reprimand entering his tone. 'This thing happened and it is a terrible thing to have happened between you three, but you and me need to know what your dad would have thought about it. That much we've got to get straight, or this whole thing is lost. You know that and I know it. Neither of us would be here doing this, if it hadn't been for your dad.' Andy had got up after saying this and stood before the painting on the easel. Eventually he turned away from the painting and said, 'It's a beautiful piece of work.'

At the back door to the lane, on his way out, Andy put his arms around Toni and hugged him. He kissed him on the cheek. 'You're in pain. They're in pain too.' He indicated the studio with a lift of his chin, the mess of empty tins and used plates and cutlery and old bread wrappings on the plan press. 'When you get sick of this come over and take a break with me.' He pinched Toni's cheek. 'Hey, don't be too downcast, you're doing the work, Prochownik!' But his show of optimism did not carry Andy's usual conviction. Andy walked out into the lane and climbed into his car and drove away.

Toni watched him go, then went back to work.

Marina telephoned that evening. She reproached him gently for being neglectful. 'I need to know how you are,' she said. 'You have to let me know what's happening. You can't just stay out of touch.'

'Nothing's happening,' he told her.

'You've still not heard from Teresa?'

'No.'

'That's unbelievable. Have you been able to do any work?'

'Yes, I'm working. Did you tell Robert?'

'We've hardly talked about anything else these past few weeks.'

'How is he?'

'He wants to see you, but I told him we should wait.'

Toni said nothing. Did she mean wait until Teresa came home? Since the day of the fight, Robert and Marina had seemed strangely remote to him. There had even been moments when he had forgotten they had come back, and had imagined them to be living in Sydney still. 'Yes, we might just give it a while,' he said. 'I'm sorry, I'm feeling a bit detached.'

'It's no wonder,' she said. 'You'd hardly be feeling normal. We'll all catch up soon enough.' She hesitated. 'Did Oriel get in touch?'

'No.'

'She wants to know what you've got for the show.'

'Andy's handling all that.'

They hung up, finally, without finding much more to say to each other, a slight awkwardness persisting between them.

.

There was a picture of a hotel and a swimming pool in the top left-hand corner of the envelope. He sat on the stool beside Nada's little table and opened it. Folded in with the letter was a square of brown paper with a coloured drawing on it; the figure of a woman in a green diamond-shaped skirt, a teardrop on each rosy cheek, above the figure the simple caption, *Mum*.

As you can see, I took the Noumea package. It's beautiful here and I feel strangely content in these surroundings. Nada is missing you, of course. The worst thing is that she does not say anything, but keeps it all inside. There's a circus school here at the hotel for the children and she and Snoopy Dog are learning to be clowns. Thankfully she seems to be enjoying it.

The temperature is around thirty to thirty-two every day and I'm swimming two Ks each morning in the pool while N is at the clown theatre. So I'm getting fit and I'm off the smokes again. I've lost four kilos.

This is my umpteenth attempt at a letter to you. I phoned once, but didn't have the courage to leave a message. I couldn't think of what to say when the machine came on.

I will always love you. And I know that you will always love me. I think we both know this. Our love is not as simple or as nice or as straightforward and perfect as I thought it was, but it is still real and it is still love.

I am coming home in time for the opening of the island show, but I don't know whether I will feel able to go. I have spoken to Roy a few times by phone. He has been incredibly supportive. I don't know if he has spoken about this to you? He has told me you only have a hairline fracture to your right arm, which is a relief. I'm glad I didn't seriously hurt you. It's lucky it wasn't your left arm! When I was telling him about our fight, Roy said something he learned in prison was that murderers are ordinary people like us. After what happened, I believe it. It is a funny thing, but he and I were able to have a good laugh about it, and I think that's when I started getting a bit of perspective on the realities of this and seeing that we have the rest of our lives to go yet.

Roy is going to do some debt collecting for me when I get back. If he can get the big accounts to pay even a percentage of what's owed the agency, I'll have some hope of getting into the clear.

There is no point in you writing to me here as I will be home before your letter arrives. I will probably go straight to Mum and Dad's. I wanted to let you know that we are both well and will be back soon, and I also wanted to say that I love you. I couldn't bear it if anything happened and I had not told you this. Nada did the picture of me last night. I'm afraid I've had a few good cries. I think it's done me good.

P.S. Don't be angry with Roy. I made him promise not to tell you we'd been talking. He's kept me in touch. It's been important.

Toni read through the letter again then folded it carefully and put it back in its envelope. It was raining heavily outside now, the studio cold, the sound of the rain hammering on the tin. He pinned Nada's drawing of the weeping woman next to her picture of himself above his dad's suit. Then he dragged the doona off the chaise and draped it over his shoulders. He was seeing Nada doing her clown training. Maintaining her dignity. Solemnly instructing Snoopy Dog. Keeping the world of her imagination safe from the real world.

They were coming back.

He realised, suddenly, that he was exhausted and could do no more. He stood looking at *The Other Family*. It occurred to him then that the picture was finished. Whatever finished meant. The *feeling* that it was finished. The *sense* that it was finished. Not that it was perfect, but that it was done with, which was not the same thing. Its story was over. The energy for it had been expended. Emptiness after the act of passion. Or perhaps it was something so different from what he had expected when he set out to paint Marina's portrait that he was not yet capable of really seeing it. There was a sense in which he was a stranger to this painting. Was there not, after all, a strange misalignment of truth and fiction in its story that might have been drawn from a place he scarcely knew? He reached and took the painting down from the easel and leaned it with its face to the plan press. He was careful with it. He cherished it. For it carried within its image the disconcerting authenticity of the unexpected and the unknown. As if another hand than his own had painted it.

He put out the light and lay on the chaise and pulled the doona up around his ears and closed his eyes. He was glad to be alone with the hammering of the rain on the roof and the howling of the sirens along High Street. He did not want to see the studio. He did not want to be reminded of the familiar shapes in the dark. He wanted to sleep, and while he slept he wanted time to pass. 'They're coming home,' he murmured into the warmth of the doona. *I will always love you. And I know that you will always love me. I think we both know this. Our love is not as simple or as nice or as straightforward and perfect as I thought it was, but it is still real and it is still love* . . . First he would paint a portrait of his father. He could see his father seated at the table in the kitchen, painting by the light of the single bulb, bending over his work in the night silence, his glasses on the end of his nose, the household objects of his meditation taking shape under his hand. But that would not be the picture. The picture would surprise him. He did not know what the portrait of his father would look like when it was finished. He knew for certain only that its title would be *Prochownik's Dream*.